Warwickshire County Council

MOBILE LIBRARY SERVICE

KCS 6/11			
Wdbrook P			
Kwnard			
26 APR 2013			

This item is to be returned or renewed before the latest date above. It may be borrowed for a further period if not in demand. **To renew your books:**

- **Phone the 24/7 Renewal Line 01926 499273 or**
- **Visit www.warwickshire.gov.uk/libraries**

Discover ● Imagine● Learn ● *with libraries*

Warwickshire County Council

Working for Warwickshire

LOST CAUSES

Other Titles by Ken McClure

LOST CAUSES

Ken McClure

Polygon

First published in Great Britain in 2011
by Polygon, an imprint of Birlinn Ltd
West Newington House
10 Newington Road
Edinburgh
EH9 1QS

www.polygonbooks.co.uk

ISBN 978 1 84697 200 3
ebook ISBN 978 0 85790 030 2

British Library Cataloguing-in-Publication Data
A catalogue record for this book is available
on request from the British Library.

Typeset in Adobe Garamond by Palimpsest Book Production Limited,
Falkirk, Stirlingshire
Printed and bound by Clays Ltd, St Ives plc

Author's Note

Twenty years ago I wrote a book called *Requiem*, a medical thriller which did not have a happy ending. In fact, there was a marked absence of scones with jam and cream, and certainly no lashings of ginger beer. Good did not triumph over evil. This has led to my being asked many times, what happened next? Although *Lost Causes* is not a sequel to *Requiem*, Steven Dunbar does have cause to revisit the events of that time and answer some of these questions.

PROLOGUE

Melissa Carlisle, daughter of Lord and Lady Pennington and wife of John Carlisle MP, looked at her husband across the breakfast table as if she were examining something she'd just trodden on. When it came to expressing extreme distaste, the upper classes were a breed apart. Melissa had been born with the ability to look down her nose, as her husband – from more modest, middle-class roots – knew only too well.

'Tell me it isn't true,' she said in a flat monotone, taking care to enunciate every syllable slowly and clearly.

'What isn't, dear?' Carlisle brushed his thinning fair hair back from his brow in a nervous gesture that caused his wife to tighten her expression even more.

'*What isn't,*' she mimicked. 'The story in the *Telegraph* this morning . . . about your expenses claim for a mortgage that doesn't exist on a second home you don't have. That's what.'

Carlisle moved uncomfortably in his seat, as if his trousers were filling with ants. 'Well?'

'It's obviously some sort of misunderstanding, an administrative cock-up somewhere along the line.'

'You mean this imaginary house belongs to someone else?'

'Well, no, not exactly . . . You must remember I was thinking about getting a flat in London to be nearer the House . . .'

'We live forty-five minutes from London and you're never in the bloody House. Are you seriously saying that you claimed for a mortgage on a flat you were *thinking* of buying?'

'A simple error of judgement. I must have looked into the

costs involved, written it down somewhere on a bit of paper and somehow it got into my expenses claim. An oversight, plain and simple . . . easily done. My God, I'm only human.'

Melissa stared at her husband for a full ten seconds. 'You disgust me.'

'Look, Melissa, it was a genuine mistake. You must see that. I'm sure that they'll see that too . . .'

'God, Daddy was right. He warned me at the time that all the nonsense about you being a future leader of the party was bullshit. He said you were nothing more than a blond, handsome puppet set up to pull in the faithful in the shires while someone else was putting words in your mouth and pulling the strings all along. And here I am, seventeen years down the line, married to a greedy, vacuous slug whose career has gone downhill every step of the way . . . like his looks. You're going to be flung out of the party over this, you cretin. What are you going to do then?'

'Look, I understand you're upset, old girl, but it was a genuine mistake,' Carlisle insisted. 'But if the worst came to the worst and the truth were to be swallowed up in some gutter press frenzy – they really are the bloody limit, you know, the press, scum the lot of them – maybe . . . Well, I was thinking . . . just maybe your father could bung a directorship or two my way? Just to tide us over?'

'You couldn't direct traffic in a one-way street.'

'I *was* leadership material,' said Carlisle, accepting that he wasn't going to win Melissa round and starting to bristle under the verbal onslaught. 'My time as health secretary was very successful. Everyone says so. I was stabbed in the back . . . but I know things, things I never mentioned at the time. They owe me.'

'You weren't stabbed in the back. You lost the bloody election because of what you and your venal pals were up to and you've been out of power for thirteen years over it. And now, just when people might have forgotten, you pop up with a mortgage that never was. Christ, the leader's going to nail you to a tree over this . . . if the voters don't get to you first.'

'I was set up, I tell you . . . but I know things.'

Melissa got up. 'I'm going away for a few days. The thought of having to play the dutiful wife at the garden gate when the hyenas arrive turns my stomach.'

She left the room, slamming the door and leaving Carlisle alone with his thoughts. They owed him: it was time to call in a few favours. Puppet, indeed. He'd see about that. He started reading the *Telegraph* article, the nervous mannerism of playing with what was left of his hair becoming more and more pronounced. 'Bastards . . . utter bastards. This country's at war and all these bastards can do is go on about a few measly quid and a genuine mistake.'

He finished reading and flung the paper across the room. He picked up the telephone and started dialling friends. Strangely, they were all unavailable.

Montrouge, Paris, 15 February 2010

The Englishman pushed a fifty-euro note into the taxi driver's hand and got out. He remained oblivious of the smiles and *mercis* resulting from such a generous tip after only a five-minute ride from the Métro station at Orléans, and looked up at the street signs. Seeing *Rue de Bagneux* on one of them, he relaxed and took out a card from his overcoat pocket, memorising the numbers on it before getting his bearings from nearby doors. He walked on for twenty metres or so before crossing the street to punch four buttons on the entry panel of number twenty-seven. A prolonged buzz followed by a heavy double click heralded the appearance of a two-centimetre gap. So far so good.

He found flat four on the second floor, above the lawyer and the dentist who occupied the two apartments on the first. There was no name on the door but there was a bell so he rang it and put his briefcase down between his feet, loosening his fashionable cashmere scarf while he waited. The door was opened by another Englishman, more portly and a full head shorter than the newcomer, but about the same age, somewhere in his mid to late fifties. 'So you found us then. Welcome.'

The new arrival was shown into a large, square, tastefully furnished room with four three-metre-high windows looking out to the north which, on a grey day in February, failed to let in much light. They got help from several elegant standard lamps placed at strategic intervals round the room.

'Good to see you again,' he said, recognising the five people sitting on sofas facing each other on either side of a marble fireplace with a coal fire burning in it. Four were men in their fifties, three of them big names in UK business, the fourth a high-level British civil servant. The fifth person was a silver-haired woman in her late sixties whose complexion proclaimed the downside of a lifelong love affair with the sun.

'Good trip?'

'As such things go these days.'

'Remind me: how did you come?'

'Air France. Birmingham to Charles de Gaulle.'

'Good. Antonia came up from her holiday place in La Motte near Saint-Raphaël. Nigel and Neil were already in Paris on business and Christopher came via Zurich. Giles drove over from Bruges after catching the overnight ferry from Scotland.'

'The short straw,' said the driver.

'It says something when we can't even risk meeting in our own country,' said the newcomer.

The host gave an apologetic shrug. 'I'm probably being over-cautious, but my feeling is that we can't be too careful after what happened back in the early nineties. We were damned lucky to walk away from that particular debacle although we did lose Paul in the process.'

Sherry was poured into seven crystal schooners and handed

round before he continued, 'I'd like to welcome you all to the first full meeting in many years of the executive committee of the Schiller Group. It's good to be back – albeit in some bizarre surroundings.' He turned to the newcomer. 'We are also very pleased to welcome our new member to the executive committee. We have all, of course, followed his progress through the ranks of our organisation as well as watching him achieve success in his own career.'

The man nodded his appreciation.

'Executive membership of our group comes, of course, with responsibilities. You will now be one of only seven people with comprehensive knowledge of our organisation and its structure, one of only seven people carrying the hopes and dreams of our ordinary members for a better nation.' He handed him a computer disk. 'This must never fall into the wrong hands.'

'Once again, I'm deeply honoured.'

'And so to business. An election looms at home and we must be ready to do our bit for our country. Thirteen long years in the New Labour wilderness has seen it descend into chaos and become a broken wreck of what it once was. Fortunately, change is on the cards.'

'It's not going to be easy,' said one of the group. 'They've turned the place into a land fit for the weak, the ignorant and the deviant, and, as if that wasn't bad enough, we're keeping open house for the sweepings of the streets of Europe and beyond. Everybody's welcome in dear old Blighty and bring your bloody family with you.'

'More than a decade wasted in the celebration of image over substance.'

'Which all the polls suggest is about to end,' interjected the newcomer. 'And presumably why we're here?'

'We're not home and dry yet,' the host cautioned. 'The electorate may be totally disillusioned with Brown and his cronies but they're still deeply suspicious of the alternatives. We should be all right if we maintain a steady course with no rising to the bait and no silly distractions in the next few months, but there's little margin for error. On the other hand, the criminal aspect of the expenses scandal seems to be hitting Labour worse than anyone else, and if those in question should get away with a defence of parliamentary privilege . . . well, they'll have to dig Brown out with a shovel.'

'One of ours is involved.'

'From the other house. Not quite the same as the brown paper bags that did for us last time.'

'I almost feel sorry for Brown,' said the woman. 'Blair left him an impossible mess to clear up and he's not exactly been helping himself. King Midas in reverse if ever I saw it.'

'Everything he touches . . .' agreed the host. There was a slight lull in the proceedings before he went on, 'It's clear that none of us underestimates the magnitude of our task but, as Confucius said, "A journey of ten thousand miles begins with but a single step." And so to specifics. All of us have now had a chance to study our new colleague's proposal and I for one would like to express my admiration for the amount of time and ingenuity that has clearly gone into the design of such a project.'

The hear hears from the others were muted.

'But it's too risky,' said one.

'There was nothing wrong with the original scheme,' said the woman. 'It was working perfectly well. It was just bad luck that that damned journalist popped up at the wrong time and ruined everything. We'll just have to be more careful this time.'

A long and at times heated argument ensued, at the end of which the host said, 'It's now decision time, ladies and gentlemen. Do we adopt our new colleague's bold project or do we make another attempt at going down the road we started on back in the early nineties?'

The newcomer sighed in frustration as the vote went unanimously against him.

'I'm sorry,' said the host. 'Tried and trusted it is.'

'Democracy in action,' replied the newcomer with a wry grin.

The host broke open two bottles of Krug champagne and they drank a toast to 'a better future for our country'.

The last to arrive was the first to leave. He shook the hands of each in turn and kissed the silver-haired woman on both cheeks. He stopped his host from getting up. 'Really, Charles, I'll see myself out.'

'Good chap,' said one as he heard the outer door close. 'Took it well, I thought.'

'Bright too.'

'Bit forgetful though,' said the host, suddenly noticing something beside the chair the newcomer had been sitting on. 'He's left his briefcase.'

'Maybe we should be having second thoughts,' someone joked.

The explosion cut short the laughter.

From the corner of the street, the newcomer watched a sheet of yellow flame erupt through the space where the windows had been as glass showered down on the Rue de Bagneux. He took out his mobile phone and made the call. 'It's out with the old,' he said.

'And in with the new,' came the reply.

ONE

Dr Steven Dunbar opened one eye and took in the time on the bedside alarm clock. It was twenty to seven, five minutes before the radio alarm would trigger and the *Today* programme on Radio Four would start the day.

'Another day of work and play,' he sighed, looking up at the ceiling and remembering with something less than enthusiasm that it was Monday.

'What time is it?' asked Tally sleepily.

'Two minutes to lift-off in yet another action-packed day in the life of Steven Dunbar, security consultant extraordinaire.'

'You go first,' said Tally. 'I don't have to be at the hospital until ten. I was there till eleven last night.'

'I noticed.'

Tally opened her eyes. 'What's up with you this morning?' she asked. 'You're even more ratty than usual.'

'It's a gift.'

John Humphrys joined them: he was laying into some hapless politician who seemed determined to avoid his question. 'Go get him, John boy,' muttered Steven, swinging his legs over the side and sitting upright. 'Crooks, the lot of them.'

Tally reached up and put a hand on his bare shoulder. 'Hey, what's the matter?'

'Oh . . . nothing. You know I'm always grumpy in the morning.' He turned, leaned back and planted a kiss on her forehead, then paused on the edge of the bed as he heard John Humphrys say, 'And now a good news story. The BBC has learned that negotiations between a cross-party group of politicians led by Conservative health spokesman Norman Travis and the heads of several international pharmaceutical companies have led to an agreement over vaccine production in the UK. Regardless of which party emerges as winner of the upcoming election, the companies will permit mass production of their products in facilities approved and licensed by the government of the day, leading to greater availability and ease of distribution in time of need. This will effectively put an end to continual squabbling between government and the pharmaceutical industry at a time when the threat of bioterrorist activity is constantly with us. Mr Travis was keen to stress that party politics had played no part in the negotiations and that what had been achieved had been done for the good of the entire nation.'

'So what are the companies going to get in return?' murmured Steven.

'What's in it for the companies, Mr Travis?' asked Humphrys.

'By not having to concentrate on production schedules, they hope to expand their research facilities and to operate in a more . . . amenable climate. We have to put an end to constant bickering over testing and licensing regulations. The pharmaceutical industry is not the enemy; the terrorists are. We are all in this together and a spirit of compromise should prevail.'

Humphrys turned his attention to a Labour health spokesman. 'The Tories have been doing your job for you, haven't they?'

'I think Norman is quite right: we shouldn't bring party politics into this. It's much too serious and, as he's already said, the new scheme will take effect regardless of who wins the upcoming election. It's the terrorist threat that should occupy our thinking. To that end we are inviting production tenders before the election so that we get vaccines on stream as soon as possible.'

'Does that mean you've given in to the companies' demands too?'

'We've looked at their requests in the light of what's just been said.'

'Well, what a day,' cooed Humphrys. 'Conservatives and Labour all lovey-dovey with an election coming up. Who'd have thought it? I'd like to explore more but we've run out of time. Over to the weather centre . . .'

Steven switched off the radio and said, 'About time too. The vaccine situation's been crazy for years.'

'People want a hundred per cent safe vaccines,' said Tally. 'They see it as their right.'

'You and I know that isn't possible,' said Steven. 'My fear is that it's going to take a terrorist attack before the message gets home. If there's a vaccine available, get it. God, look at the time. No gold star for me at the end of the month.' He got up and padded through to the bathroom.

Tally – Dr Natalie Simmons – watched him disappear, admitting to herself that she'd been expecting something like the undercurrent of frustration Steven was showing. He loved her – she had no doubts about that – but he'd also given up a job he'd loved in order to come and set up home with her in Leicester, and she still wasn't sure that he believed he'd made the right decision. She wanted to think it had been a considered commitment, made after a great deal of thought, but she knew differently. Steven had been angry and disillusioned at the time of his resignation: it had been a spur-of-the-moment thing, although, to be fair, disillusionment had been threatening for some time before that. On the other hand and on the bright side, he had already rebuffed several requests from London urging him to reconsider and come back.

Since leaving the army, where he'd served with the Parachute Regiment and Special Forces, Steven had been employed as a medical investigator with the Sci-Med Inspectorate, a small unit attached to the Home Office which investigated possible crime and wrongdoing in the high-tech world of science and medicine – areas where the police lacked expertise. It was a job he'd been extremely good at but it had taken him into a number of dangerous situations where on more than one occasion his life had been in danger. Tally had met him during one such investigation so she had first-hand experience of the risks. She had been terrified and had no wish to ever find herself in that position again . . . or even try to form any serious relationship with someone who might be.

Steven had fallen for Tally and had initially hoped that he could convince her that being in danger was the exception rather than the rule, and that it would be perfectly possible for him to combine his Sci-Med career with a normal relationship. Tally, who had her own career to pursue and was currently a senior registrar in paediatric medicine in a Leicester children's hospital, disagreed and was quite adamant that she couldn't live in constant fear of the danger her partner might be in. She'd made it clear that that kind of uncertainty was no basis for a relationship and they had ultimately parted over it.

Some time later, when Steven found himself totally disillusioned with the outcome of his last assignment when, in the 'public interest', the bad guys had got away with it – yet again, as he saw it – he had resigned. He had contacted Tally and told her what had happened. There would be no going back, he assured her. He had never stopped loving her. Would she consider making a life with him if he resigned from Sci-Med? Tally had agreed without hesitation and had suggested that he come and live with her in Leicester while he looked for a new job. At least one of them would be working.

Although himself a qualified doctor and an expert in field medicine – the medicine of the battlefield – Steven had known that it would be difficult if not impossible for him to find his way back into civilian medicine, having never really been involved in it before at any level. He'd joined the army – what he'd really wanted to do all along – almost as soon as he'd completed his hospital registration year after university. He had been one of those students who'd been steered towards medicine by ambitious parents and teachers. Unlike many, he'd found the courage to rebel before the die had been irrevocably cast.

Now, largely because he needed to find something that paid a salary, he'd taken a job as a security consultant with a pharmaceutical company with research labs located on a science park shared with Leicester University. The security was more concerned with intellectual matters than with the guarding of gates. It was vital that the company's projects be kept safe from the prying eyes of competitors, so the screening of research and support staff as they came and went was an important factor. Thorough background checks had to be carried out on incoming staff, and privacy agreements in line with contractual obligations had to be signed and adhered to by those who were bound for pastures new. All very vital and all very boring.

Steven did his best to shut out such thoughts. After all, the job had enabled him to set up a new life with Tally and would in time allow him to see more of his daughter Jenny and play a bigger role in her life. Steven had been married before, to a nurse he'd met in Glasgow during the course of an early Sci-Med assignment, but Lisa had later succumbed to a brain tumour, dying when Jenny was little more than a baby. After her death – perhaps the blackest and most unhappy time of his life – Lisa's sister Sue and her husband had taken Jenny to live with them in the village of Glenvane in Dumfriesshire, and she had been there ever since, brought up with her two cousins, Peter and Mary. Steven had visited as often as he could, every second weekend when possible.

Sue and her solicitor husband Richard had always assured Steven that they regarded Jenny as one of their own, and that she could stay as long as she was happy with them. They'd even let it be known that giving her up would be traumatic for all of them after so many years – Jenny was settled and happy at the local primary school – but Steven still harboured dreams of family life although he recognised that Jenny herself would have to have the final say. He suspected, however, that his dream might well become unattainable before any such decision had to be made, as Tally had no plans to give up her own career. The demands of the medical ladder would almost certainly involve a geographical move when she began to think about applying for a consultant's post, and perhaps more than once: not ideal for Jenny.

Steven was aware of Tally giving him sideways looks at the breakfast table. 'What's up?' he asked.

'Are you beginning to have regrets?'

'About what?'

'You know damned well.'

'Not for a second,' said Steven softly. 'I made my decision. It was the right one. I love you.'

Tally remained unconvinced. 'I know you. I can sense when you're restless, unsettled, a bit unhappy . . .'

'I'm not unhappy. I'm living with the woman I love. I've got a good job. The sun's shining. How could I possibly be unhappy?'

Tally smiled, deciding to believe him but aware that it might be because she wanted to. 'You'd better get a move on.'

'Yep, you never know who may be planning to steal the aspirin . . .' Steven got up from the table.

Tally looked down at her coffee cup. There it was again, the little aside that hinted at a lack of self-respect in the job he was doing. That could be serious: it could eat away at him unless she could persuade him to see things differently. His job was responsible and important, but how to make him see that was another matter. Most people had little or no trouble convincing themselves – and others – that their job was meaning-ful and worthwhile even if it was only a case of coming up with a fancy title for what they actually did, but Steven was different. He really had lived in a different world. He had lived life on an edge where harsh reality had to be faced and bull-shit and imagery had no place. He had served with Special Forces all over the world, operating in appalling conditions in jungles and deserts to save the lives of comrades, experiencing the joy of bringing them back from the brink and the anguish of losing them.

Sci-Med investigations had, of course, been less demanding in terms of life and death scenarios but had still brought him into conflict with those who would stop at nothing to achieve their ends. How did you go about convincing a man like that that an office job was important in his scheme of things?

'I'll try to get home at a respectable time tonight,' she said. 'Maybe we could catch a film or something?' *Anything out of the ordinary.*

'Good idea,' said Steven. 'See you later.'

He picked up his briefcase in the hall and left for work, running down the stairs rather than taking the lift in an effort to keep fit now that he was chained to a desk for much of the time. He walked round to the car park and got into the Honda CRV that had taken the place of his Porsche Boxster – a sacrifice he'd had to make when his government salary cheque had stopped and the spectre of unemployment loomed large. The hiatus had only lasted a month or so but the feeling hadn't been pleasant.

In truth, he hadn't sold the Boxster. It had been put into 'suspended animation' at the mews garage belonging to his friend Stan Silver in London. Silver, an ex-Regiment soldier himself – although not at the same time as Steven – was the man who had supplied the Porsche in the first place. It had been he who had suggested storing the car for a while to see how things worked out. He had offered to loan Steven a more modest vehicle until he found himself a job, when they could talk again.

No decision had as yet been made about the Porsche, although Steven had started paying Stan for the use of the Honda.

It had been Tally who had suggested the Honda from the cars on offer; it was more of a family car, she'd said, and if he was serious about being a family man . . . *well, look at all that space in the back.* My God, he'd thought, he'd be wearing Pringle sweaters and taking up golf next. No, suicide was higher up his list of things to do than golf. The Honda started first time; it always bloody did.

Steven had his own parking bay with a white board on the wall saying *Head of Security*. It always made him smile. To his way of thinking, the last thing you should be advertising was where the head of security parked his car. But there was no doubting that things were different in the civilian world, so he didn't say anything. From what he'd seen in the three months he'd been in the job, no one would have any reason to harm him anyway.

His office was on the sixth floor, bright and airy with light wood furniture and an abundance of potted plants. The wide windows had Venetian blinds, necessary in the afternoon when the sun moved round to that side of the building, but it was a dull, grey morning so he opened them fully and looked out over the campus. People in white coats were hard at work in the university labs across the way, as they would be downstairs in his own building, clearly visible in the harsh, white fluorescent lighting that illuminated their domain.

A knock came to his door but before he could say anything it was opened by a short woman in her mid thirties, hair tied back in a severe bun, and dark-framed glasses on her nose. She was Rachel Collins, one of the company's legal team who specialised in intellectual property. She had the office next door. She smiled and said, 'I thought I heard you come in. Have you checked your email yet?'

'No.'

'There's a special meeting at ten this morning with the top brass. You and I have been instructed to attend.'

'Sounds exciting,' said Steven in a voice that suggested otherwise. 'Maybe they've discovered a cure for cancer downstairs.'

'I think we would have heard about *that*,' said Rachel with a smile. 'The conga in the corridors would have been a small clue.'

'How long have you worked for Ultramed, Rachel?'

'Eleven years. Why d'you ask?'

'I'm still trying to get a feel for things. Any big discoveries in your time with the company?'

Rachel screwed up her face, seeking an alternative to 'no'. 'Can't honestly say there have been any *big* discoveries,' she replied, stretching the word 'big'. 'Lots of little things, stuff for indigestion, athlete's foot treatments, hay fever pills, bread-and-butter stuff, not much better than the remedies they're replacing, if truth be told, but with a shiny new box and an ad campaign aimed at GPs they bring in a bit. No really big earner.'

'I guess big earners don't come along all that often.'

'And that's why drugs are so expensive,' said Rachel. 'Lots and lots of research that went nowhere has to be paid for. Anyway, see you at the meeting.' She turned to leave but stopped and turned back as she reached the door. 'How are you liking it here?' she asked, her tone suggesting that she really didn't know the answer.

'Fine,' said Steven. 'Absolutely fine.'

'Good.'

Steven returned to gazing out of the window, wishing it had been true. He was a very long way from being 'absolutely fine'. He had known it would be difficult; he had done his best to prepare himself for the feelings he knew were bound to come. The one he had at the moment, that of being trapped, had been odds-on favourite to make an appearance from the outset but he was determined not to give in to it despite the urge he felt right now to run downstairs, go out through the door and keep on going till he dropped.

The first antidote was to think of positives. He thought of Tally and the life they were having and would have together. He thought of Jenny, his little girl who now had a father in an ordinary respectable job rather than one that could result in her becoming an orphan. The second counter-measure was to think of negatives, those that had made him resign from Sci-Med in the first place. The creeping suspicion, built up over the years, that he didn't work for the good guys after all; that there were no good guys, only various shades of in-between. Our democratic government was a warren of ulterior motives, alternative agendas, horse trading and compromise, connived at by a bunch of greedy self-serving twerps whose egos knew no bounds and whose only duty was to themselves.

He was now away from all of them and their devious machinations but he did miss the intellectual challenge of the job, that of figuring out what the hooks and crooks were up to and then going to war with them. Someone in the SAS had once told him that you don't know you're alive until you're very nearly not, and they were right. Everyone who had experienced danger over a long period of time knew about 'the feeling', that heightened sense of awareness which perhaps only drugs could simulate. When it stopped you were relieved, but if it didn't come back at some point you'd start to miss it, and miss it badly. Formula One drivers, rock climbers, downhill skiers, all knew about 'the feeling'. Retiral might seem like a good idea at the time but after a year or so, God, you missed it. You just had to go back.

Steven's game plan was to think of his time with the military and with Sci-Med as a drug addiction from which he was now withdrawing. It wouldn't be easy but it could be done. He would struggle to keep his twitchiness and bad temper under control while he fought his demons, and in the end he would come through and emerge as a better person: a loving, contented husband to Tally if she'd have him as such and a caring considerate father to Jenny, even if she chose to remain in the north. *Enough navel gazing.* He turned on his computer and checked his mail for details of the meeting.

TWO

Sci-Med Inspectorate, Home Office, London

'I have Chief Superintendent Malloy on the line for you, Sir John,' said the voice of Jean Roberts, his secretary, from the speaker on John Macmillan's desk.

'Put him through.'

'John? I don't think I'm going to make lunch today. Something's just come up.'

'A pity, Charlie. I was looking forward to seeing you again. It's been ages.'

'It has,' agreed Malloy, 'but the French authorities have been in touch. I don't know if you heard anything about a gas explosion in Paris?'

'I read something in the papers.'

'Turns out it wasn't gas; it was a bomb and it looks like at least some of the victims may have been British. Fragments of British passports were found in the clean-up.'

'Ah,' said Macmillan. 'So someone else's mess has just become yours. Any idea what's behind it?'

'Not right now, but the *gendarmerie* has ascertained that the flat was let to an Englishman named Charles French on a short-term agreement. Apparently it wasn't the first time, according to the letting agency. He'd used the place on a number of occasions when he was in Paris on business.'

'What kind of business would that be?'

'The agency had no reason to know that and didn't ask, but

we matched the name up with a missing person report. If it's the same chap, he's Charles French, CEO of Deltasoft Computing, a Cambridge graduate and pillar of the community, by all accounts.'

'Did the passport fragments yield anything?'

'We've managed to identify one holder so far. There was enough of the name left for us to match it up with a Lady Antonia Freeman who has been absent from her holiday home in the south of France near Saint-Raphaël where she likes to spend the winter months. Her housekeeper reported her missing; apparently she'd no idea her ladyship had gone up to Paris.'

'Strange. What was that name again?'

'Antonia Freeman.'

'Rings a vague bell . . .'

'Let me know if anything comes to you,' said Malloy. 'I think our best bet is to match up what we've got with passport control and missing person reports.

Anyway, sorry about lunch. How are you fixed for next week?'

'That should be fine,' said Macmillan. 'I look forward to hearing more.'

Macmillan pressed the intercom button. 'Jean, I've rescheduled my lunch with DCS Malloy for the same day and time next week.'

'I'll put it in the diary, Sir John. All right if I go to lunch?'

'Of course.'

'Don't forget you have a recruitment meeting at two thirty.'

'Ah, yes. Thanks, Jean.'

Macmillan got up and walked over to the window to look out at the rain while he thought about the meeting Jean had reminded him of. He'd been avoiding considering a replacement for Steven Dunbar until it was absolutely certain that he wouldn't be returning, but sadly it seemed that that moment had come. Steven had twice turned down his overtures and still appeared adamant about not coming back. Macmillan knew why, of course, and understood Steven's frustration at watching the guilty walk free so often – he hated it himself – but surely, through his anger, he must be able to see why no charges could have been brought at the end of his last investigation. It was just not in the national interest. He'd felt sure that Steven would come round eventually, as he'd always done in the past, but apparently not this time. He was now working as some kind of security consultant, living in Leicester. God, what a waste.

Sci-Med was Macmillan's baby. He'd seen the need for a different sort of investigator in a high-tech world. True, the police had special squads, such as those that dealt with fraud and crime in the art world, but when it came to science and medicine they lacked expertise. It had taken him several years to persuade the government of the day to agree with him that such a unit was necessary, and that it should be independent, but in the end he had succeeded. It had now been operational for fifteen years.

There was no doubt it had been a success, as several governments had been forced to admit, although perhaps they would have liked Sci-Med to have been a little less independent on occasions where success had also brought embarrassment when the great and the good had been exposed as being rather less then either. As this embarrassment had not been confined to any one party, history had worked in Sci-Med's favour, ensuring that any attempt by the rulers of the day to clip the unit's wings would be vigorously opposed by Her Majesty's Opposition, whoever happened to be in power. Macmillan had often pointed out that it was the opposition who kept Sci-Med in business, not the government.

Steven had been Macmillan's top investigator, a doctor and a soldier with a proven record of being good at both, and he wouldn't be easy to replace. Sir John had asked two of his other investigators, Scott Jamieson and Adam Dewar, to come in and help him assess possible candidates but he would be doing it with a heavy heart. Another course of action open to him would, of course, be . . . retirement. After all, he had the knighthood and had passed the sixty milestone where most senior career civil servants went off to grow roses and write their memoirs, but he couldn't quite bear the thought of giving up the reins of Sci-Med just yet. It meant so much to him . . . if not his wife, it had to be said. She would be delighted to see him walk away from it all to spend more time with her. Given half a chance, she'd have him on some round-the-world cruise, dancing bloody rumbas with her blue-rinsed pals and listening to their bloody boring banker husbands telling him how they saw the crash coming all along. Jesus, he wasn't dead yet.

The rain had stopped and the sky was brightening. He'd lost his appetite for lunch but he'd walk over to the club anyway if only to smell the wet grass in the park. Apart from that, something Charlie had said was niggling away at him. He'd mentioned that the dead woman was Lady Antonia Freeman. Macmillan felt that the name should mean something to him, but for the moment he couldn't think why.

The meeting with Scott Jamieson and Adam Dewar was a relaxed affair, during which they narrowed down the list of potential candidates for Steven Dunbar's replacement to three: two were medics, one a science graduate, all in their mid thirties. It was Macmillan's practice never to recruit people who hadn't yet proved themselves in other jobs, so new graduates were not considered. Both medics had served in Afghanistan with distinction. One was an A&E specialist, the other an orthopaedic surgeon. Both had been called into action through their association with the Territorial Army. Once derided as weekend soldiering, membership of the TA now meant almost certain active service overseas. The science graduate, with a first in biological sciences from Heriot-Watt University in Edinburgh, had seen service in Iraq with the Military Police, where he had shown himself to be a more than competent investigator in uncovering a medical supplies scam.

'Are you sure Steven won't be coming back?' Scott Jamieson asked.

'I think his mind is made up.'

Dewar seemed almost embarrassed about saying what was on his mind. 'You know, I'm not at all clear . . . why he left.'

'Come to that, me neither,' added Jamieson.

'And I'm afraid I can't tell you,' said Macmillan. 'Don't take that personally. I would trust the pair of you with my life, but there are some things that the fewer people know about them the better, and Steven's last assignment was most decidedly one of them.'

'But as no court case was forthcoming at the end of it, we might guess that that was the reason?' said Jamieson.

'Let's move on.'

'Yes, boss.' Jamieson smiled.

'Check your diaries: let me know any dates that aren't suitable and then I'll ask Jean to send out invitations for interview. No hurry: sometime in the next few days.'

'Still hoping?' said Dewar.

As Macmillan was clearing his desk at the end of the day, he suddenly remembered why the name Antonia Freeman should mean something to him. Her husband had been Sir Martin Freeman, an eminent surgeon in his day. It was a long time ago, back in the early nineties, but he had died in the middle of an operation. He'd been operating on a woman who'd had a bad facial deformity from birth, attempting to give her a new face using a revolutionary new technique, when he'd collapsed and died in theatre.

There had been some other scandal surrounding the whole affair whose details he couldn't remember, but what he did remember was thinking at the time that that was exactly the kind of situation that cried out for an organisation like Sci-Med. In the morning, he would ask Jean to see what she could come up with about the case. It might just be a trip down memory lane, but his widow had just got herself blown to bits in Paris. The niggle had gone; he felt a whole lot better.

The Black Dahlia Restaurant, Chelsea, London

A tall, elegant man sipped gin and tonic and thumbed through the wine list while he waited for the others to arrive. He'd chosen the restaurant because it had a small private dining room, ideal for the five of them. Officially they were the competitions committee of Redwood Park golf club, and he was the secretary, James Black. Unofficially, they weren't, and he wasn't.

Toby Langton was first to arrive, a slightly stooped man with an unruly crop of light brown hair, and clothing that suggested an academic, which he was. When he spoke it was in a languid drawl but with an underlying confidence that tended to present opinion as fact. Constance Carradine was next, a woman in her mid thirties, 'power-dressed' as expected of a prominent figure in the City of London. She wore a well-cut navy blue suit over a white blouse, and a pale blue chiffon scarf at her throat. Her dark hair was cropped short and she wore fashionable small-framed spectacles that only served to amplify an already piercing stare. Finally, Rupert Coutts and Elliot Soames came in together, having met in the car park. Both wore dark Savile Row business suits, individualised, in their minds at least, by the ties they wore: regimental for Soames, an ex-Guards officer who now headed an asset management group; university for Coutts, a top-level career civil servant.

'Good to see you all,' said Black after they'd ordered drinks. When they arrived, the waiter, dressed in black but wearing a white apron and looking as if he'd stepped out of a nineteenth-century French painting, asked if they would like to see menus.

'Give us thirty minutes,' replied Black, and the man left.

'I haven't seen anything in the papers,' said Coutts.

'Nor I,' said Langton.

'There was a small piece in the *Independent*,' said Constance Carradine. 'Suspected gas explosion in Paris suburb kills five.'

'Actually six, but it'll take them a while to figure out who they all are,' said Black. 'After all, none of them were supposed to be there and wouldn't have told anyone where they were going. As to what they were doing there . . . that will remain anyone's guess.'

'Please God,' murmured Soames.

'French was meticulous about security. We're safe.'

'It's all a bit of a shame really,' said Constance Carradine. 'I mean, they were the ones who set the whole thing up all those years ago.'

'And they did a good job in their day,' said Black. 'But their day was over. They had their chance before the New Labour nightmare began and they blew it. One prying journalist got nosy and they had to shut the whole thing down before the party twigged what was going on. They had no option but to lie low until the dust had settled, and by that time scandal had destroyed the party and an election was lost. So were the subsequent two. They wanted to go down that same old route again. Can you believe it? They turned our plan down. We've spent ten years putting it together and getting everything in place and they turned it down. They had to go.'

'So here we are,' said Langton. 'The new executive of the Schiller Group, the guardians of all we hold precious.'

'I take it we all saw the *Telegraph* this morning, and the Carlisle story?' said Coutts.

'What an arse,' said Soames.

'He is a worry,' said Black. 'It was never very clear how much he actually knew at the time. He was such a posturing idiot that no one told him anything if they could avoid it.'

'But he was such a pretty boy,' said Constance. 'Shame he had the intellect of a cabbage. Now he's starting to look like one.'

'Well, he served his purpose as the charming front man of his day. I sometimes wonder what would have happened if French and co. had taken him all the way to the top.'

'Doesn't bear thinking about.'

'There's a story going around that he's been trying to telephone people high up in the party,' said Black. 'No one's talking to him, of course. He's about as popular as bubonic plague, but he seems to think he has something to bargain with . . . something to stop the leader pulling the rug out from under him. We're by no means past the post in this election. We don't need strange stories doing the rounds, even if they come from a discredited clown like Carlisle. We could be back in the wilderness.'

'He's a loose cannon,' said Langton. The others turned to face him. 'If he did know more than we think he did, he might well see this as the time to use it.'

'Blackmail, you mean?'

'It was more a revelation to the press I was thinking of. If the leader shows him the door, what's he got to lose?'

'Maybe we should . . . help matters along?' suggested Coutts.

There was a long silence in the room until Constance Carradine said, 'I think that might be a very good idea. There will be lots of very angry constituents out there; no telling what they might do. It would also give me the chance to test out the new chain of command.'

'Very well,' said Black. 'It's agreed, unless anyone has objections?' Thinking there were none, he was about to continue when Langton spoke again.

'I really don't think it a good idea to go down the angry constituents route,' he drawled. 'It would only amplify the nature of the crime in the eyes of the public – *he made them so angry they felt they had to take matters into their own hands*, et cetera – that would do the party no good at all.'

'Good point,' said Black.

'What would you suggest?' asked Constance, irked at having her idea shot down.

'Something that would elicit public sympathy for Carlisle would be preferable.'

'Like?'

'I'll leave that in your capable hands, Connie,' said Langton with a smile.

Black decided to move things along. 'Connie's already mentioned putting the new regime to the test,' he said. 'How about the rest of you? Have you used the information from the disks? Elliot, what's happening with our finances?'

'Absolutely no problems there,' replied Soames. 'I used the contact number and gave the password. I told them I had taken over as trustee of the Wellington Foundation from Lady Antonia Freeman. It was accepted without question. I requested statements and they arrived the following day. Things are looking good, very good indeed.'

'Excellent. Always nice to have money in the bank.'

The others reported similar success in touching base with people designated as operational contacts.

'We have to hand it to Charles French,' said Black. 'He did an outstanding job in setting up the network. But the old guard has gone. We are now the only people who know just how many members we have, how many people there are out there who share our views and care enough to change things, organised as cells within cells within cells . . . people all prepared to do their bit for their country.'

There was a knock on the door and the waiter entered.

'So we're all agreed about the changes to the fourteenth hole and the ladies' tee on the fifteenth?' said Black.

'Absolutely.'

'Would you like some menus now, Mr Black?' asked the waiter.

'You know, I think we would.'

THREE

Melissa Carlisle arrived back at Markham House, the wedding present from her father where she and John had lived all the years of their marriage, the last ten of them in complete misery as far as Melissa was concerned. She watched the taxi crunch off down the gravel drive to be let out by the two policemen on the gates – there to keep the small posse of cold, miserable press photographers at bay. If they were expecting tea, they could swivel.

She felt very low. She had spent the last few days being lectured by her father, who insisted that women like her did not leave their husbands at times like this. It mattered not one jot that John was a useless waste of space. She hadn't taken his advice at the time, and now it was far too late. It was her duty to stand beside her husband in his hour of need. That's what people of her sort did. Argument had proved useless. Times might have changed but core values hadn't, her father had pronounced before packing her off back home as if she were a rebellious teenager not wanting to return to school after the holidays. Her mother had kept quiet throughout.

Melissa unlocked the front door, thought about announcing that she was back, then changed her mind and flung her keys down on the hall table. The noise echoed upwards. She walked through to the kitchen where she switched on the kettle and stood looking out of the window at the grounds while she waited for the expected *Is that you?* to come. It didn't.

Melissa wondered whether he was out but his car was there,

a grey Range Rover sitting in front of the garage. She made her tea and took it through to the drawing room where she picked up the morning paper and sat down to read it. She found she couldn't concentrate: she certainly didn't want to but she kept wondering where he was. In the end she threw down the paper and walked out into the hall. 'John,' she called, trying to make it sound as flat and uncaring as possible. God, it was awful what so much loathing did to you, she thought. 'John?' There was no reply.

She went upstairs and checked his study before knocking on the door of his bedroom – they'd had separate rooms since the business involving his secretary some years before. There was no response but she looked in anyway, considering he might have climbed into the bottle and passed out as he often did when problems came to call. The room was empty. The bed was made . . . but it was made properly, the way Mrs Allan, their cleaner, did it. But this wasn't her day . . . and neither was yesterday.

Melissa walked slowly up to it and smoothed the top cover unnecessarily. The bed hadn't been slept in for the past two nights. Just what the hell was he up to? What parliamentary 'researcher' was he pouring his heart out to this time, before pulling her pants down? But his car was there. Where the hell was he?

Melissa cursed as she opened the back door and saw it had started to rain heavily. She pushed it to while she put on wellington boots and a Barbour jacket before stepping outside and hurrying over to the garage and stable block. 'John, are you there?'

She found John in the stables. He was hanging from a roof beam.

Melissa felt her heart miss a beat as she stood there transfixed by the sight of his face. It was blotchy purple and white, and his swollen tongue was lolling out of the side of his mouth, making him look like some hideous gargoyle on the wall of a medieval cathedral. His body was turning slowly in response to the draught coming in from the open door. Above him the rain battered mercilessly on a small skylight.

'Oh, Christ,' she murmured as she moved in closer to remove the envelope pinned to a rail. It was addressed to her. In it, John apologised for all the pain and distress he had caused, not only to her but to his constituents as well. He understood their anger but hoped that in time they would come to see that it had been a genuine error of judgement.

Melissa looked up at the body, her eyes showing a mixture of frustration and anger. 'A suicide note . . .' she murmured, 'and you bloody *typed* it.'

Steven was sitting with his feet up, reading the paper, when Tally got home at six thirty. 'Here as promised,' she announced. She was slightly flushed from hurrying.

'Well done,' said Steven. He got up and gave her a hug. 'A whole evening to ourselves. What takes your fancy, dinner or a movie?'

'Why don't you choose? I've been the one working late all the time.'

'Dinner,' said Steven. 'We haven't had the chance to sit down and talk for ages.'

'Okay, I'll shower and make myself smell nice while you decide where we're going.'

Steven's suggestion of Italian was warmly received by Tally. 'Any particular reason?' she asked.

'I thought we might go to Bar Firenze. We enjoyed it last time: noisy, cheerful, chaotic, and Italians make great sweets.'

'And I can flirt with the waiters.'

'While I have a second sweet.'

'As if I would,' said Tally, sidling over and putting her hands on Steven's shoulders, 'when I've already got the best.'

'Madam is too kind,' said Steven, kissing her lightly on the lips. 'Come on, hurry up. Time and pasta wait for no man.'

'So how was your day?' he asked as they sipped an aperitif. He thought he saw a questioning look appear briefly in Tally's eyes. 'Isn't that what people like us say?'

'Yes,' she conceded, disappointed at the implication that he might be playing a part. 'I suppose it is. My day was hectic, stressful, frustrating and thoroughly unsatisfying as they all are these days in a health service that's falling to bits. I spend half my time dealing with management demands that I tick boxes and meet targets stipulated by politicians who don't actually give a damn about anyone but themselves but are determined to create the impression that they do. It's all about image. Substance doesn't matter as long as things look right on the surface.'

'I wish I hadn't asked. But if that's the case, it does leave a rather obvious question begging to be asked, doctor . . .'

Tally looked thoughtful for a moment, as if considering a slap-down, but then decided that the question did merit an answer. 'Because . . . there comes a time, through all the shit and management crap, when it's just me and a sick kid and I'm the one who can make the difference . . . and when I've made it and the kid walks off the ward, trailing his little Thomas the Tank Engine suitcase behind him and Mum and Dad have that look in their eyes – that special look – there's just no feeling like it.'

Steven swallowed and nodded. 'Fair enough.'

'How was *your* day, doctor?'

Steven gave an apologetic shrug, trying to avoid giving an answer after what had gone before, but Tally's expression made it plain she was waiting for one. 'I attended a management meeting this morning. The company knew about the agreement over vaccine production we heard about this morning on the radio. It's considering a big change in emphasis.'

'You mean it's going to tender for the manufacturing contract?' asked Tally.

Steven nodded.

'You're right; that is a big change in emphasis. I hope they've thought it through.'

'Although it's not a party political thing, they seem to think that the fact it was a Conservative initiative might well help the party's cause in the election. They see that as a good thing.'

'I suppose it might even influence me,' said Tally. 'How about you?'

'I won't be voting.'

Tally could see by Steven's expression that he meant it, and they'd been down this road before. 'Well, I won't give you a lecture on what people have suffered in the past so that we can have the right to vote,' she said. 'I know you have your reasons.'

'Correct. I detest the lot of them.'

Tally gave a little smile. 'I won't even argue that there must be some good ones. I will simply drop the subject and move on.'

'Good.'

'What do you think about the company's plan?'

Steven thought for a moment. 'They want to do the opposite from the big guys. They want to change the emphasis from research to production. Less risk equals more happy shareholders. The contract will have to go to tender but they sounded like they really want it; they were talking about coming up with a very competitive bid, cutting every last cent to win it.'

Tally paused while Steven refilled her glass. 'Where does the head of security fit into all this?' she asked.

'We're not going to be the only company hoping to land the contract. Knowing what the other guys are bidding could be a huge advantage. It'll be my job to ensure that our figure stays a secret.'

Tally nodded. 'And if your company lands the contract and

the emphasis shifts away from research . . . where would that leave you?'

Steven smiled as he filled his own glass. 'I suppose I could be out of a job if the research element of the company disappears completely, but maybe they'll find something else for me to do, cleaning the lavatories or something.'

'Pathetic, Dunbar.'

'It was, wasn't it? I'll have to work on my self-pity. What do you say to another bottle?'

'*Grazie mille, signore.*'

FOUR

Lark Pharmaceuticals, Canterbury, Kent

Dr Mark Mosely parked his dark green Jaguar in his designated parking spot, and pulled his collar up against a biting east wind as he crossed to the glass front doors, which slid open on instructions from the infrared detector above them.

'Morning, serfs,' he said as he made his way past the potted palms of Reception to the lifts.

The two receptionists smiled dutifully at the daily joke and chanted their 'Good morning, sir' like primary school children.

Mosely was in a good mood. The announcement about the vaccines agreement was good news for everyone in the industry and heralded a new era in operating conditions for companies like his. It should do much to reduce the mountain of regulations that had built up over the last ten years.

The clock showed nine thirty; it was time to carry out his weekly inspection of the manufacturing floors.

The line managers would be waiting for him on Level 3 as usual to conduct him round their domains. After that he would have his weekly meeting with the quality controllers and then lunch in the canteen with the workers to listen to any minor grievances they might have . . . just as he'd done for the past two decades. In the afternoon he would inspect the loading bays and talk to the transport manager about delivery schedules. There was also the ongoing discussion about additional fleet vehicles to deal with. He knew the transport manager favoured

Mercedes vans but he himself would prefer vehicles that were at least assembled in the UK.

The main event of the day was to be a meeting with representatives from Oxfam and three other major charities at three p.m. to discuss the quantities and distribution of vaccine supplies for Third World countries, and to appraise the latest reports from the World Health Organisation, especially projections for future needs.

Lark Pharmaceuticals was a private, non-profit-making concern set up by a charitable trust some twenty years before. It made a profit from one half of its business – the manufacture of diagnostic kits, antiseptic creams and antihistamine compounds – and this was used to fund the other half, which manufactured vaccines for Third World countries at rock-bottom prices, something that attracted much favourable publicity for the company in a world that was deeply suspicious of the motives driving drug companies. The walls of its reception area were adorned with the many awards it had received from humanitarian organisations.

Mosely was going through his mail when the phone rang. He could see the call was coming from level B2.

'Everything is ready. We need to talk.'

'This evening. Seven p.m.'

Sci-Med Inspectorate, Home Office, London

John Macmillan left the office and walked across the park to keep his postponed lunch date with Charlie Malloy. He saw a few snowdrops on the way but they failed to convince him that winter was anywhere near ending. A 'barbecue summer' that wasn't had been followed by a 'warm, wet winter' that had turned out to be the coldest in many years, leaving him feeling nothing but frustration with weather forecasters.

Leonard, the club's doorman of many years, welcomed him

into the warmth and took his coat. 'Chief Superintendent Malloy is already here, Sir John,' he said. 'I've put him in the lounge.'

It was John Macmillan's custom to invite contacts in government and administration to have lunch with him on a rotational basis – not people at ministerial level but fairly high-level players who knew what was going on. It was his way of getting a feel for things, hearing the latest rumours and often putting two and two together. Sci-Med investigated what they saw fit, and were therefore very dependent on information gathering. Much of it was done by computers using programs developed over the years to seek out reports of unusual happenings in science and medicine, but the human touch was also very important.

'Good to see you, Charlie,' said Macmillan, entering the lounge and shaking hands. 'How are things?'

'A bit calmer this week, although we've been left with a bit of a headache. You remember the supposed gas explosion that turned out to be a bomb?'

'And you had identified two of the dead as British?'

'That's right. Turns out all six of them were.'

'What was it? Some kind of club or business meeting?'

Malloy shook his head. 'They didn't travel together. In fact, they seemed to come from all over the place to meet their death in Paris on a cold afternoon in February.'

'The woman you mentioned last week, I remembered why her name struck a chord. Her husband was Sir Martin Freeman, a groundbreaking surgeon in his day who went out on a bit of a low. He collapsed and died in the middle of an operation.'

'Good God, the stuff of nightmares,' murmured Malloy, his expression mirroring his words.

'So what was she? A doctor like hubby or a nurse who got lucky?'

'Actually neither. In fact I think it was a case of Martin getting lucky. Antonia came from a very well-to-do family whereas Martin got his shoulder tapped for being good at his trade.

Story was she and her family didn't let him forget it either. Not the nicest of people, by all accounts.'

'That would fit with her not having many friends, then,' said Malloy. 'I can't say my chaps have been finding her sorely missed. Thanks for your input.'

'How about the others?'

'Actually, identification wasn't too difficult.'

Macmillan frowned. 'How so?'

'The rest of the dead were all big hitters and quickly reported missing. One was chairman of a merchant bank, another was a top-level civil servant, and the other two were captains of industry. The strange thing was that none of their families knew they were in Paris.'

Macmillan let out a low whistle. 'So why go there?'

'Because they didn't want to be seen here?' suggested Malloy after a moment's thought and a long sip of wine.

'I do believe tonight's star prize goes to Chief Superintendent Malloy,' said Macmillan. 'Do you think I could be kept in the loop on this one, Charlie? For some reason, it's making me feel uneasy and I'm not sure why.'

'No problem. Is your Steven Dunbar back with you yet or is he still in a huff?'

Macmillan smiled. 'I wish it were only a huff, Charlie. I really do.'

'So what went on there?'

Macmillan adopted a dignified pose. 'In the interests of the state, I can't tell you, Charlie. I'm sorry.'

'Heigh-ho, I've been round that block a few times. The bottom line's always the same. Some high-up bugger's got away with something.'

Macmillan didn't argue.

Jean Roberts looked up as Macmillan came in. 'Nice lunch, sir?'

'Interesting. Jean, have you had a chance to do anything yet about the information I asked for on Martin Freeman's last operation?'

Jean brought out a red folder from her desk drawer. It seemed to weigh quite a bit as she struggled to lift it with one hand. 'There was actually quite a lot going on at the time,' she explained.

Macmillan accepted the file in amazement. 'A thorough job as always, Jean,' he muttered.

He spent the remainder of the afternoon reading through the file recording the events of 1992 when Martin Freeman had died while operating on a severely disfigured patient at College Hospital, Newcastle. Another surgeon, Dr Claire Affric, who had been assisting Freeman at the time, had taken over and completed the operation but press access to the principals at all stages afterwards had been very limited, and there had been rumours that the bandaged figure finally put before the cameras to assure everyone that all was well was not the patient, Greta Marsh, at all. The whole unhappy saga did little to calm Macmillan's unease. Instead, it triggered off more memories.

A very good investigative journalist had been covering the case at the time, he recalled. He worked for one of the nationals and had been successful in uncovering some NHS funding scandal before he went north to look at the Greta Marsh affair. Kincaid, that was his name, James Kincaid. He'd never returned from that assignment up north. He and a nurse from a local hospital had been found dead. The explanation had been that Kincaid had become interested in another story concerning a drugs racket, and had paid the price for interference along with the nurse, who'd become his girlfriend.

Macmillan read that Kincaid and his girl had not been the only victims of what the papers had called the northern drugs war. Paul Schreiber, a pharmacist who had been involved in setting up a new health initiative at College Hospital, had also died along with two male nurses when thieves had carried out a raid on the hospital pharmacy. Yet another victim of the war had been a local GP named Tolkien, who'd been running a drug rehabilitation clinic in the area.

Macmillan rested his elbows on the desk and cupped his chin in his hands to read on. The violence had not been confined to the north. Kincaid's editor in London had also been murdered, supposedly in case Kincaid had passed on any of his findings to him.

Something stirring at the back of his mind made Macmillan look back a couple of pages to the piece on Paul Schreiber. It wasn't the murder that had caught his attention, it was the bit about his being involved in 'a new health initiative'. He leaned over and pressed the intercom button. 'Jean, what was the name of that Tory MP who committed suicide the other day?'

'John Carlisle, sir.'

Ye gods, that was it. Carlisle was the figurehead at the time of . . . Macmillan willed the name to come to him. The Northern Health Scheme, that was it. John Carlisle had been health secretary back then and had been credited with introducing a revolutionary, computerised new health initiative in the north of England, which by all accounts had been hugely successful.

But then . . . what? Macmillan found to his embarrassment that he couldn't remember much more. Carlisle had seemed to fade from popular view although only a few months before he had been touted as a possible future leader of the Conservative Party. The new, computerised health scheme had also disappeared. 'How very strange,' he said aloud.

'What is, Sir John?' asked Jean Roberts's voice. Macmillan had left the intercom on. He switched it off without apology. His mind was now on other things, spreading its horizons. It was all a very long time ago and the Tories had been voted out of office in '97, but the fact that Carlisle's career had come to such an abrupt end in the preceding parliament, and such a hugely successful health initiative had ground to a halt without explanation now struck him as very odd.

'Jean, I need all you can get me on something called the Northern Health Scheme, operating around the early nineties in the north of England at a time when John Carlisle was Secretary of State for Health.'

'How soon, Sir John?'

'Yesterday.'

He knew that there would be no Sci-Med files on the subject as this was before the inception of the unit, but Jean would use press archives in the first instance and augment them with government information where necessary. He got the first of her results an hour later.

He couldn't have told anyone what he was looking for as he leafed through the pages; he didn't know himself, but he knew that he'd recognise it when he found it, and a few minutes later he did, in the list of people responsible for the running of the short-lived Northern Health Scheme introduced in November 1991. Apart from John Carlisle, one Charles French of Deltasoft was there: the Charles French who had just been blown to bits in Paris . . . along with Antonia Freeman.

'Hell and damnation,' whispered Macmillan, tapping his pen on the desk in a gesture of annoyance as something else occurred to him. He looked back at the material on Martin Freeman to make doubly sure. Yes, it was the same hospital: College Hospital, Newcastle.

Macmillan looked into the middle distance for a long time before realising that the dull headache that had been plaguing him for the past few days was getting worse. In fact, it was becoming unbearable. Beads of sweat broke out on his forehead as he held his hands to his temples.

'Jean, I need some help in here . . .'

FIVE

'You seem down,' said Steven, watching Tally play more with her food than eat it. It had gone eight o'clock on Tuesday evening and Steven had prepared dinner, although 'prepared' was perhaps an exaggeration: he'd opened two M&S ready meals and heated them up. Steven didn't cook, never had. Food had never played a big part in his life and he couldn't quite understand all the fuss about it, particularly the hours devoted to it on television.

'Things on my mind.'

'Am I allowed to ask what?'

Tally gave a slight shake of the head as if reluctant to go further, but then she reconsidered. 'It's my mother,' she said. 'She's finding it difficult to cope. Independence in the community with support or whatever they call it is just not working out.'

Steven made a face.

'A home would kill her. She's always said so.'

'Most people do,' said Steven, aware that his words could be construed as callous but still feeling it needed pointing out. 'It really doesn't have to be that bad.'

'How many of these places have you seen?' snapped Tally.

'Not many.'

Tally's stare demanded more.

'None.'

'She's my mother, Steven. The woman who brought me into the world, comforted me when I was down, encouraged me when I was unsure, cheered for me when I won things, found excuses for when I didn't. She made me what I am. I wouldn't be comforting other people's kids on a daily basis if she hadn't done that for me. Don't you understand?'

'Yup, I had one just like her,' said Steven.

Tally digested the comment for a moment, acknowledging the truth of what Steven was saying but unwilling to give ground. She rested her head in her hands, considering other ways to get her point across. 'I just cannot bear the thought of putting my mother into one of these places where she'll end up watching daytime fucking television until she dies. No one deserves that.'

'Which brings us to the alternatives.'

Tally leaned forward and let her fingers slip through her hair to the back of her head. 'And there aren't any . . . Right?'

'My work situation is not good enough for you to give up your job to look after your mother,' said Steven.

'I know, I know . . . but thanks for the thought. Look, I don't want to discuss it any more tonight. My sister Jackie's coming up from Dorset at the weekend. We'll talk about it then.'

'I think you once mentioned having two sisters,' said Steven. 'But you never got round to telling me their names.'

Tally smiled. 'I suppose there's still quite a lot we don't know about each other.

'Then we shouldn't get bored.'

'If you say so,' said Tally, relaxing a little. 'You'll like Jackie. She's fun.'

'Anything else on your mind?'

'Yes, the constant struggle to get medication approved for our cancer kids. I know health budgets are not bottomless pits but come on, children are our future. We should be doing our best for them, not making endless assessments as to the *likely outcome of therapy* before loosening the purse strings. There are too many people pursuing too many agendas.'

'Maybe an election will clear the air and make things easier.'

'Do you really believe that?'

'No, I just thought I'd try to cheer you up.'

'You're impossible.'

'It's a gift.'

'Another one?'

'You're right. I do seem to have more than my fair share. Still, what can one do?'

Tally made to throw a cushion at him, but was interrupted by the phone ringing. She read the caller display and paused before picking up. 'It's John Macmillan,' she said.

'I'm out,' said Steven.

Tally answered while Steven started clearing away the dinner things. 'I'm sorry, Lady Macmillan, he's just stepped out for a moment,' she said as Steven left the room on his way to the kitchen. 'Can I help?'

Steven returned from his chores to hear Tally saying, 'Oh, I'm so sorry. Of course I will. He'll be back shortly. I'll get him to call you . . . Yes . . . Goodbye.'

Steven's eyes asked the question.

'John Macmillan's in hospital. He collapsed. It's a brain tumour, and it's not looking good. He's asked to see you.'

Steven sank down into a chair and rubbed his forehead lightly with his fingertips.

'You have to go.'

Steven was finding it difficult to think straight. He and John Macmillan had had a difference of opinion but that didn't alter the fact that Macmillan was probably the most decent, honourable man he'd ever met. They thought the same way about practically everything. They had often argued but it was usually just a case of Macmillan using the wisdom of his years to temper Steven's impatience to get on with things. He had walked away from the Sci-Med job but there had been nothing personal in it and John knew that. It had been he who had saved Steven from the boredom of a meaningless nine-to-five life in some humdrum job when he left the services; it had been he who had rescued him from the . . . life he now lived.

Steven tried to block out that last thought and closed his eyes tightly.

'You okay?' Tally asked.

Steven nodded. 'I'll phone John's wife.'

He drove to London in the morning, having been assured that there was no point in his driving down the night before. The doctors had told Lady Macmillan that John had had a good day and was sleeping peacefully. He was awake when Steven was shown into his room in the King Edward VII Hospital, and managed a small smile.

'How are you feeling?'

'I've felt better.'

'They tell me you'll be out of here in no time.'

'I think not,' croaked Macmillan.

'It's malignant?'

'They don't know yet. Either way it has to go. We're talking fifty-fifty surgery.'

Steven nodded and swallowed. 'I'll make sure no fat lady is found singing round here for the foreseeable future.'

Macmillan put his hand on Steven's wrist and gave it a slight squeeze. 'At the risk of sounding like a recruiting poster, your country needs you,' he said.

'Not me,' said Steven. 'It's Sci-Med it needs and that's all your doing.'

'That's why I wanted to see you.'

Steven shook his head. 'No good, John. Unlike you, I'd reached my limit. I'd had enough. It was time to stop getting into fights I couldn't win. I needed . . . something else.'

'Have you found it?'

'I love Tally.'

'That isn't what I asked.'

'Change takes time.'

'You were the best. You *are* the best. I need you to head Sci-Med if I don't make it, otherwise it was all for nothing.'

'That's nonsense and you know it.'

Macmillan chose to stare directly at Steven without reply.

'And unfair.'

'All that's required for evil to triumph is that good men do nothing . . .'

'You have Scott Jamieson, Adam Dewar. They're both experienced men. They could do the job perfectly well. You know they could.'

'I don't want *perfectly well*. I need the best for Sci-Med.'

'I'd lose Tally.'

This proved effective as a stopper. Macmillan seemed to lose animation and sank back on his pillow. A veil of tiredness swam over his eyes. 'There's a reason I need the best,' he said. 'Will you hear me out?'

'Of course.'

'Almost twenty years ago something happened which no one ever got to the bottom of. Something tells me it may be about to happen again.'

'What?'

'I don't know.'

'You don't know,' repeated Steven flatly.

'A journalist named Kincaid went up north to cover a story about a new surgical technique. He never came back. His attention was diverted to another story while he was up there, something that resulted in him and his editor and a number of other people being killed. It was the time of something called the Northern Health Scheme.'

Steven looked blank.

'It was the brainchild of a Conservative politician named

John Carlisle, health secretary at the time and a man thought to be destined for greater things, the same John Carlisle who took his own life a few days ago after a scandal over his expenses.'

Steven made a face.

'Another founder member of the Northern Health Scheme, Charles French, was blown to bits in an explosion in Paris a couple of weeks ago along with the wife of a surgeon who was working at the same hospital at the same time.'

Steven frowned. 'But if all that was twenty years ago . . .'

'Eighteen, but we've had three Labour governments since then.'

Steven couldn't follow Macmillan's line of thought and was finding it all a bit much to take in. There was plenty he wanted to ask but he could see that Macmillan was very tired so he prepared to leave.

'Give it some thought, Steven, that's all I ask . . .' murmured Macmillan without opening his eyes.

'I will, John. Get some rest.'

Steven decided to check his flat in Marlborough Court before driving home. He had chosen not to sell it before his move to Leicester but to hold on to it for as long as possible, giving property prices a chance to recover. Tally had agreed it made economic sense.

It was cold inside, familiar but seeming strangely foreign as he checked the rooms. He turned the mains water on and let the taps run and splutter for a bit to clear the airlocks before parking himself in his favourite chair by the window.

The flat was one street back from the river but he had a view of it through a gap in the buildings across the way. He had watched a lot of river traffic pass by from this seat while he'd wrestled with the puzzles that Sci-Med had thrown his way. He'd also looked up at a lot of stars while letting gin and tonic take the edge off his day. But that was all in the past. He'd moved on.

As he entered the outskirts of Leicester, a time check on the radio suggested that Tally would not be home for another couple of hours, so he decided to call in at work before going home to see if there was anything that needed his attention, and to catch up on any urgent messages, not that he could recall ever having had one of those in his new job. He had rung in earlier to say he wouldn't be in but hadn't said why.

Rachel Collins met him coming out of the lift. She was on the point of leaving for the day. 'Are you okay?' she asked.

'Fine, thanks.'

'We thought you might be ill.'

'No, a friend is.'

'Oh, good. Oh, God, I mean not good about your friend but, you know . . . The chief exec was looking for you earlier.'

'Thanks, Rachel.'

Steven planked himself behind his desk and started going through his mail, all of it routine and largely comprising extra reference checks he'd made on new employees who'd started in the past couple of months. None of the checks had thrown up problems. He hadn't really imagined they would. There was an internal letter from the chief exec's office listing the names of people from the accounts and statistics department who had been charged with preparation of the company's bid for the government vaccine initiative now that it had become a reality. Steven was reading the names when his door opened and the chief executive, Lionel Montague, walked in as if modelling a black cashmere overcoat and contrasting red scarf. All that was missing was a 360-degree twirl. 'I was about to leave the car park when I saw your light was on. I tried to get you earlier.'

'I had to go to London.'

A frown crossed Montague's face. 'In connection with what, might I ask?'

Steven could sense the man was spoiling for an argument but didn't fully understand why. He hadn't had much to do with him since his arrival, although he had noted on occasion that Montague's name seemed to inspire either respect or fear in other staff members, and he wasn't sure which. Once again he had the familiar feeling of being an outsider in a world he didn't fully understand. 'In connection with the fact that my friend and former employer is dying. He asked to see me.'

'You know, I really shouldn't have to point out to senior staff like yourself that their first duty is to this company. Personal matters come second. Do I make myself clear?'

'Depressingly.'

Montague bridled at Steven's choice of word but chose not to push things further.

'How can I help you?' asked Steven, already regretting the use of it. The art of biting his tongue had yet to be fully mastered.

'What d'you mean?'

'You said you were looking for me earlier.'

'Oh, yes. I wanted to talk to you about security screening of the accountants we are tasking with the preparation of our bid.'

'I've just read who they will be,' said Steven, holding up the internal note.

'It's absolutely imperative that nothing leaks out. I can't stress that enough.'

'Absolutely.'

'And it will be your job to see that it doesn't.'

'Right.'

'Just so we understand each other.'

'We do,' said Steven calmly.

'And consider what I said earlier about conflicts of professional and personal interests.'

'I will.'

Montague exited, leaving Steven staring at the closed door. He was experiencing inner conflict over the choice of a word to describe Montague. A toughie, but just another challenge to be faced in the wonderful world of commerce. He turned to his computer and started going through his email.

SIX

'How was he?' asked Tally, when Steven got in just after seven.

'Not good.'

'Do they know if it's malignant yet?'

'No. I had a word with his doctor afterwards who showed me the scans. They're going to have to remove it but it's not going to be easy. They've told John fifty-fifty.'

Tally's eyes asked the question.

'On a good day.'

'Could you have a conversation with him?'

'Yes, he was very tired but quite *compos mentis*. He wants me to take over at Sci-Med if the worst should come to the worst. I declined.'

'How did he take that?'

'He was . . . disappointed. He seems convinced that something awful is about to happen.'

'The one-last-mission gambit,' said Tally.

'Maybe,' said Steven, impressed as always by Tally's understanding of the games people play.

'It must have been hard to turn down a dying man, especially a good friend. What reason did you give?'

'I couldn't afford to lose you.'

The reply stopped Tally in her tracks. She swallowed and unconvincingly changed the subject. 'You're back late.'

'I went to the London flat to make sure it was okay and then called in at work on the way home to go through the mail – shouldn't have bothered. Got my wrist slapped by Lionel

Montague for putting personal considerations before work and swanning off to London, as he saw it.'

'What?' exclaimed Tally, her eyes widening like saucers. 'But you're . . . No, no, no, this is all wrong. This shouldn't have happened.' She started to pace around the room as if wrestling with some inner conflict.

'Hey, it's no big deal,' Steven tried to assure her, feeling alarmed and not quite understanding her reaction.

Tally shook her head. 'No. It's not just this. I've been kidding myself. This is all wrong. I've been hoping against hope that our life together could work but it's not going to. You're not like other people, Steven. You really *are* special . . . and I thank you for trying to change for my benefit but I can't allow it any longer. You must tell John that you'll go back to Sci-Med.'

Steven was stunned. 'But what about us? We made a bargain. I agreed to walk away from it all.'

'We can't be the kind of "us" I hoped for. I'm just going to have to accept that; we'll have to work round it. You are Steven Dunbar, the kindest of the kind, the bravest of the brave, and the fact of the matter is that one day with you is worth a lifetime with any nine-to-five, arse-kissing, pen-pushing emasculated excuse for a man who'd put the company before the wishes of a dying friend – the sort of man I was trying to turn you into and I'm so, so sorry.'

Steven felt her warm, wet tears on his cheek as he held her close. 'Maybe we should sleep on this and talk about it in the morning.'

'No,' said Tally, pulling away slightly and trying to regain her composure, wiping her cheeks with her palms and smoothing back her hair, which was still tied back the way she wore it to work. 'I've decided.'

With Steven's pharmaceutical company suitably compensated by Her Majesty's Government for taking their employee away without notice, he endured an excruciating farewell sherry party in Lionel Montague's office, smiling his way through jokes about his having found life in the private sector a bit too tough and scuttling back to the safety of public sector life.

'Tosser,' whispered Rachel Collins at his elbow.

Steven's smile simply became broader. He was just so happy to be leaving. He felt as if he had wings on his heels as he ran down the stairs for the last time and drove out of the car park. He and Tally went out to dinner at the French restaurant they'd used when they'd first met, an easy relaxed affair now that neither was playing a part and all their cards were on the table. They'd never felt closer, despite the fact that Steven would set off for London in the morning.

'Did you hear how Sir John was today?' Tally asked.

'No real change. He's holding his own.'

'No doubt boosted by the imminent return of his star investigator.'

'All I've agreed to do is take a look at the thing that was worrying him.'

Tally took Steven's hands in hers. 'You don't think he could have faked the whole thing just to get you back, do you?' she said earnestly.

'Of course not,' exclaimed Steven, and then was relieved to see it had been a joke as the smile appeared on Tally's face at his reaction.

'Good, otherwise he'd have another thing worrying him and she'd have a scalpel in her hand.'

Next morning Steven drove straight to the flat in London and parked the Honda in the basement garage, taking his gear up in the lift. Only two journeys were required; he'd left as much as possible in Leicester in an effort to minimise the change. The heating gurgled and protested for a bit but finally sorted out its problems and settled down to a steady hum before he left for the Home Office. He had changed into a dark suit and tie, Macmillan's stipulated dress code; he wouldn't be there but somehow it seemed only right.

'How nice to see you,' exclaimed Jean Roberts when Steven appeared in her office. 'I couldn't believe it when I heard the rumours about your coming back; I'm so glad they were true.'

Steven and Jean had known each other a long time, and it was good to be exchanging pleasantries again. Jean asked to be brought up to date on Jenny and her life in Scotland, and Steven got the latest details about the Bach Choir, of which Jean was an enthusiastic member. When they reached a natural hiatus, Jean asked, 'Will you be using Sir John's office?'

Steven shook his head. 'No I'll use the small one for the time being. Let's not give up on him yet. Apart from anything else, I've only agreed to take a look at the thing that's been concerning him most. I take it you have some notes for me?'

'Quite a lot, actually.' Jean pulled out several files from her desk drawer. 'In the absence of any specific requests from Sir John, I had to go for blanket cover.'

'Wow,' said Steven, surveying the pile. 'Where do I begin?'

Jean smiled. 'How much do you know?'

'Let's see. Almost twenty years ago, a journalist went up to Newcastle to cover a story and never came back. He, his editor and several others died. Officially the story he was covering was about an operation that went wrong in a hospital where a new health scheme was being introduced at the time – the very successful brainchild of the then health secretary, John Carlisle. The scheme was abandoned for some unknown reason, Carlisle dropped off the radar and ended up taking his own life last week. Someone else connected with the scheme was recently blown to bits in Paris. How am I doing?'

'I think you've grasped the main points very well.'

'But most of this was nearly twenty years ago,' said Steven. 'What triggered John's interest?'

Jean appeared thoughtful. 'Looking back, I think it was a

lunch he had with Detective Chief Superintendent Malloy. He came back from that wanting details about the operation you mentioned. Apparently the surgeon's wife was one of those who died in Paris too, and the name had rung a bell with Sir John. It just seemed to go on from there.'

'Thanks, Jean. Maybe I'll go see him again before I make a start on this.'

'Give him my best.'

John Macmillan was resting with his eyes closed when Steven arrived at the hospital, causing him to pause at the door. He was wondering whether or not to just leave when Macmillan seemed to sense someone was there and opened his eyes. 'Steven.'

'How are you feeling?'

'Like I have a brain tumour.'

'Stupid question. Have they scheduled the operation?

'Next week.'

Steven sat down beside him. 'It's going to take more than a clump of cells to fell the John Macmillan I know.'

Macmillan smiled serenely, as if he knew better. 'Have you seen Jean?'

'I've just come from the Home Office. She gave me what she thought were the relevant files – all of them.'

Macmillan managed a chuckle. 'Sorry there are so many.'

'So where should I start?'

'Carlisle's death. There was always something odd about the man. I think he could be the key to whatever's going on.'

'A dead man?'

Macmillan closed his eyes and gave a slight nod as if acknowledging the problem.

'What do you mean by odd?' Steven continued.

'Meteoric rise, spectacular fall, something not quite right with either.'

'Okay, I'll run with that,' said Steven gently, sensing that Macmillan had no heart for further talk. 'We'll talk after the op.'

He turned at the door to look back at the sleeping man. A lump came to his throat.

When he got back to the flat and had made himself some coffee, he took Macmillan's advice and separated the material on John Carlisle from the files. It took about fifteen minutes to do this, followed by another hour of reading it, before he found himself agreeing with John Macmillan. There was something very odd about the man. He seemed to have appeared on the political landscape from nowhere. A poor lower second from Cambridge had been followed by several jobs in the City – none of which had lasted longer than a few months – and then he'd popped up as the Conservative candidate for Ryleigh in the Cotswolds, a safe Tory seat. Why was that? Why had he been gifted a safe seat when there must have been tremendous competition for such a prize?

It was much more usual for would-be MPs to cut their teeth fighting no-hope seats in their opponents' heartlands, proving their resilience and commitment to the cause before being adopted by a constituency which afforded them at least a chance of winning. But not John Carlisle. He materialised from nowhere, a new, unknown candidate in a constituency where they'd elect a cardboard cut-out if it was wearing blue, and won the seat with a majority of over ten thousand.

Steven could see from contemporary press cuttings that Carlisle had been a strikingly good-looking man in a pretty-boy sort of way – all white teeth and floppy hair. He could imagine Tory matrons taking to him well enough but even so . . . it all seemed far too easy. The man said nothing in the House for the first year but then started to exhibit an interest in the National Health Service and produced over the course of the next eighteen months a string of suggestions as to how it could be modernised and improved – an interest and expertise that again appeared to have come from nowhere. A year later, after a cabinet shuffle, he was made health secretary, and launched an ambitious modernising scheme in the north of England to much acclaim.

Reading through yet more press cuttings from the time, Steven found that few had a bad word to say about the Northern Health Scheme, although one or two local GPs had expressed concern over a perceived lack of freedom to prescribe as they saw fit. Steven followed this up but there was little to support the GPs. Under the scheme, a computer made the final judgement about which drugs the patients were to be given, but it was clear that the computer did not just pick the cheapest option. A sophisticated software program examined the doctors' recommendations, sought alternatives and examined the merits of all, based on published research, before making the final decision about what to give the patient. If two drugs had equal merit in the literature, it would supply the cheaper one.

The computer was unbiased, which was more than could be said for prescribing physicians who could be influenced by shiny advertising and pharmaceutical company hospitality. When the computer had made its choice, the drug was supplied from a central pharmacy quickly and efficiently, to be either administered in the hospital or collected by the patient. The need for bits of paper floating around the system and people interpreting them had been eliminated at a single stroke, as had the need for queuing at chemists while prescriptions were filled. Doctors in College Hospital and the surrounding GP practices simply punched in details of their patients and their recommended medicines, and the computer did the rest.

Steven found himself admiring the system. Like many good ideas, it had simplicity at its core and, as a bonus, the money saved through streamlining the process was ploughed back into the budget. Unlike the situation in many health authorities, no drugs were off limits in the Newcastle area, even the most expensive anti-cancer ones. If the computer accepted the diagnosis and the doctor's recommendation, and could find no better alternative, it would supply the drug. Everyone appeared to be thoroughly satisfied with the new scheme, and voices were raised in favour of its being extended across the nation. The only question lingering in Steven's mind as he got up to make more coffee was why on earth that hadn't happened.

As he read on, Steven could see that the fate of the Northern Health Scheme was inextricably linked to the fortunes of its designer, John Carlisle. At the height of its success, Carlisle was being mooted as a future Tory leader, and then, without any discernible reason, it all seemed to wither and die. The Northern Health Scheme was wound up – the 'end of its experimental period', according to the press releases. Carlisle was switched to another ministry in which he became totally anonymous before being dropped from cabinet altogether, and becoming an equally anonymous backbencher, finally hitting the skids and being exposed in the expenses scandal before taking his own life – the meteoric rise and fall, as John Macmillan had said.

Daylight was fading fast and Steven had nothing to eat in the flat, so he thought he'd eat at a new Thai restaurant he wanted to try. After that, he would call Tally to swap tales of the day, and then spend the rest of the evening going through the files. If he felt up to it, he might wind up by going late-night shopping at an all-night supermarket to stock up with the essentials of life: bacon, eggs, cheese, bread, gin, tonic, beer and lots of frozen ready meals.

SEVEN

It was two a.m. before Steven stopped reading. He put out the light and rested his head on the back of his chair to look up at the clouds drifting across the moon. Although he agreed there was a puzzle in John Carlisle's sudden change of fortune and in the abrupt ending of an excellent and innovative health scheme, he couldn't quite understand why John Macmillan was so worried about it. An awful lot of water had passed under the bridge since those far-off times, even if Carlisle's suicide was more recent.

There was the Paris bomb, of course, and the past involvement of one of the dead in Carlisle's health scheme – maybe a second if Lady Antonia was in some way implicated – but that didn't give him a handle on anything to cause alarm.

It was unfortunate that Macmillan hadn't been able to be any more specific about his fears. It all seemed to be down to gut feeling, but John Macmillan's gut feelings were not to be taken lightly. If Macmillan smelt a rat it was time to get out the traps. But even extrapolating to the worst possible scenario and considering for a moment that the Paris deaths had been linked to the health scheme, why would anyone want to kill those people twenty years after the event? Steven yawned. He'd had quite enough for one day. It was time to turn in.

A new day started with bacon sandwiches and coffee, something that made Steven glad he'd gone shopping the night before, even though it was something he didn't enjoy doing. He saw late-night visits to supermarkets as something akin to visiting restaurants at the end of the universe, but at least his fellow travellers had been few and far between and the check-out was quick.

He'd steeled himself to spending the whole morning reading through more of the files, this time concentrating on the other things that had been happening in the north of England at the time of the health scheme, hoping to find a connection, see some link, discover some synapse that might trigger the same feeling in him as the one that had made Macmillan uneasy.

It was impossible not to feel horror at the story of the surgeon, Martin Freeman, dying in the middle of an operation, leaving his junior the nightmare of completing a very far from routine operation. It was easy to understand why it had attracted the attention of the nation's press at the time, among their number the journalist James Kincaid.

Freeman's patient, Greta Marsh, had reportedly gone on to make a good recovery and been able to give a press conference – although heavily bandaged – to assure medical observers of the operation who feared that her sight might have been damaged beyond repair that their fears were groundless. But then all hell had appeared to break loose.

Kincaid had been murdered in cold blood along with a nurse who was with him at the time; his killers were thought to be members of a powerful drugs gang. The same gang had been blamed for the death of Neil Tolkien, a local GP involved in a drug rehabilitation scheme in the area – Steven smiled wanly at the name, thinking how different the Shire was from the environs of Newcastle in the early nineties. The gang was blamed again for the death of the head of pharmacy of the Northern Health Scheme, Paul Schreiber, along with two male nurses when they had all been caught up in a raid on the hospital pharmacy.

Steven frowned, not least at the causes of death involved.

Kincaid and the nurse, Eve Laing, had been shot, but Tolkien had been injected with bleach. One of the male nurses had been stabbed, and Schreiber and the other male nurse had perished in a lab fire. Kincaid's editor, a man named Fletcher, had been murdered too but he had been shot in London, supposedly to stop any revelation of Kincaid's story about the drug barons of the north.

'What drug barons of the north?' murmured Steven as he failed to find any report of a successful trial and conviction relating to any of the horrors he'd been reading about. Seven murders and not one arrest? If he had been looking for the reason for John Macmillan's unease, he felt he'd come some way along that road. Why had no one been brought to justice? Surely there would have been a public outcry . . . but apparently not. When the dust settled, the Northern Health Scheme had just faded away, and John Carlisle's career had followed suit, along with what the papers had been calling the drugs war. Life had seemingly returned to normal for the good folks of the Newcastle Health Trust area in record time.

A new Conservative government was returned in '92, and a new health secretary was appointed. The Northern Health Scheme 'experiment' was declared over, and relative calm prevailed for the next five years before the public voted the Tories out and New Labour came to power. Now, after nearly thirteen years, and with an election looming, it looked like time for change again. And this scenario had coincided with the death of two people, maybe three, who had been involved in a health initiative in the early nineties. Coincidence, or was there more to it?

Steven felt he'd been cooped up in the flat for too long, and sitting in the one position had given him a sore back. The sun was shining so it was easy to give in to the urge to go for a walk by the river. There was a lot to think about, and he hoped the fresh air might clear his head. What he needed was some kind of working hypothesis, but for the moment he felt as if he could have been looking for the unifying theory of the universe; there was always going to be a bit that didn't quite fit. Macmillan had mooted the idea that John Carlisle might be the key, so he concentrated his thoughts on him.

Supposing Carlisle had always been the dishonest character he'd recently been shown to be, and supposing he had been involved in something not quite kosher at the time of the health scheme, was it conceivable that he had been found out and marginalised by his own party who had then mounted some kind of cover-up to avoid a scandal? The incoming Conservative administration back in '92 could have shifted him sideways – as indeed they had – and kept him quiet with threats of what they were holding over him, but that wouldn't explain why they had dismantled the new health scheme when it had been working so well.

It didn't make sense. Politicians didn't turn their backs on success, and the scheme had clearly been a big asset. Surely the bright thing would have been for the new health secretary to continue with it and roll it out across the whole country to popular acclaim. Instead, they had abandoned it, labelling it as an 'experiment' – a failed 'experiment' if they were abandoning it. He must be missing something.

Maybe it had had something to do with the health scheme itself, was Steven's next thought, some scam running in parallel, something to do with drug supply or pricing, perhaps? It only took a moment to conclude that this was an even more preposterous theory. Even if Carlisle had been the most venal of men, he would hardly have been likely to jeopardise a then brilliant career, with everything to play for, including leadership of his party, for a bit of cash on the side. That was a non-starter.

As he turned for home, Steven concluded that he needed to know more about John Carlisle. He needed to know what the man had really been like. Right now he was floundering between a prospective leader of his party and possible future prime minister, and a dishonest little nobody caught fiddling his expenses. The man was dead but he had a widow and she lived down in Kent.

That idea was stillborn. Tory wives were notoriously loyal where outsiders were concerned. Standing by their man came more naturally to them than to Tammy Wynette. What he needed was a few words with one of Carlisle's opponents, a contemporary who, after all this time, might provide an unbiased appraisal. He would ask Jean Roberts to find someone who'd been on the Labour health team back then and, if possible, set up an interview.

Three days later, Steven drove up to Yorkshire for a meeting with Arthur Bleasdale, retired Labour member of parliament for Knowesdale, and the man who had shadowed John Carlisle and his successor until his own retiral just before the '97 election. He decided to drive up because he wanted to stop off in Leicester on the way back.

'Good of you to see me, Mr Bleasdale,' said Steven as he was shown into a large bay-windowed room at the front of a solid stone villa on the outskirts of Knowesdale by Mrs Bleasdale.

'Don't get that many visitors these days, lad,' said Bleasdale, getting up stiffly from his chair to shake hands. 'Sit yourself down.'

Steven found himself taking an immediate liking to the man, who he guessed was in his early to mid seventies, a victim of arthritis judging by the gnarling of his hands and the stiffness of his movements, but with a full head of white hair and clear blue eyes that didn't need glasses. His accent and the fact that he looked Steven straight in the eye when addressing him suggested honesty and forthrightness.

'What can I do for you?'

'I'm sure you must have heard about the death of John Carlisle,' said Steven.

'Aye, I did.'

'You must have known him quite well.'

'You could say. I shadowed him for a couple of years back in the early nineties or thereabouts.'

'At the time of the Northern Health Scheme?'

'That's right.'

'What did you think of the scheme?'

'Couldn't say so at the time, but bloody brilliant, worked like a dream. I was reduced to asking why they hadn't done it sooner,' recalled Bleasdale with a staccato laugh. 'Couldn't think of anything else to criticise.'

'Then you were a fan of John Carlisle?' said Steven, immediately realising his error and adding, 'Well, not exactly a fan, you were political opponents of course, but an admirer of his abilities?'

'No, I was never that,' said Bleasdale, leaving Steven faintly puzzled.

'But you thought his scheme was brilliant.'

''Twas, but it weren't his,' said Bleasdale.

'I'm sorry?'

'It were never John Carlisle who thought that up, lad. I wouldn't have put money on him doing the four times table. Thick as a plank.'

'A government minister?'

'Who avoided interviews like the plague. Any time he appeared in public he was reading a prepared speech. Someone else was pulling the strings, you take my word for it.'

Now he was getting somewhere, Steven thought. 'Would you happen to know who?'

Bleasdale shook his head. 'I don't even think the people in his own party knew the whole truth of what was going on.'

'Not even his cabinet colleagues?'

Bleasdale broke into laughter. 'Sounds bloody ridiculous when you put it like that, doesn't it, but I don't think so. There was a certain reticence about asking or saying too much about Golden Boy at the time, as if . . . it might not be good for one's own . . . career? I don't know. But they just seemed to accept they had a cabbage sitting beside them and got on with it.'

'Why on earth would they put up with a situation like that?'

'Because whoever was behind Carlisle was so bloody good,' said Bleasdale. 'The Northern Health Scheme was brilliant and probably the reason for the Tories getting back in '92. Apart from that, Carlisle's good looks were bringing in a shedload of votes for them. The shire ladies got moist at the very sight of him.'

Steven smiled. 'But then it all went wrong?'

Bleasdale looked thoughtful. 'Aye, it did. Although for the life of me I can't think why.'

'No idea at all?'

'I remember some kind of drugs war broke out in Newcastle at the time: people died and suddenly it was all over. Carlisle was shifted to some ministry dealing with European trade regulations and the new woman with the health portfolio abandoned the scheme. If I'd stayed on after '97, I'd have cheerfully pinched the idea and reintroduced it without a second thought,' said Bleasdale with a chuckle that Steven found infectious. 'I'd be sitting in bloody Lords right now.'

'Why did you leave Parliament?'

Bleasdale gave a shrug. 'Party changed, lad. Blair arrived. New Labour was old Tory as far as I was concerned. I was having none of it.'

Steven nodded. 'Looks like the country might just be about to agree with you. Thank you for your help, Mr Bleasdale. I'm much obliged.'

'It's Arthur, lad. Now, before you go, what's Sci-Med's interest in all this?'

Steven asked Bleasdale if he'd read about the Paris flat explosion.

'Aye, I did.'

'At least one of the murdered victims had something to do with the Northern Health Scheme, maybe two, and then John Carlisle takes his own life . . .'

Bleasdale nodded. 'You know, I wouldn't have thought he'd have had the nerve. Takes courage to do that, lad. All that stuff about easy way out is bollocks. Doesn't sound like Carlisle at all.'

Steven made a mental note.

'Quite a few people died in Newcastle too,' said Bleasdale thoughtfully. 'People in and around College Hospital.'

'In the drugs war,' said Steven in a tone that made Bleasdale acknowledge the doubt in it with a slight shrug before stating the obvious.

'Well, it were all such a bloody long time ago.'

Steven got up to go. He shook hands with Bleasdale, thanked him again and told him not to get up.

'Let me know how you get on, lad.'

Steven arrived at Tally's flat just before nine p.m. 'How are you?' he murmured in her ear as they embraced.

'Knackered.'

'Pity.'

Tally withdrew slightly. She smiled and said, 'Not that knackered. Drink?'

They settled down on the couch, sipping gin and tonic, Tally snuggling in to Steven's shoulder, Steven's heels resting on a footstool. 'Well, tell me all about it,' she said.

'I'm all at sea,' Steven confessed. 'I'm still not sure what I'm supposed to be investigating.'

'I knew it. It was all a trick to get you back.'

Steven dismissed the notion with a smile. 'There are a lot of puzzling things but I don't see how they fit together as yet.'

'Try me. I was always good at jigsaws.'

Steven told Tally what he'd been doing and about his meeting with Bleasdale.

'You know, this reminds me of a film I once saw,' said Tally. '*The Manchurian Candidate*, all about a Communist plot to get their man to the presidency of the USA.'

'I remember,' said Steven. 'Frank Sinatra was in it. I don't think John Carlisle was brainwashed though, just dumb.'

'A handsome front man of no discernible substance,' said Tally. 'Not that unusual in politics, when you come to think of it.'

'No,' conceded Steven. 'But the people behind Carlisle were so good that no one in the party made a fuss, and as their secret agenda seemed to be modernising and improving the National Health Service out of all sight, why would they? And then something went wrong and it all disappeared in a mess of un-explained deaths.'

'I thought you said a drugs war broke out?'

'That was the official story.'

'You don't believe it?'

'There were never any arrests.'

'I have a suggestion,' said Tally after some thought.

'Mmm?'

'Let's go to bed.'

EIGHT

'I didn't ask about your mother,' said Steven, suddenly feeling guilty as the thought came to him at breakfast. 'Did your sister come up at the weekend?'

Tally nodded. 'Don't worry. You had a lot on your mind with what was happening to John and other things. We've agreed to look at homes. I'm going to see one this evening.'

Steven nodded, not knowing how to respond. He wanted to say it was probably for the best but could see how much Tally was hurting at the idea. 'I hope it's the right one.'

Tally got up to start clearing away the dishes. 'John's big day,' she said.

'The operation's scheduled for eleven.'

'Let me know when you hear something, but it'll have to be a message on my mobile.'

Steven said he would. 'Just leave those,' he said as Tally started to wash up. 'I'm in no hurry. I'll do them before I go.'

'There's a meeting of senior medical staff this afternoon,' she said, drying her hands. 'I think it may have something to do with that new vaccines agreement with the pharmaceutical companies we were talking about.'

'Why should that affect you?'

'I think we're going to be asked to suggest priorities,' said Tally, putting on her jacket and coming over to kiss him goodbye.

'I suspect the defence of the realm people will have first bite of that particular cherry,' he said.

'No harm in letting our views be known. We're not all

pessimists when it comes to bio-attack. Let's not forget weapons of mass destruction. Are they still looking?'

Steven smiled. 'Love you.'

'Love you too.'

Steven drove back to London, wondering what his next move should be, but thoughts of John Macmillan and the two possible outcomes of the operation kept interfering with his train of thought. If John died, would he really consider taking over? Come to that, would he get the chance? He might be John Macmillan's preferred successor, but if Macmillan wasn't around to have the final say, Government, new or old, might see an opportunity to interfere, and he had put up a few backs over the years. In fact, more than a few if he were honest.

But if John should pull through and take up the reins again, would he go or would he stay? Tally had insisted he return to Sci-Med but rightly or wrongly she'd been feeling guilty at the time, and that could change when she found herself under the stress and strain of 'not knowing' – the feeling she'd always feared. There was also his reason for having resigned in the first place – a matter of principle which didn't seem so clear-cut now that he had experienced life in that bloody awful job at Ultramed.

'Shit, I don't know,' he exclaimed out loud as he entered the outskirts of the capital. There were just too many variables . . . as was the case with his current investigation. He decided to dump the car at his apartment and head over to the Home Office to wait out the operation with Jean Roberts.

Jean broke into a big smile when he appeared. 'I'm so glad I'm not here on my own this morning,' she said. 'How did you get on up north?'

'Bleasdale was very helpful. Thanks for setting the meeting up. Turns out Carlisle was a man of straw.'

'Most men are,' said Jean. 'Present company excepted,' she added quickly.

Steven smiled. He knew Jean had never married and wondered if her comment had been born of past bitterness. He decided not to pursue the matter as he saw the hands of the clock reach eleven o'clock. 'Good luck, John,' he said.

'Amen to that,' said Jean.

Steven found himself imagining the smell of burning bone in the theatre as the surgeon's trephine removed a segment of John Macmillan's skull to allow access to the brain. He tried to dismiss the image and asked, 'Jean, how did John know that the Charles French murdered in the Paris explosion was the one involved in the Northern Health Scheme?'

Jean looked thoughtful. 'The name, I suppose.'

'You think he remembered that a man named Charles French was part of the Northern Health Scheme all these years ago?'

'No, I don't think it happened that way . . . Let me see, DCS Malloy told him about Charles French renting the Paris flat and being one of the victims . . . Antonia Freeman was also identified, and Sir John remembered who she was . . . then John Carlisle took his own life and I was asked to come up with information on the health scheme. He would have seen the name in the stuff I gave him about that.'

'Right,' said Steven. 'That makes sense. What do we know about French?'

'Largely what DCS Malloy told Sir John. He was a Cambridge graduate, chief executive of Deltasoft Computing and a pillar of the community.'

'Carlisle was at Cambridge,' said Steven, thinking out loud.

'You think they might have known each other when they were students?'

'Worth finding out.'

'Right. Actually, I've just remembered something else. It wasn't just Charles French's name John would have seen in the old info, it was the company name as well. French was running Deltasoft at the time of the health scheme.'

71

'You're absolutely right. I should have picked up on that. Well done, Jean. So his contribution presumably would have been in the provision of software to run the operation.'

'Seems logical.'

'Quite a contribution when computers weren't what they are today . . . Maybe our man of substance behind the man of straw.'

'What would you like me to do first?' Jean asked.

'See if Charles French and John Carlisle were at Cambridge at the same time. We'll take it from there.'

'Will do,' said Jean. She looked up at the clock. 'Too soon to phone?' she asked.

'I think so. Brain surgery takes time.'

Steven phoned at one thirty and was told that Macmillan was still in theatre. He suggested that Jean go to lunch and waited until she returned before checking again. The operation was over: the surgeons were optimistic that they had managed to remove all the tumour, which had proved to be benign, but only time would tell the extent of collateral damage caused by its excision. For the moment, he was stable and sleeping peacefully.

'So far so good,' said Jean, but both were considering what 'collateral damage' might mean, without actually mentioning the subject.

Steven went out to get a sandwich and some fresh air while Jean started to make enquiries about Carlisle and French's university days. She had an answer when he returned.

'They were at Cambridge at the same time, but at different colleges.'

'Same course?'

'No. Carlisle left with a lower second in history; French took a double first in maths and physics.'

'So they might not have known each other,' mused Steven.

'I'm working on that. My source says she'll call me back in a couple of hours.'

'Okay. I think I'll go over to the hospital and see if I can have a word with John's wife.'

'She could probably do with a bit of moral support.'

Steven didn't stay long at the hospital because there was nothing to be done except wait, and that was best left to family. Once he had assured John's wife that the thoughts of the people at Sci-Med were with her, and had enthused about the fact that the tumour was benign and the surgeons had got all of it out, he left and went back to the flat in Marlborough Court.

Jean phoned as he was making coffee. 'They did know each other,' she said. 'Both were members of the Conservative club throughout their time at Cambridge.'

'Well done, you. Now we're getting somewhere.'

'There's more. French had a falling out with other members of the club at the start of his final year and left to set up a breakaway faction, taking quite a few of the others with him. My source also seems to think there was some trouble involving the police at a later stage and French appeared in court, but she doesn't have details. Would you like me to run with it?'

Steven thought for a moment before saying, 'No, I think I'll ask Charlie Malloy about that. I wanted to talk to him anyway about the others who died in Paris. Jean, I've been thinking. Maybe I would like to have a word with John Carlisle's wife after all. Do you think you could set that up?'

'Will do.'

Steven called DCS Malloy.

'I heard you were back,' said Malloy. 'Unfortunate circumstances, though. How is he?'

Steven brought Malloy up to speed on John Macmillan's condition.

'Good bloke, your governor.'

'He is,' agreed Steven. 'Charlie, that bloke Charles French who died in Paris, did he have a record?'

'A record? Well, he was a victim, not a suspect. I'm not even sure if we ran a check once we'd identified him. We probably had no reason to once we'd established he was the millionaire boss of a computing company and a pillar of his local community.'

'I think he might have got into some trouble when he was a student in Cambridge.'

'That wasn't yesterday,' said Malloy.

'No, it was a very long time ago,' agreed Steven. 'And maybe you could run record checks on the others killed in the blast too?'

'If you think it necessary . . .'

'I'd be obliged, Charlie. I'm clutching at straws here, I admit, but this is John's thing and if he thought it worth pursuing . . .'

'Fair enough. I'll be in touch.'

The phone rang almost as soon as he put it down. It was Jean asking him if he could meet Melissa Carlisle at her home, Markham House in Kent, at eleven the following morning. 'She's going abroad the day after and doesn't know when she'll be back,' Jean explained.

'Absolutely fine.'

At seven p.m., just as he was beginning to think that it would be the following day before he heard back from CS Malloy, Steven got a call.

'You were right. French picked up form back in 1975. Apparently he was heavily into politics at university, but fell out with the Conservatives and went on to set up a rival group that went from strength to strength under his leadership. It was their practice to invite various right-wing speakers to their meetings, something that annoyed their fellow students no end. When French and his pals asked along a South African politician not noted for his liberal views on race, the lefties set up a protest rally and succeeded in stopping the meeting. French lost the plot and went after one of the protesters. He laid into him like a man possessed, according to witnesses. The chap ended up

74

losing an eye and French was charged with causing grievous bodily harm.'

'Not the best start in life for either of them,' said Steven.

'French got off with a fine,' said Malloy.

'*What?*'

'The judge was minded to see what happened as the passions of youth getting a bit out of hand. He saw no good reason to destroy the future career of a brilliant student.'

'Who was the judge?' Steven wrote down the name. 'Anything on the others in Paris?'

'Pure as the driven snow, unless you count giving large sums of money to the Conservative Party as criminal.'

'I'm much obliged to you, Charlie.'

Ending the call, Steven looked at the judge's name on the pad in front of him, the phrase *passions of youth* running through his head. 'Seems a bit lenient for the loss of an eye, m'lud,' he murmured as he turned on his laptop and set up a Google search for his lordship. This revealed that the good judge had not enjoyed a reputation for leniency during his career. On the contrary, he had been renowned for the harshness of his sentencing. One observer had noted that the frustration of not having hanging and flogging among his options had left him with a grudge that he took out on everyone unfortunate enough to be tried before him and found guilty.

'Then why go easy on French?' muttered Steven, giving birth to the cynical thought that perhaps his lordship was a Cambridge man himself . . . No, that wasn't the case, Steven learned as he looked through his personal details. The judge had died back in 1988, leaving behind him a wife, Matilda, and a daughter, Antonia, who was married to a surgeon, Sir Martin Freeman. There were no grandchildren.

Steven stared at the screen. The judge who'd let Charles French off with a fine had been Antonia Freeman's father?

NINE

Steven called Tally to talk over the day's events.

'I got your text,' said Tally. 'It's good news about the tumour, and that they managed to get all of it.'

Steven agreed. 'Now it's a case of waiting to see how much trauma was caused to the surrounding brain tissue.'

'I take it they're not hazarding a guess?'

'You know surgeons.'

'Mmm.'

He told her what he'd come up with during the day.

'Sounds like you're making progress.'

'Placing Carlisle and French at Cambridge at the same time was a plus,' he agreed, 'as was establishing their common interest in right-of-centre politics. Antonia Freeman's father popping up as the judge who let French off on a GBH charge was a bit of a showstopper, though. I didn't see that coming.'

'So, what was going on there, d'you think?'

'Difficult to say. I'm inclined to think there must have been some good reason for it . . . something I've yet to establish. Something *else* I've yet to establish,' Steven added.

'And then French and the judge's daughter end up being blown to bits in Paris together some twenty years later,' said Tally. 'Just where do you go with that?'

'First, I want a word with Carlisle's wife. I'm going to see her tomorrow.'

'His widow,' Tally corrected. 'What do you think she can tell you?'

'If French was really the brains behind her husband. Suppositions are like thin ice; it would be nice to have something solid under my feet.'

'Good luck,' said Tally, her tone reflecting the doubt she felt.

'I know it's a long shot, but it's worth a try. How did your meeting go?'

'It was just a case of filling in the details of what the new scheme would mean, and asking for our views. The government's in the process of putting the manufacturing contract out to tender. After that, they'll commission a whole range of vaccines – a sort of central supply – the idea being that once it's up and running we shouldn't have last-minute rushes like the one with swine flu, and the public will be less exposed to the risk of epidemics.'

'Was I right about the MOD having first call on what vaccines should be produced?'

'Yes, and surprise surprise, it's a secret. '

'I guess they made the difficult decisions, took the tough choices . . .'

'That sort of thing.'

'Well, as long as they don't start arguing over details and get it up and running soon,' said Steven.

'We can agree on that.'

'And on that happy note . . .'

'Do you think you'll manage to get up at the weekend?'

'I certainly plan to, unless fate gets in the way.'

'Don't fall for the grieving widow tomorrow.'

Steven returned to thinking about his investigation. He was accumulating pieces of a puzzle but assembly was being hindered by having no notion of the picture on the box. He needed a sense of order. He got out a notepad and started to write down what he knew.

John Carlisle, Cambridge-educated but no great intellect – interested in politics – good-looking front man for brighter folk – made it to cabinet rank with a little help from his friends, and given credit for designing the Northern Health Scheme but probably didn't. Faded into obscurity, and took his own life after being exposed as an expenses cheat.

Charles French, Cambridge-educated, brilliant – a double first – very interested in politics, involved in an unsavoury incident leading to criminal charges but got off thanks to an exceedingly lenient judge, set up Deltasoft, a software company which was involved in the Northern Health Scheme, went on to become a big player in the computer world and a pillar of the community, according to Charlie Malloy. Murdered in Paris.

Antonia Freeman, wife of surgeon, Sir Martin Freeman, operating at the same hospital where the Northern Health Scheme was trialled and at the same time but, perhaps more important, daughter of the judge who let Charles French off on a charge of GBH. Murdered in Paris.

Steven doodled with his pen at the corner of the page while he went over what he'd written. French hadn't been completely 'let off', he reminded himself: he had been fined. No big deal as a punishment perhaps, but enough to give him a criminal record for a particularly nasty offence, something that would almost certainly have come back to haunt him had he tried to pursue a political career of his own. On the other hand, there was nothing to stop him operating as a backroom boy, out of the public eye and away from press interest.

Everything pointed to French's being the brains behind Carlisle. They were at university together, had both been in the Conservative club, and, later, French's company had supplied the sophisticated software for the innovative health scheme up in Newcastle.

Steven found that this conclusion raised more questions than it answered. However bright French had been as a student, and subsequently as a software designer, he had not been in any position to arrange a safe seat for Carlisle or smooth his progress through the parliamentary ranks. Others had been involved . . .

person or persons unknown. It wasn't the Northern Health Scheme that was the link connecting these people; there was something else, something bigger, some group or association that included a high court judge and people in positions of real power. The Northern Health Scheme was something they had been involved in but it wasn't the be all and end all.

Steven relished the intellectual freedom this conclusion gave him. He could now widen his thinking to include the others who'd died in Paris and see what it all added up to. He shuffled his way through the bits of paper he'd been accumulating and found what Charlie Malloy had told Macmillan about the Paris dead. Apart from Antonia Freeman and Charles French, they comprised three big names from the world of business and a senior civil servant. He didn't have names to hand but Charlie had also mentioned large donations to the Conservative Party. He had enough to go on to form a working hypothesis. What these people had in common was right-wing politics, perhaps even extreme right-wing politics.

The obvious common ground for them would be the Conservative Party but the way the John Carlisle story was shaping up suggested not. Everything pointed to their working outside the mainstream of the party. Twenty years ago they had used John Carlisle as a front for their association, presumably to promote their aims, which were what exactly? A toughie, thought Steven. All he had to go on was the success they'd made of the Northern Health Scheme. He smiled as he found himself looking at an extreme right-wing faction that had greatly improved the National Health Service in the north of England at a time when everyone believed the Tories were very much for getting rid of it. Maybe they all lived in Sherwood Forest as well, he thought, as he threw down his pen.

There were, of course, the deaths in the north at the time to consider, the victims of the 'drugs war', which now looked even more fanciful. There had been another reason for all these deaths, and the fact that no prosecutions had been brought . . . Steven felt a chill run up his spine as he wondered just how much power these people were capable of wielding. His desire to find out what had made John Macmillan so uneasy had now been granted in spades. He didn't understand what had really been behind the Northern Health Scheme but, whatever it was, it was a fair bet it had had nothing to do with care and concern.

Steven saw he was following in the footsteps of James Kincaid, the journalist who'd been murdered along with his nurse girl-friend. It wasn't the drug barons he'd fallen foul of: it was 'them'. He must have come too close to what had been going on and paid the price with his life, as had his editor.

Steven wondered if this had been true for all who'd died back then. But there was a possibility they hadn't all been on the same side – the old hostage-situation dilemma where outside rescuers had no way of telling the good guys from the bad when they stormed the building. Steven's train of thought slowed and finally hit the buffers when he was forced to recognise that the people who'd been behind the operation twenty years ago – Carlisle, French and the others in the Paris flat – were in no position to reprise whatever it was they'd been up to. They were all dead.

An act of vengeance? Had someone carried a grudge for all these years and taken retribution on a cold winter's day in Paris, or had it been down to something else? Could the Paris killings have been the result of internecine strife? If so, had the group or organisation or whatever it was been wiped out or had it just been reborn?

Steven revisited Antonia Freeman's father's leniency towards Charles French. It made sense now. Antonia's father had been by all accounts as far right as it was possible to get. He must have recognised a kindred spirit in French, possibly even recruited him and his right-wing breakaway group to a bigger, more organised body, one that did have the wherewithal to get John Carlisle into a position of influence and power.

Steven suddenly saw how he could eliminate the possibility of an act of vengeance in Paris. Charlie Malloy had highlighted the secret nature of the meeting. The individuals concerned had gone to great lengths to leave no trail of their movements or indeed inform anyone where they were going – not even close family. But the person who had set the bomb must have known in advance where the meeting was being held, and prepared accordingly. The bomber had been one of those who'd been invited to the meeting. He or she had been one of 'them'. The chances were it had not been revenge; it had been a coup.

'Shit,' said Steven under his breath as he saw the magnitude of his task grow. He didn't know who 'they' were; he didn't know how big the organisation was and he didn't know what they were planning. He decided his only option was to learn from the past. He might be dealing with a case of history repeating itself if there was to be some kind of revival of the Northern Health Scheme, so he'd have to try to find out what Carlisle and his colleagues had been up to back in the early nineties. 'A stroll down memory lane,' he murmured as he called it a night.

Markham House looked impressive, Steven thought, as he got out of the car to use the phone at the side of the gates. He only managed a brief look, however, before turning away from a bitter wind which was whipping sleet into his face. 'C'mon, c'mon,' he complained, as no one up at the house seemed keen to answer the buzzer. He pressed twice more before an upper-class female voice said, 'Yes, who is it?'

'Steven Dunbar, Sci-Med Inspectorate.'

'You'd better come in.'

'Yes, I'd better,' murmured Steven, shrugging his shoulders in discomfort as rain-water found a way inside his collar to trickle down his back. The iron gates swung open and Steven drove up to the house.

TEN

Melissa Carlisle's expression could best be described as neutral, Steven thought, as she held the door open and gestured that he should come in. The fact that she kept her right hand on it suggested that she had no intention of shaking hands, so he stepped smartly inside and waited.

'This way.'

He followed her into the drawing room and sat down on the chair that she indicated to him by way of a languid hand motion.

'I don't have much time. I'm leaving the country tomorrow.'

'Holiday?' Steven asked.

'South Africa. A period of recovery.'

'Ah yes, your sad loss.'

'I've never heard of the Sci-Med Inspectorate, but I assume it's John you've come here to discuss; the woman who telephoned me made it clear I didn't have much choice in the matter. We get more like a police state every day. What is it this time? Ye gods, my poor husband isn't cold in his grave. What exactly does the great voting public want now? His eyes?'

'As I understand it, your husband committed suicide after making a fraudulent expenses claim over a property he didn't actually own, and being found out,' said Steven.

'A complete misunderstanding.'

'Rubbish.'

'I beg your pardon,' exclaimed Melissa, assuming an expression of wide-eyed disbelief.

'As you don't have much time, Mrs Carlisle, I though we

should cut to the chase,' said Steven, who had decided before coming that his only chance of success might be to go on the offensive. 'I'm not interested in expenses claims. I'm not the press, and I am not under any obligation to report our conversation to anyone. What I need to know is just how a man of limited intellect, by all accounts, reached cabinet rank, received universal acclaim for the design of a revolutionary health scheme he didn't actually design, and then plunged into obscurity before topping himself over a seedy little expenses fiddle.'

There was a long silence, during which Melissa stared at Steven unflinchingly. Just as he thought his gamble wasn't going to pay off, she broke eye contact and said, 'His suicide surprised me too. I didn't think he'd have the balls.'

Steven remembered that Arthur Bleasdale had said much the same thing. It set off alarm bells, but he maintained an expression that indicated he was waiting for more.

'Christ, I don't know how he ever became a minister,' said Melissa. 'He was unbelievably thick.'

'But he had the looks and the right accent,' said Steven. Another gamble.

Melissa broke into a small smile. 'You don't mince words, do you, Dr Dunbar? But you're right. It was something I learned too late. He was an empty shell, the mouthpiece of others.'

'It's the others I'm interested in,' said Steven.

'I don't think I can help you there. I wasn't privy to what arrangements he had. I was the dutiful little woman in the background, as befitted my role in the party.'

Steven smiled. 'Does the name Charles French mean anything to you?'

'He and John were at university together. John maintained they were friends but I could never see it.'

'How so?'

'I first met John when he was a young MP. He was handsome and charming and I fell for him. I suppose I just assumed he had ability, so I ignored certain warning signs, including the advice of my father who thought he was an idiot. Charles was introduced to me as one of John's researchers but I got the impression that he lacked respect for John. He always had an air of quiet superiority about him.'

'How did he feel about you?'

'He seemed to like me. Encouraged the relationship between John and me.'

'Saw you as a suitable wife?'

'It could have been that.'

'Do you think Charles French could have been the brains behind John?'

'He was certainly much brighter than John,' said Melissa, looking doubtful. 'But he was young, the same age as John. He couldn't have had any influence within the party, so I don't see . . .'

'Could he have been part of a larger, more influential group, d'you think?'

'You know, I recently asked my father about that. Mistake. I thought he was going to have a heart attack. I don't think I've ever seen him so angry. Demanded to know what had made me ask.'

'What did?'

'John and I had a fight. I said some very cruel things. Told him exactly what I thought of him, and how the party were going to fling him out on his ear. He seemed to suggest they couldn't because he "knew things" and "they" owed him.'

'For what?'

'I don't know. I was past caring by that time. I'd had enough of listening to his drivel. I stormed out and went home to my mother and father's place.'

More alarm bells. Two people who knew him well didn't think Carlisle had the balls to take his own life, and now the suggestion that he might have been considering some kind of blackmail. Steven asked, 'I know it seems insensitive, but do you think I could see where John died?'

Melissa appeared taken aback but simply said, 'I suppose so.' She led the way through to the back of the house, where she donned a jacket before opening the door and crossing to the stable block. 'I found him here, hanging from that beam.' She pointed. 'What exactly are you looking for?'

'How he did it,' replied Steven, deciding not to beat about the bush.

'It's not rocket science: even John managed it,' said Melissa bitterly. 'He tied the rope to that beam, looped it round his neck and jumped off. Look, I really don't see the need for this. It's positively macabre . . .'

'Jumped off what?' Steven interrupted.

'The top rail of the stall, I suppose.'

'Why the top rail?'

'Because of the . . . height he was off the floor when I found him.'

'Quite a gymnast.'

Melissa fell silent as she took Steven's point. She examined the route her husband would have had to take to get onto the top rail of the stall, and thought about the physical ability it would have demanded. Then she shook her head.

'Unless there was a stepladder . . .' suggested Steven.

'No,' said Melissa. 'No stepladders, no chairs, no boxes. Nothing. You think he was murdered, don't you?'

'I'm not sure.'

'But he left a note . . .'

They returned to the house. 'Where do we go from here?' asked Melissa, sounding very subdued.

'In the circumstances, I suggest we do nothing for the moment. Go to South Africa for your "period of recovery".'

Melissa nodded, and Steven sensed her relief, although her expression betrayed nothing.

'Apart from Charles French, do you remember anyone else who was around your husband at the time of the Northern Health Scheme?'

'He was a minister. Lots of people.'

'No inner circle?'

'Paul Schreiber, I suppose. I think he was in charge of pharmaceuticals. And Gordon Field, the hospital manager.'

'No one else?'

'I'm not sure if you could call her inner circle, but a very unpleasant woman named Freeman kept popping up. She was the wife of a surgeon at the hospital but she behaved as if she had some kind of official position, although I never worked out what exactly. The others were very respectful towards her.'

'Lady Antonia Freeman,' said Steven.

'That's right. Do you know her?'

'She's dead. So is Charles French.'

Melissa swallowed. 'I knew about Charles.'

'These "things" that your husband said he knew. Are you absolutely sure you don't know what he was referring to?'

'Positive. He'd never mentioned anything like that before.'

'Good.'

Melissa looked surprised, but then she understood. 'You mean there are some things it's better not to know?'

'Enjoy your holiday.'

Steven left Markham House feeling satisfied with what he'd established. He called Jean Roberts from the car. 'Jean, I need as much information as you can dig up on two people from the old Northern Health Scheme: Paul Schreiber and Gordon Field. Schreiber was concerned with the supply of medicines, and Field was the manager of College Hospital at the time.'

'I'll see what I can do, but—'

'It was a long time ago. Yes, I know. Do your best. I also

need more information about the people who died in Paris – not French or Freeman, the others.'

'Very well. Have you heard how Sir John is?'

'Not yet. I'll let you know.'

First Steven called Charlie Malloy. 'I know this isn't your bag, Charlie, but I'm beginning to have doubts about John Carlisle's suicide. Any chance of someone taking a discreet look at the circumstances surrounding it – and I mean discreet?'

'You know, Dunbar, I'm beginning to wish you hadn't come back,' joked Malloy. 'I'll see what I can do. What exactly's your problem with it?'

'His jump-off point. According to his wife, his feet were about five feet off the ground. That meant he had to have come off the top rail of a horse stall. There was no chair or ladder around so he would have required considerable arm strength to get up there. If he'd been a fit Royal Marine, fair enough, but he wasn't.'

'I'm not sure how we could prove something like that now,' said Malloy.

'We couldn't. So if nothing comes of your foraging maybe we'll just keep it as our secret.'

'Fair enough. Let's both forget we just said that.'

Steven called the hospital and was told that John Macmillan was stable and comfortable. He had not been allowed to regain full consciousness yet. That would probably happen tomorrow. 'Good luck, old son,' he murmured as hung up.

ELEVEN

Steven did not make much progress over the next three weeks. The information which Jean came up with on the Paris flat victims only served to confirm Charlie Malloy's cursory assessment of them: two names in the business world, a merchant banker and a senior civil servant. None of them had a criminal record or had been associated with any scandal considered newsworthy by the press.

Paul Schreiber, however, had thrown up a more interesting CV. He had been head of a pharmaceutical company before being implicated in a price-fixing scam and forced to resign. He had remained as a major shareholder in the company, Lander Pharmaceuticals, with a big say in its running. He had been responsible for supplying the medicines requested by Charles French's software. He had died in a fire along with a male nurse in the pharmacy department of College Hospital.

Gordon Field, the hospital manager, also had a bit of a shady past, having had some involvement with a dodgy PR company before reinventing himself in health care administration. Not much to go on, thought Steven, although Field, as far as he knew, was still alive . . . somewhere. A big plus in this investigation.

Carlisle, French, Freeman, Schreiber, Field . . . as fine a body of people as you could ever hope to meet, thought Steven. And the only thing on their mind had been the improvement of health services in the north-east. Not.

Charlie Malloy's 'discreet' inquiry into Carlisle's suicide had not come up with anything new either. The pathologist had been in no doubt that he'd died of a broken neck, sustained after falling a fair distance with a noose around his neck. How he had managed to get up high enough to achieve a drop of a 'fair distance' was not something that could now be investigated. People often managed feats of considerable strength under conditions of extreme stress, Malloy pointed out.

'There was one thing that came up, though,' he added. 'The suicide note he left behind was typed – or rather printed. The signature was his but the letter hadn't come from either of the two printers in Markham House. Not much, but something to bear in mind, I suppose.'

'Thanks, Charlie. I appreciate it.'

While Steven hadn't made much progress in the recent weeks, John Macmillan had. He'd been home now for four days and was reportedly in good spirits, although still very tired after the trauma of major surgery. His wife had noticed no worrying loss of mental faculty as yet, but it was still early days, and the mere fact that he recognised her was considered encouraging.

The national vaccine production agreement had also progressed. A quick government decision had been made on the tenders submitted and a manufacturer chosen. Merryman Pharmaceuticals, a company sited in the Midlands, would be tasked with providing the nation's vaccine supplies. Steven felt a small twinge when he read this as it meant that his old company, Ultramed, must have failed in their bid. His regret was to turn to irritation, however, when Lionel Montague phoned him personally to complain.

'Merryman must have known what our bid was,' Montague fumed. 'We pared our tender to the very bone and they still undercut us. We were even prepared to make a loss in the first year in order to get the contract.'

'Maybe they did the same. Why are you telling me this,

Lionel?' said Steven. 'I don't know what your bid was, and I don't know anything about the contract.'

'You work for the government, and this is some kind of government stitch-up. They must have favoured the Merryman bid.'

'Frankly, Lionel, that's ridiculous. I don't know the first thing about government contracts, but why would they do that? I'm sure they don't care who makes the vaccines as long as they do it well and come up with them as quickly and as cheaply as possible. They've obviously given the contract to Merryman because they came up with the best package.'

'You'll never convince me of that.'

'Then I won't even try.'

'I'm not going to let it rest here.'

Montague hung up, leaving Steven looking at the phone. 'Thank you and good night, Mr Angry,' he murmured.

On Friday afternoon he called Jean Roberts to say that he was planning to be away for a long weekend. He was driving up to Leicester that evening and then going on up to Scotland to see his daughter, leaving on Saturday morning. He'd come back on Monday.

'A long drive,' said Jean. 'Is there anything you'd like me to do?'

'The journalist who died up north, Jim Kincaid. Do you think you could see if he has any relatives still alive?'

'Will do. Anything else?'

'The manager at College Hospital – Gordon Field. Can you check if he's still in that line of work – or even alive, for that matter?'

'I'll give it a go.'

'Thanks, Jean. Now I understand why John thought . . . thinks so much of you.'

Jean laughed. 'I didn't realise he did.'

'It'll be the Scottish genes in him,' said Steven. 'Saying anything nice is a sign of weakness.'

As he put down the phone, Steven reflected on what Jean had said about the long drive. She was right. Tally was working this weekend, so she couldn't come up to Scotland with him. It was time to get the Porsche back on the road. He called Stan Silver at the mews garage who said to give him a couple of hours.

'I take it this means you're back in the service of the nation?' said Silver, who was working on the front brakes of a Saab convertible, spanner in hand, when Steven parked the Honda and walked towards him.

'For the time being. My ex-boss has just had brain surgery, and I'm back holding the fort.'

'Noble causes follow you around like a puppy, Steven,' said Silver, lifting a brake caliper clear of the disc.

Steven didn't respond. They'd known each other a long time. He valued the fact that Silver always said what was on his mind without considering first. Sometimes it didn't make for easy listening.

'She's all gassed up and ready to go,' he said now, nodding to where the Boxster was sitting.

'We have to settle up first.'

'Nothing to settle, mate. Band of brothers and all that.'

Steven nodded and smiled. 'Thanks, Stan. I owe you.'

'Try to look after it. Any plans for taking your motor across fields and through rivers like you usually end up doing, and I'd stick with the Honda if I were you.'

'No such plans, Stan. Church on Sundays and running Tally to her French class.'

Steven started the Porsche and revelled in the sound. He took a last look at the staid, comfortable and utterly dependable Honda before smiling and spinning the wheels of the Boxster as he took off. He looked back to see Silver laughing and waving in the rear-view mirror.

* * *

'I got the Porsche back,' said Steven, not long after he'd arrived at Tally's place. It was weighing on his mind.

'I thought you might,' said Tally, who had her back to him at the time, preparing dinner.

'And?' he asked tentatively.

Tally turned her head and smiled. 'And nothing. It suits you.'

'Have I told you lately that I love you?'

'Not nearly enough.'

Steven put his arms round her waist from behind and kissed her on the side of her neck. 'I love you, Tally Simmons.'

'Of course you do. You're hungry, and then you'll want sex.'

'Why do I get the feeling I can't win?'

'Because you can't. Open the wine, will you?'

He told her about the call from Lionel Montague.

'Silly man. Why call you?'

'I guess he needed someone working for the government to yell at. What d'you know about Merryman?'

'A perfectly reputable company. I see their name on quite a lot of things – more than I do Ultramed's, if I'm honest.'

Steven nodded. 'I guess he was just pissed off over losing the contract. It was such a big deal for him.'

'And presumably for Merryman too,' said Tally. 'As long as someone starts making vaccines soon; that's all I care about.'

The conversation moved on to Steven's investigation and how he felt it was grinding to a halt. 'I mean, I think John was right. There was something very fishy about the Northern Health Scheme and the forces behind Carlisle, but I can't see how to make a twenty-year leap into anything that could be happening now.'

'Well, the way things are going, you'll be able to talk it over with John himself soon,' said Tally.

'You're right,' agreed Steven, finding something to smile about. 'Against all the odds . . . So what's been happening in your life?'

'Apart from the usual skirmishes with them upstairs over

money, not a lot. Although my sisters and I have decided on a home for Mum. She seemed to like it well enough, and it checks out as being well staffed, clean and comfortable. I still feel guilty, though. It's an act of betrayal . . .'

'Don't,' Steven soothed. 'You're doing the right thing. If we win the lottery we'll move to a place in the country and have her come and live with us. This is only temporary.'

'Idiot.'

TWELVE

Edinburgh, Friday 30 April 2010

At eleven p.m. a large Citroën Picasso drew into one of the car parking bays surrounding Charlotte Square. The driver, a middle-aged Asian man, got out and slid the passenger door back. 'Ready?' he asked the two younger men in the back.

'Ready,' they replied in quiet, tense voices.

'Welcome to Edinburgh. This way.'

The older man led them across a busy street and paused at the west end of George Street, one of the broad thoroughfares in Edinburgh's New Town that ran west–east, parallel to Princes Street. By day it showed a respectable Georgian façade to the world. On a Friday night it was a street full of light and noise. It was the time when the café bars and clubs, located on the ground and basement floors of buildings with banks and offices above them, came into their own. Business ruled the daytime, pleasure the evening. Their doors were so continually being opened and closed that the inside ambience spilled onto the street. On the street itself, laughter, yells and screams rent the night air as groups of people moved like multicellular organisms seeking ever-new sources of sustenance and entertainment.

'Western society,' said the older man. 'Come see. Observe.'

The three men joined the throng on the streets, pausing only to allow drunks to stagger across their path or people walking backwards and sideways to do the same. One girl stumbled and fell as she exited a doorway. She rolled over onto her back, her legs spread, her underwear showing under the briefest of skirts as she laughed hysterically. Her two friends seemed too drunk to help her up but joined in the laughter. The three men skirted round the trio, only to come to a halt again when confronted with a group of youths arguing with a policeman.

'Your last chance,' the constable warned. 'You either leave the street now or you're bloody nicked.'

'Fuck that, we've no' done nothin'!' argued one, struggling against his companions as they tried to pull him away.

'You've annoyed me. Now, I'm going to count to three . . .'

The youths started to move off and the Asian men continued on their way. A hen party dressed as nurses came towards them, strung out across the pavement, singing loudly but out of tune. The imminent collision was averted by a group of businessmen emerging from one of the café bars. They wore suits and carried briefcases but were clearly drunk, having probably been in the bar since the end of the business day. They broke into raucous laughter at the sight of the 'nurses' and started making lewd comments.

It was more their accents than the comments that antagonised the girls. 'In your dreams, tosser,' said one.

'I've seen better talent come out of a skip,' added another.

The bride, wearing L plates on her front and back, brought her knee up sharply into the groin of one man silly enough to get too close.

'Fucking cow,' gasped the man, collapsing to the ground.

'Whoops,' said one of the bridesmaids, stepping on his fingers as she passed.

The Asians, who had moved off the pavement to stand between two parked cars, remained unnoticed observers in the night until, after another hundred metres or so, a drunken youth who had been urinating unsteadily in a doorway turned and saw them. 'Looks like the Pakis have arrived,' he announced to his waiting friends.

'What do they fucking want?' slurred one, who sported a

trail of vomit down the front of his V-neck pullover. 'Don't bloody drink, do they?'

'After our birds, I reckon. Can't see what their bloody own look like under these bleedin' blankets they put over their heads, can they?'

The Asian men did not respond but continued their walk.

'That's right, pal, get back to your corner shop.'

'Poppadom, poppadom,' chanted another.

The crowds began to thin and the noise faded as the men left the revellers behind. The older man stopped and turned. 'Well,' he said, 'do you think that is the way Allah intended us to live?'

'No,' agreed the younger pair vehemently, one still shaking with suppressed anger at having to ignore the taunts of the youths they'd passed. 'Disgusting,' said the other, shaking his head, clearly affected by what he'd witnessed.

'You have been chosen to sweep the filth away, my brothers, clean society of such depravity, bring truth and light to the darkness, spread morality and the rule of law – a law that cannot be flouted because it is *his* law. Allah is great.'

The younger men echoed his words before being led through quieter streets and alleyways back to the car. They drove to a small, detached bungalow in a quiet suburban street in Corstorphine, three miles west of the city centre, where they took care not to disturb the neighbours when closing the car doors.

In a room at the back of the house the older man sat down and indicated that the other two should do the same. 'You are young. I took you there tonight to show you,' he said. 'Just in case you had any doubts. You were both born in this country but you did not fall prey to the evil you saw tonight. Your faith has kept you pure. Your brothers have always been with you. And now I must ask you. Are you ready to take your place in the fight?'

Both younger men agreed that they were, although they sounded nervous and a little uncertain.

'It is a great honour to be chosen,' they were reminded.

'Only two of us are here in Edinburgh. There were eight when we started out,' said one.

'Evil is all over this land. Your brothers will act at the same time but not in the same place.'

'What must we do?'

'Read your Koran. Your training will begin the day after tomorrow.

Similar tours for another six young Asian men, illustrating the UK at play, were drawing to a close in Manchester, London and Liverpool.

On Saturday morning, Steven bade Tally a fond farewell as she left for work.

'Are you going to stop over on your way back?' she asked.

'You bet. Why don't we go out to dinner?'

'A reason to live,' she teased. 'See you Sunday. Give my love to Jenny. Tell her I'll see her soon.'

Steven tidied up and had a last cup of coffee before setting out for Scotland. He was about two hours into the journey when the phone rang, and he moved over to the inside lane, slowing down to hear the call through the car speakers on Bluetooth. It was Jean Roberts.

'It's Saturday, Jean,' he joked. 'Your day off.'

'Yes, well, I found out last night that James Kincaid, the journalist you asked about, does have a relative. He has a married sister living in Newcastle. I thought, as you were up in Scotland this weekend, you might like to stop off there on the way back.'

'Good thinking, Jean. I'm obliged,' said Steven, already starting to do mental calculations about his return journey on Sunday if he were to include Newcastle in his itinerary. 'I'm on the motorway right now. Could you email or text me the address and I'll pick it up later?'

'Consider it done.'

'Daddy, you've got Tarty back,' exclaimed Jenny when she saw that Steven was driving the Porsche again. The name was derived from the adjective her aunt Sue had used when she'd first seen the Boxster. 'A bit tarty, isn't it, Steven?' For some reason the name had stuck. 'I like Tarty,' enthused Jenny. 'I mean I liked Tin Drawers too' – Sue's name for the Honda, which she regarded as more staid – 'but I think I like Tarty better.'

Neither Jenny nor her cousins Mary and Peter understood the connotations of the names, which made them all the more amusing for the grown-ups, whose only fear was that the children would come out with them in public. It hadn't happened yet.

'It's ages since I saw you, Daddy.' Jenny took Steven's hand on the way into the house and announced, 'He's brought Tarty with him.'

'So I see,' said Sue, trying to keep a straight face as she came over to embrace Steven. 'Richard's in the study, catching up on paperwork. He'll be down in a minute. The market's been picking up a bit.' Richard was a lawyer in Dumfries, special-ising in property work.

'And how has her behaviour been, Aunty Sue?'

'Excellent.'

Jenny beamed.

'And her school work?

'Excellent too. Her teacher is very pleased, as to our amaze-ment were Peter's and Mary's teachers too.' Sue tousled Peter's hair. 'It was parents' night last Tuesday.'

Steven swallowed and quickly smiled to conceal the momen-tary frisson of regret. 'In that case, why don't I take these three star pupils to the cinema in Dumfries this evening? We could catch the early performance and be home by . . . ten o'clock?'

The children's eyes widened with excitement at the prospect of being up late, and enthusiastic appeals were made to Sue, who took her time coming to a decision.

'After all, it isn't a school night . . .' prompted Steven.

'Are you sure you're not too tired after such a long drive?'

'No, but now the bad news. I'm afraid I'll have to leave early tomorrow morning, so we won't be able to go to the swimming pool this time.'

It had become traditional that Steven took the children to Dumfries swimming pool when he came up for the weekend, and then treated them to a pizza and ice-cream lunch. 'I could make it up to you tonight with popcorn and ice-cream . . .'

This attracted loud approval.

'Oh well, I suppose,' agreed Sue as Richard came into the room asking what all the noise had been about.

'Good show,' he said, smiling at Sue when she told him. 'Let's go down the pub. It's been ages.'

Steven set off for Newcastle before eight on Sunday morning, hoping to have a word with Lisa Hardesty, James Kincaid's sister. According to Jean's notes, she was married to Kevin Hardesty, and had been expecting her first child at the time of her brother's death. He was going to call on spec rather than phone ahead to arrange a convenient time. He often found that it worked better: it didn't give people time to prepare what they were going to say or, perhaps more important, what they weren't. He punched the Hardestys' post code into Tarty's satnav and let it take him there.

THIRTEEN

The Hardestys lived on a neat housing estate on the west side of Newcastle. It comprised a mixture of detached and semi-detached houses of the type found in the suburbs of any British city. The Hardestys lived in one of the three-bedroomed detached types. Steven found himself going into estate-agent mode as he looked at its neat garden and hedges. Desirable property in much sought-after area . . . double glazing, gas central heating . . . master bedroom en suite . . .

A three-year-old Vauxhall Astra was parked on the driveway in front of the garage door, so he thought his chances of finding someone in were looking good. Sure enough, the bell was answered by a fair-haired, smiling woman somewhere in her forties who struck Steven as being a round peg in a round hole. Suburban life clearly suited her.

'Mrs Hardesty?'

'Yes, that's right. How can I help?'

Steven liked the way she said it. There was no suspicion that he might be selling something in her voice.

'I hope I haven't caught you at a bad moment, Mrs Hardesty,' he began, going on to say who he was and showing his ID.

'I'm sorry, I don't see what you could possibly want with—'

'I'd like to talk to you about your brother James.'

'James died a long time ago.'

'I know.'

Looking confused, Lisa Hardesty said, 'Please . . . come in.'

She led the way through a tidy lounge into a small conservatory where she invited Steven to sit down on one of the cane armchairs.

'You're alone?' he asked.

'My husband and son are off to the football. They're big Newcastle supporters. Now, what's this all about?'

'I'm interested in just how James came to die.'

'He was shot, for God's sake,' exclaimed Lisa. 'You must know that. He was murdered along with Eve, his girlfriend. She was a lovely girl.'

Steven nodded. 'I'm sorry. I should have said I'm more interested in *why* he was murdered.'

'After all this time,' Lisa said sadly. 'According to the police, he got caught up in a drugs war. Drugs war my backside.'

'That was the official story,' said Steven quietly, excited at what he was hearing and hoping for more.

'Jim was in big trouble. He came to me for help. But it wasn't from any "drugs barons", as the papers called them. It was from the people at the hospital, the Londoners. He got on the wrong side of them.'

'The Londoners,' Steven repeated.

'They'd set up a new health scheme, centred on College Hospital.'

'And your brother got on the wrong side of them . . .'

'I know it sounds stupid, but Jim was in fear of his life.'

'You said he came to you for help. Did you help him?'

A look of regret come into Lisa's eyes; maybe even guilt, Steven thought. 'No,' she said. 'My husband didn't want us to get involved. Jim asked if Eve could stay with us for safety's sake, and I had to turn him down. I never saw either of them alive again.' Lisa looked round for a box of tissues and dabbed at her eyes.

'Do you have any idea who these people were?'

Lisa shook her head.

'You said he got on the wrong side of them. What did that mean? What did he do?'

Lisa blew her nose. 'I only know Jim got friendly with a local GP called Neil Tolkien. They both thought something nasty was going on at the hospital. Jim thought our father died because of them and their newfangled health scheme. He was worried about his daughter too.'

'Your brother had a daughter?'

Lisa nodded. 'Kerry. She was brain-damaged after an operation when she was a baby, and lived in a care home. Her mother, Jim's estranged wife, didn't bother with her much – she'd built a new life – but Jim always thought she had the capacity to get better if she got the right treatment, bless him. Used to sit with her for hours when he was up here, but of course he couldn't be here all the time.'

'Is Kerry still . . . ?'

'No, she died a couple of months after her dad. Pneumonia, they said. Maybe it was for the best, poor love. She didn't have much of a life.'

'Correct me if I'm wrong, but I got the impression that everyone liked the new health scheme when it was introduced.'

'You're right, they did. There was no waiting around. Your doctor ordered up your treatment on the computer and it arrived within the hour.'

'But Jim saw something else?'

'I don't think he trusted the people at the hospital. He and Eve thought they covered up the outcome of an operation that went badly wrong.'

'The one where the surgeon died?'

Lisa nodded. 'There was a lot of press attention over that, and Jim thought they wheeled out an actress with bandages over her face at a press conference to assure everyone that all was well and get rid of the reporters.'

'Did he manage to prove that?'

'I'm not sure. It never made the papers, maybe because he got sidetracked by something else. Then Dad got cancer – he'd been a miner and his chest was never right after that – and had to have an operation. Jim didn't think he'd been given the right medicine afterwards. Maybe it was just anger and grief on Jim's part, but on the other hand Dr Tolkien had doubts about what was happening to his patients as well. I think that's why they teamed up. Eve had reservations too – she was a nurse – and they all ended up paying the price.'

Steven found it difficult not to react to what he was hearing. It was the script of a nightmare. He could see that Lisa was still upset but was reluctant to stop questioning her. 'You said your brother and Dr Tolkien teamed up. Eve too. Was anyone else on side?'

Lisa thought for a moment before saying, 'I think there was, now you come to mention it. Holland, somebody Holland. I think he had something to do with computers at the hospital. '

'Anyone else?'

'I don't think so.'

'Mrs Hardesty, I'm sorry for disturbing your Sunday and bringing back such painful memories, but you've been most helpful.'

'It's nice to know someone's interested in Jim's death after all these years. No one was at the time.'

'I thought you weren't coming,' said Tally when Steven arrived at her apartment the wrong side of seven thirty.

'Sorry, I had to go to Newcastle. A quick shower and I'll be right with you. Where shall we go?'

'Look, we don't have to go out,' said Tally sympathetically. 'I can rustle up something here and you can relax and get your breath back . . .'

'No, we're going out.'

'Oh, right,' said Tally with a smile at Steven's insistence, 'but I'll do the driving. You look as if you could do with a drink.'

They drove to a popular Indian restaurant where they had no trouble getting a table on a Sunday night. The place was about half full, and muted sitar music set the atmosphere as they sat under chandeliers, surrounded by red flock wallpaper.

'Why did you go to Newcastle?' asked Tally.

Steven told her about his trip to see James Kincaid's sister and what she'd been able to tell him.

'You know, this is shaping up into something really nasty,' said Tally.

Steven agreed. 'But at least I can now sort out the good guys from the bad among the dead.'

'But as to what they were up to . . .'

'I'm a way off that yet,' said Steven. 'The system was supposed to be foolproof but Kincaid thought they had killed his father by giving him the wrong treatment and Neil Tolkien thought the same about some of his patients.'

'From what you've told me, there didn't seem to be much margin for error,' argued Tally. 'If a doctor prescribed a certain drug, a computer checked that the treatment was appropriate, and only stipulated a cheaper alternative if it had been clinically proved to be as good. Then the automated pharmacy department was instructed to supply it. What could go wrong?'

'You'd think it would be a safer system than the usual one,' Steven agreed.

'Mind you,' Tally began thoughtfully, 'I think you once told me that Tolkien was involved with drug addicts . . .'

'What's on your mind?'

'What did Kincaid's father die of?'

'I understand he had long-term chest problems because of his occupation and he'd just developed cancer. They operated but he didn't live for long afterwards.'

Tally topped up Steven's glass. 'I suppose we have no way of knowing that the drug addicts were the patients Neil Tolkien was worried about, but if they were . . . we could be looking at lost causes here.'

'How d'you mean?'

'An old man, chronically ill and now with cancer . . . a number of addicts with associated problems like HIV and AIDS . . . people who were costing the NHS a lot of money with no real prospect of getting better . . .'

'God, I see what you're getting at,' said Steven. 'Although I wish I didn't . . . Kincaid was worried about his daughter too. She was brain-damaged and in long-term residential care. She died of pneumonia a couple of months after her father.'

'Just a thought,' said Tally.

'And a brilliantly awful one too,' said Steven quietly, his mind reeling with the implications. 'I'm going to see if I can lay my hands on hospital and GP records at the time, if they still exist. See if I can spot a pattern along those lines. The early deaths of lost causes.'

'It would be absolutely horrible if it were true . . .' said Tally, pausing.

'But?'

'Sounds terrible to say it, but it would be . . . historical. This was all nearly twenty years ago and the perpetrators – if that's what they were – are all dead.'

Steven looked at her, wondering for a moment whether to just agree or to tell her more. His natural inclination was always to keep things to himself, but this time he decided there had to be one person in his life he had to trust absolutely. 'Maybe they're not all dead,' he said. He told her of his suspicions regarding the identity of the Paris bomber. 'It could have been some kind of coup,' he finished. 'He was one of them.'

'It could equally be they were planning to set up the same thing again and the bomber decided to put a stop to it.'

'Maybe, maybe not, but my fear is it could be business as usual under new management.'

'Okay, now I understand why you must find out everything about what happened twenty years ago,' said Tally. 'If we're on the right lines, we know the crime and we know the motive – to save money. What we don't know is how they did it.'

'God, I'm tired.'

'You look it. Let's go home.'

Tally had to leave before Steven in the morning. 'Last night was a landmark,' she said after she kissed him goodbye.

'How so?'

'A landmark in our relationship. It was the first time we ever went to bed without making love.'

'God, I'm sorry. I don't know . . .'

Tally put a finger on his lips. 'Don't be. It was nice. You held my hand, told me you loved me and went out like a light. I believed you. I slept like a log.'

FOURTEEN

'How was your weekend?' Jean Roberts asked when Steven arrived at the Home Office in the early afternoon.

'The trip to Newcastle to see Kincaid's sister was well worth it,' he said. 'Kincaid was investigating the Northern Health Scheme along with the GP Neil Tolkien. They both thought people were dying who shouldn't have been dying. The drugs war story was a cover-up. Lisa Hardesty is convinced that the people running the scheme killed her brother because he figured out what they were up to.'

'And what were they up to? I thought people were very much in favour of it,' said Jean.

'The majority were,' Steven agreed. 'But from what Lisa Hardesty told me, her brother suspected there was a downside to the scheme, a lethal one.'

'I don't think I understand.'

'James Kincaid's father was long-term sick. He developed cancer and died shortly after his operation.'

Jean's expression indicated that she didn't think that was too unusual.

'A number of Neil Tolkien's patients met a similar fate – died when he hadn't expected them to. It made him suspicious.'

Jean pursed her lips but still didn't comment.

'James Kincaid had a daughter in long-term care because of brain damage. She died of pneumonia.'

'Are you suggesting they were murdering people?' asked Jean, looking shocked.

'Selectively,' said Steven. 'There's a strong possibility they were killing off "lost causes", as Tally called them.'

'But how? That sounds like something the Nazis would do.'

'I don't know how. I don't even know if we'll be able to prove it after all this time.'

'It's hard to see where you'd begin.'

'Medical records. We need to look at the records of people who were treated under the Northern Health Scheme, in particular the people who might have been regarded as lost causes . . .'

'As defined by?'

Steven thought for a moment. 'Likely to be a long-term drain on public resources.'

'Assuming we can access these records – and that's a big if after all this time – we're going to need help. It sounds like a big undertaking.'

Steven nodded. 'Bring in all the help you need, but check if we can get the records first. Start with the College Hospital records department and then try the local GP practices, beginning with the one Neil Tolkien was a partner in. He was also involved in some drug rehabilitation initiative, but I doubt if that still exists. These places tend to come and go.'

'I take it we'll have full Home Office backing on this?' said Jean.

'You bet.' Steven smiled as he felt an unspoken question in the air. 'I'm going over to see John now,' he said. 'I think he's well enough to make the handover to me official. I'll ask him to sign the relevant paperwork.'

'Tell him I was asking for him. Oh, I nearly forgot. I came up with something this morning you'll be interested in. You asked about Gordon Field, the manager at College Hospital in the early nineties. I found him.'

'Well done.'

'He's in Leigh Open Prison doing eighteen months for fraud.'

Steven gave a sigh of resignation. 'Well, at least I'll know where to find him.'

He found John Macmillan doing the *Times* crossword. The Sci-Med director was sitting in a wing-backed armchair in dressing gown and slippers, his feet resting on a footstool in front of a coal fire. His head was still bandaged but his eyes were bright and alert. 'Come in, Steven. Good to see you.'

'I don't believe it,' exclaimed Steven. 'You've just had serious brain surgery and you're doing the *Times* crossword?'

'Don't be fooled. I used to do it regularly in twelve minutes. I've been stuck on four down for the past two hours.'

Steven smiled at what appeared to be a genuine complaint. He could see that the puzzle was already three-quarters done.

'Help yourself to a drink. I would have asked you to stay to dinner but my wife is away, staying with our daughter for a few days. I thought she needed a break from me so there's just the agency nurse and the housekeeper at home.'

Steven poured himself a gin and tonic. Macmillan declined with a slight wave of the hand. 'So how are things going?'

'I think you were right to have . . . concerns over recent events in Paris and the death of John Carlisle,' said Steven. 'I share them. In fact, I'm going to have to expand the investigation. I need our arrangement to be put on a more formal basis. I need something on paper.'

Macmillan nodded. 'Stating that you are now head of Sci-Med?'

'No, stating that I'm officially *acting* head of Sci-Med pending your return. The way things are I just might need a big stick to wave at authority. I'd be happier knowing there's one in the cupboard. So would Jean. She sends her regards, by the way.'

'Consider it done,' said Macmillan. 'I'll put something down in writing and send it over in the morning. Now, are you going to bring me up to speed?'

Steven did so. He was genuinely delighted to see Macmillan apparently almost back to his old self. He sat, listening without interruption, looking off into the middle distance, as was his habit, but, as Steven knew only too well, taking absolutely everything in. When he'd finished, Macmillan continued to sit in silence for a few moments before saying, 'No wonder the Northern Health Scheme was so bloody efficient. They didn't address problems: they buried them.'

'That's certainly what it looks like,' Steven agreed. 'But it's going to take some work to prove it and establish exactly how they did it.'

'If all this should turn out to be true, the meeting in Paris could have been the first step in starting up the whole thing all over again.'

'Presumably the prospect of a change of government and an easier administration to infiltrate brought their long hibernation to an end.'

'But something went wrong. Instead of conducting a secret meeting in Paris, away from prying eyes, they ended up dead. Any ideas?'

'The killer had to be one of their own,' said Steven, giving his reasons for thinking so, and adding, 'Apart from anything else, you don't go around with a lump of Semtex in your pocket on the off chance . . .'

'Quite so,' Macmillan conceded.

'I'd like to think that one of them had an attack of conscience and decided to put a stop to things for once and for all, but . . . there are alternative explanations.'

'Like?'

'Internecine strife? A policy disagreement? A takeover bid?'

Steven went on to tell Macmillan of his doubts surrounding John Carlisle's suicide. 'It looks to me as if someone went for a complete wipe-out of the old guard, including Carlisle.'

'In order to do what?' mused Macmillan.

'Now ain't that the big question. I suppose it could be the same thing again. It could have been that the others in Paris weren't keen to try that. The scheme seemed to work well enough the first time. If it hadn't been for James Kincaid and his interfering little band, it could well have spread across the whole country, the end result being . . .'

'A leaner, fitter, richer nation,' said Macmillan with a wry smile. 'Right-wing politics do have that unhappy knack of appealing to plain, ordinary common sense, don't they? It's only when you start uncovering the pits full of bodies that you see the reality.'

A middle-aged woman in nurse's uniform knocked and entered. 'Excuse me, gentlemen. Time's up, Sir John,' she said, pointing to the face of the watch hanging on the front of her dress. 'You don't want to overdo things when you've been doing so well.'

'Sorry, Steven,' he said. 'Keep me informed. I'll get that letter to the Home Office in the morning.'

James Black, the new head of the Schiller Group in his guise as the secretary of the competitions committee of Redwood Park golf club, had called a meeting at only four hours' notice, so he wasn't sure how many would make it to the private function room at the usual restaurant by the suggested time of eight p.m. In the event all had arrived by twenty past.

'I take it we're not about to be given good news,' said Toby Langton.

A murmur came from the others.

'Nothing we should be greatly concerned about, but I thought it best you should know. Sci-Med has started to take an interest in the old Northern Health Scheme.'

'And we shouldn't be concerned?' exclaimed Constance Carradine. 'That's the last thing we need.'

'What in God's name made them do that?' asked Rupert Coutts.

'Take it easy,' said Black. 'They're not exactly knocking at our door. They probably looked at the identities of the dead in Paris to see what they had in common, made the connection to John Carlisle . . .'

'And came up with the Northern Health Scheme,' completed Elliot Soames. 'I don't like it.'

'How much do they know?' asked Langton.

'What is there to know?' said Black. 'The scheme was very popular and highly successful in its time. Everyone behind it is now dead. *Sic transit gloria mundi* and all that.'

'I still don't like it,' said Constance. 'Sci-Med have a reputation for picking away at things.'

'How did you find out about this?' asked Toby Langton.

Black hesitated before answering, knowing that his reply would not help to settle nerves. 'A contact in the police forensic service told me that Sci-Med weren't convinced Carlisle took his own life.'

'Jesus Christ, they're really onto us,' said Coutts.

'Whoa,' said Black. 'The pathologist's initial report was confirmed.'

'Thank God for that.'

'I heard that the head of Sci-Med was seriously ill,' said Soames.

'He is.'

'So who started asking questions about Carlisle?'

'Someone called Dr Steven Dunbar, Sci-Med's chief investigator apparently.'

'Do we know what made him suspicious?' asked Constance.

'I understand he went to see Carlisle's wife.'

'Do we know why?'

'No.'

'Maybe we should ask her?'

'I considered that,' said Black. 'She's out of the country, in South Africa, getting over the demise of John. Look, I think we're worrying unnecessarily here. There's nothing to connect French and the others and what they did to us. They're all dead.'

'I suppose you're right,' said Coutts. 'Still, the thought of Sci-Med nosing around is . . . disconcerting.'

'It's my bet their interest is over,' said Black. 'They probably felt obliged to take an interest in the Paris deaths and the suicide of an ex-health secretary and now it's over.'

'If you say so,' said Coutts. 'But it wouldn't do any harm to keep an ear open.'

'We should certainly do that,' agreed Black. 'But they're an independent lot. Tend not to advertise what they're up to.'

'What do we know about Dunbar?' asked Constance.

'Rumour has it he's good at his job, but it's my understanding that he'd actually left Sci-Med but came back to stand in for Sir John Macmillan when he fell ill. Probably just holding the fort. Going through the motions. Perhaps now you'd like to hear how things are going with our plans?'

FIFTEEN

'There are no official hospital records from the time of the Northern Health Scheme,' said Jean Roberts. 'The practice Dr Neil Tolkien was a partner in ceased to exist fifteen years ago. No record of patient reallocation was kept, and no one can remember anything about the drug rehabilitation scheme he was involved in. All thoroughly depressing.'

'Damnation,' said Steven. 'But you said "official" hospital records?'

'I thought you might latch on to that,' said Jean with a smile. 'Apparently hospitals like to get rid of records as soon as they possibly can, so when the legal requirement time for keeping them passes they simply don't exist on the system any more. That doesn't actually mean that they've been destroyed. They're often not, a bit like deleted items on the hard disk of a computer. They're still there; they just don't have a label any more and you can't reference them.'

'And?'

'There's a reasonable chance that the files still exist in physical form somewhere in the basement of College Hospital. Apparently it's a warren of cellars and tunnels that people use for storage when they're pressed for space upstairs. My informant couldn't guarantee that what you're interested in will be down there but there's a chance.'

'Then I'd best take it,' said Steven. 'Perhaps you could inform College Hospital of our interest and get me permission to rifle through their cellars?'

'Of course.'

'And I'd like to go see Gordon Field some time. Where exactly is Leigh Open Prison?'

'Yorkshire. Do you want me to approach the governor?'

'Please. I plan to visit him some time in the next few days.'

Steven drove up to Leicester on Sunday and stayed overnight at Tally's place. 'What do you think the Lib Dems are going to do?' Tally asked as she and Steven did the washing up after dinner. She got the expected grunt in response. 'You don't care, do you?'

'Correct.'

'Oh, Steven, I know you've had a lot of bad experiences with politicians, and I know you don't like them, but all the same . . .'

'You don't know the half of it.'

'Maybe not, but it won't change unless you make it.'

'Human nature doesn't change, Tally. It's the driving force behind everything, always has been. It's circumstances that change.'

'What does that mean?'

'Today's freedom fighters are tomorrow's corrupt rulers. Yesterday's idealists are today's self-interested liars. It's circum-stances that change. The selfish gene will always out. People will grab the best for themselves.'

'Gosh,' said Tally, as if she'd just heard more than she bargained for. 'What are *you* planning on grabbing, Steven?'

'Your bottom . . . just as soon as I'm finished these dishes,' said Steven, trying to keep a straight face.

'Oh well,' said Tally. 'No use trying to fight human nature, I suppose . . .'

Steven had the usual trouble finding a parking place near a big city hospital. The situation was exacerbated by College Hospital's being the oldest hospital in the city, built at a time when two legs were the most common form of transport. He was on his second circuit of the area when he saw reversing lights go on on a silver estate car up ahead, and paused to let the driver reverse out before slipping into the space, feeling the inevitable sense of achievement such success always brought.

'I'm expected,' he told the receptionist when she asked about an appointment. This prompted a phone call to 'Mrs Rutherford' before he was told that someone would be down shortly. He used the time to look around him, seeing what he expected: a mixture of Victorian architecture and bland, modern signing to departments not yet dreamt of when the place was built, tiled walls and corridors that stretched into the distance like the set of a nightmare and possessed that smell which all hospitals had.

He saw a young man in a suit pause at the desk to ask something, and the receptionist pointing in his direction.

'Dr Dunbar? I'm Paul Drinkwater. The hospital manager asked me to give you his apologies – he has a meeting. I'm to give you all the assistance you need.'

Steven shook hands and said that all he required was access to the basement area.

'I hope you've brought a boiler suit with you,' said Drinkwater. 'It's pretty dirty down there.'

'Didn't think of that.'

'Out through here.' Drinkwater led the way out of the main building and across a cobbled courtyard to a small group of buildings signed as *Works Department All Trades*. Steven was introduced to the clerk of works, Dennis Drysdale, a short, stocky man, who Drinkwater told him would show him the way down. 'If you need anything else, I'm on extension 117.'

Steven, who had thought that accessing the basement would simply mean opening a door and descending some stairs, followed Drysdale on another short safari across uneven cobbles to a pair of wooden double doors in the wall of the main building. Drysdale unlocked the padlock on them and said, 'All yours.'

Steven peered down a narrow, sloping walkway which looked like the entrance to a mine, the stone walls lit at intervals with caged bulkhead lights.

'Let me know when you're finished and I'll lock up again,' said Drysdale. 'Otherwise the winos and smackheads will move in.'

At least it wasn't cold was Steven's first thought as he walked down the slope to an intersection with corridors leading off in three directions. He opted for the middle one, calculating that it would take him under the centre of the hospital where, with luck, he would find more than long stretches of featureless corridor designed mainly for housing the supply pipes for the hospital's services. Hot water and steam were uppermost in his mind as the temperature seemed to rise with every yard of progress. He had to stoop to avoid contact with the pipes but could still feel the heat on his face.

His spirits rose when he saw the corridor widen to accommodate a series of arched cellars, some with doors, some without. He could see piles of old furniture in one and what looked like antiquated anaesthetic equipment in another. Old steel bedheads and oil lamps made him feel as though he'd entered a museum. Long-skirted nurses in frilly caps and frock-coated surgeons flitted across his imagination.

He thought the last door might be locked when he tried it but it yielded to his shoulder and the slight echo the noise provoked suggested he was entering a much bigger space. It was in darkness, the bulkhead lights outside only illuminating the first few feet, so he ran his hand up the wall and found a bank of old-style metal light switches. To his surprise and relief, they worked.

The cellar was about the size of two tennis courts, although the openness of the space was broken by a regular series of brick pillars holding up the hospital above. Piles of wooden chairs and tables near the entrance impeded his progress, but once past them he found exactly what he'd hoped to find: rows of shelving reaching up to the ceiling and laden with cardboard file holders. A cursory opening of one of them revealed the patient notes of Mrs Matilda Gardner, who had been treated for gallstones in 1976.

The big question now in Steven's mind was whether or not the notes had just been piled there haphazardly or whether they were in any kind of order. If the former, he was looking at a career, and one he had no wish to embark on. He stood in the eerie silence of the underground cavern, looking for any helpful signs on the shelving, his spirits falling as he failed to find any.

He walked towards the nearest row, already starting to calculate just how many people it would take to sift through the mountains of files and put them in chronological order. Then something caught his eye and he ran his fingers along the bottom edge of one of the shelves. To his joy, as the dust and grime cleared a little, he could just about make out something scrawled in black pen: two numbers and a dash: 75 –

With hope rekindled, Steven collected an armful of files and took them back to the cellar entrance where he dumped them on the floor while he fetched a table and a chair from the pile, and set them up as an impromptu office where he could sit and look through the files. It only took a few moments to establish that the ones he'd picked up were all from patients who'd been in the hospital in 1975. There was order among the feared chaos.

Steven put back the '75 files and started hunting for more pen markings on the shelves. He felt his pulse-rate rise as he came across '91 –'. Another armful of folders and a few minutes sitting at his reclaimed dusty desk and he had established that he was looking at files from patients treated in the hospital at the time of the Northern Health Scheme. He now had to decide whether to make arrangements for people to come here to sift through the records or to organise transport to take the files back to London.

It only took a few moments for him to plump for London. Sci-Med had a network of consultants, agencies and contacts they could call in at a moment's notice. Jean Roberts would be able to come up with a team of people with the necessary skills to analyse medical records and report on their findings. They could be doing that while he went to pay Gordon Field a visit in prison. He had phone calls to make.

Steven paused at the door to examine the metal light switches. He hadn't seen these for years but they looked the same as the ones his grandmother had had in her house in Keswick. He was thinking about her and picturing the front room with its piano and lace curtains when he heard a sound suggesting that someone was outside in the corridor.

'Hello, is anyone there?' he called out.

There was no reply.

He couldn't quite convince himself it had been his imagination so he tried again.

Nothing.

Steven shrugged and switched out the chamber lights before closing the door and crossing the cellar junction, preparing himself for the stooped journey back along the pipe corridor he'd come in through. He felt the heat on his face as once more he came into close proximity to the supply pipes, carefully steering a middle course so that he didn't touch them. Maybe it was the slight unease he felt about thinking he wasn't alone that heightened his alertness, but when he thought he saw a movement a few metres ahead he instinctively dropped to his knees and put his hands up in front of his face.

At the same moment a valve opened and high-pressure steam shot out, scalding the back of his hands and filling the tunnel with deafening noise and the sulphurous smell of a boiler-house. Steven cried out in pain as he rolled away. He crawled along the floor under the steam jet until he was past the open valve, where he was just in time to see a running figure up ahead.

'You son of a bitch,' he yelled out, as anger vied with pain and sent him off in pursuit. He could see it was a male figure, tall – like him it had to stoop to avoid hitting its head – dressed in denims and trainers . . . and getting away.

Steven stopped running. Get a grip, Dunbar, he thought. Think about your hands. He remembered seeing occasional taps set in the wall on the way in so he turned all his attention to finding one of them. When he did, he'd found a supply of cold water. He held his hands under the flow and experienced instant remission from the pain although he knew it would return when he removed them. He held them there long enough to catch his breath and regain rational thought. In spite of the pain, he'd been lucky. Had he not dropped to his knees so quickly the steam would have caught him full in the face. As it was, he needed to seek medical help as soon as possible to minimise the damage. At least he was in a hospital.

'What the hell!' exclaimed the clerk of works, Drysdale, when he saw the backs of Steven's hands.

'Steam burns,' said Steven, hurrying past to get to A&E.

SIXTEEN

Drysdale appeared again in the company of Paul Drinkwater as Steven was finishing in A&E.

'What on earth happened?' asked Drinkwater.

'Someone opened a steam valve in the tunnel as I was leaving.'

'Christ, they were quick off the mark,' said Drysdale, a comment that made the other two look to him for more.

'The winos,' said Drysdale. 'And the junkies. They see the tunnels as a nice warm place to kip down. That's why we keep the access doors locked, but of course they were left open while Dr Dunbar was down there.'

'Oh, I see,' said Drinkwater. 'You think one of them must have come across Dr Dunbar and seen him as the face of authority?' He turned back to Steven. 'How bad is it?'

'They'll mend,' said Steven, holding up his bandaged hands and feeling slightly woozy because of the painkillers he'd been given. 'It could have been a lot worse.'

'Dare I ask if you found what you were looking for?'

'I did. That's why I'd like the doors to be locked and kept that way until I can arrange transport for the files I'm interested in.'

'Of course,' said Drinwater. 'Dennis, can you see to that?'

Drysdale nodded. 'No problem. Mind you, if there's a heating problem somewhere in the hospital . . .'

'No one goes down there alone,' said Steven. 'I'll arrange with the local police for an officer to be present to accompany anyone who has to go down in an emergency.'

Drysdale nodded. 'Very well.'

They were interrupted by the arrival of a well-dressed man in his late forties whose dark suit and silk tie suggested management. 'Dr Dunbar? I'm so sorry. I've just heard what happened. I'm Clive Deans, the hospital manager. I'm sorry I couldn't welcome you earlier, and now this. Absolutely awful. What can I say?'

'You'll excuse me for not shaking hands,' said Steven.

'Look, maybe you shouldn't drive. Why don't you use the hospital suite we use for relatives? It's empty at the moment. You can get a good night's rest, and if you need any more painkillers you'll be in the right place.'

'Thank you. I think I'll take you up on that.'

He was shown to the suite and given a couple of internal telephone numbers to call if he needed anything. Deans left him alone, still apologising for what had happened, and Steven used his mobile to start making calls, phoning Jean Roberts first.

'Jean, I've had a bit of an accident. There are a number of things I'd like you to do.'

'Doesn't sound like an accident to me,' she said, after obliging him to tell her what had happened.

'Be that as it may, I'd like to get the records back to London as quickly as possible. We'll need a courier service and we'll need a team of analysts to work on them when they arrive. I also need you to arrange with the local police to mount guard on the cellars in College Hospital until we get the records out. Anyone who has to go down there must be accompanied, and no papers are to be removed.'

'Understood. Are you calling a code red on this?'

Steven hesitated for a moment. He'd often requested a code red – official approval for a full investigation with a number of Home Office powers being invoked – but never found himself in a position to actually sanction one. 'Not yet,' he said. 'Let's request co-operation at the moment. If we don't get it, we'll start thinking about a code red.'

'Very well. 'I'll keep you informed of the arrangements. Do you still intend to visit Gordon Field in prison?'

'I'm going to drive over there in the morning.'

'Take care, Steven.'

For some reason Steven found Jean's parting words thought-provoking. He wasn't entirely convinced that he'd crossed the path of a down-and-out in the tunnel. He wanted to believe it, because any other explanation implied that it had been an attempt to stop him or his investigation and indicated that someone had a powerful reason for ensuring that sleeping dogs were left that way. However, he had no wish to share these thoughts with anyone else at the moment – least of all Tally, because of the alarm he'd cause – so his injuries were put down to the accepted version of events when he phoned her.

'Oh, you poor thing. How bad?'

'No lasting damage, but bloody painful at the time. I've had them dressed and taken a couple of painkillers so I'll get a good night's sleep and be out of here in the morning. I'm going to see Gordon Field in Leigh Open Prison in Yorkshire.'

'Sounds like a nice day out,' Tally joked. 'Will I see you later to kiss your hands all better?'

'I may have to come back here.'

'Of course, the transfer of the files. Oh, well . . .'

'Then maybe I'll take a day off. Maybe you could do the same. We could go somewhere?'

'I'll see what I can do.'

Leigh Open Prison was located in a remote part of the Yorkshire moors, far enough from transport links to deter thoughts of earlier-than-planned release for the fleet of foot should the idea occur. George Plumpton, the governor, a large man with a florid face and an obvious penchant for tweed, welcomed Steven to 'our humble abode' with the offer of tea and ginger biscuits, which he accepted. 'So, it's Gordon Field you're here to see?'

'It is.'

'Not planning to go ten rounds with him, are you?' said Plumpton, alluding to Steven's bandages.

'I was rather hoping I wouldn't have to. In fact, I was hoping he'd be a model prisoner?'

This prompted a laugh to escape Plumpton's mouth before it was entirely free of biscuit, and he wiped the crumbs from the scatter area. 'They all are. Mainly middle-class chaps with jobs that brought them too tantalisingly close to other people's money and, in a moment of madness – as their defence counsel would maintain – they gave in to temptation and changed the course of their lives.'

Steven nodded. 'Have you noticed anything out of the ordinary about Field?'

'Like what?'

'Does he have strong views about anything? Politics? The system? The unfairness of it all?'

Plumpton shook his head. 'Far from it. Some of them seek to atone for past mistakes by going too far the other way, if you know what I mean. They find religion and decide to bring it to the rest of us, devote themselves to lame ducks and good causes, but Field just keeps his head down, does what he's told and serves his time without comment.'

'Thanks,' said Steven. 'That's helpful.'

He was shown to an interview room where Field was already waiting. He said who he was and sat down opposite the prisoner. 'Mr Field, I'd like to ask you about your time at College Hospital in Newcastle.'

'What would you like to know?' replied Field in well-modulated tones.

Steven eyed him up, looking for signs of dumb insolence,

but found none. 'Exactly what were you and French and Schreiber up to?'

Field recoiled a little and Steven thought he saw nervous uncertainty in his eyes. 'What d'you mean? I was the hospital manager. I did my job. End of.'

Steven shook his head. 'No, no,' he said with a smile. 'We both know that's a bunch of crap. I think you were involved in something that's going to end up with you moving to a very secure prison indeed, where Leigh will just be a distant memory of holidays past.'

'I swear to God I had nothing to do with whatever these bastards were up to.'

'I'm not God and I'm not interested.'

'Okay, look, I admit I played a part in the Greta Marsh deception but I didn't have much choice. You didn't say no to French and that bloody woman Freeman.'

'Greta Marsh was the patient being operated on when her surgeon died?'

'That's right. They didn't want any publicity. That bloody Freeman woman didn't seem to give a fuck about her husband dying. All she and the others were interested in was making the press go away. College Hospital was to be about good news, nothing else.'

'Tell me about the deception.'

'Greta was left blind and brain-damaged. She was shipped off to an institute called Harrington Hall, and French and his buddies hired an actress to take her place at a press conference to assure everyone that Greta was okay.'

'And James Kincaid?'

'Who?'

Steven kept quiet and just stared at Field until he said, 'Oh, the journalist, right? He kept popping up like a bad smell.'

'So you killed him.'

'No, I had nothing to do with that,' insisted Field, beginning to panic. 'I admit I was involved in scaring him off after he broke into Harrington Hall and got a bit too close to the truth for comfort, but that's as far as it went. As God's my witness . . .'

'So what were French and his pals up to? The thing you had no part in . . .'

'I don't know. I was an outsider. They didn't tell me anything I didn't need to know. As far as I could see, they seemed to be doing a pretty good job. They ran a very efficient operation that all the staff and patients liked . . .'

'But?'

'Somehow, they weren't exactly the sort of people you'd expect to be doing that sort of thing, if you know what I mean. They weren't natural candidates for the caring professions.'

Steven understood his meaning very well. 'And John Carlisle, where did he come into it?'

'The health secretary?' said Field, appearing amused. 'He popped up at intervals with his entourage and took any credit that was going. He smiled a lot and made the right noises. Did what politicians do.'

'You said French and Schreiber ran a very efficient operation. What exactly did they do in a practical sense?'

'French oversaw the computing side of things, Schreiber organised the pharmacy and liaised with the supply company.'

'Which was?'

'Lander Pharmaceuticals. I think Schreiber had some connection with them.'

'And Antonia Freeman? What did she do?'

'Lady Antonia? God knows, but everyone seemed shit scared of her, like she was the real boss.'

'Of what?'

Fields shrugged. 'I dunno. It's funny. They seemed like a bunch of individuals but they weren't, if you know what I mean?'

'No.'

'Well, they seemed to have access to . . . back-up services. They knew where to hire an actress to play Greta Marsh. They knew where to come up with heavies when Kincaid had to be warned off. Things like that. It was like they weren't alone. Little helpers just appeared when they needed them.'

Steven nodded, thinking about someone to open a steam valve. 'Thank you, Mr Field. I don't think I need to take up any more of your time.'

'Take up as much of my "time" as you like,' said Field. 'You do believe me, don't you?'

'Yes, I do,' said Steven, getting up to go. He did not add that one of the main reasons for believing Field was the fact that he had been left alive when all the others hadn't.

Steven was half an hour into his journey back to Newcastle when Jean Roberts phoned. The courier company had been briefed and would be on site at College Hospital at four p.m. if that was convenient.

Steven checked his watch and said that it would.

'I've also recruited a team to start work as soon as the records arrive. They're people from the Department of Health, and the permanent under-secretary insists that Sci-Med foots the bill.'

'No problem.'

'And one other thing. I've managed to trace a doctor who worked with Neil Tolkien at the time of the Northern Health Scheme. She was one of the voluntary team who worked with heroin addicts at the time. Her name is Mary Cunningham; she's still a GP in the area with a practice in Lamont Avenue.'

'Excellent. I'll look her up.'

It was just after six p.m. when Steven watched the second of two courier vans leave College Hospital for London, laden with the medical records of patients treated between 1990 and 1992 when John Carlisle was health secretary and the sun was shining brightly on his career. Drysdale, the clerk of works, was on hand to lock up the cellars and return the trolleys the couriers had been using, and Paul Drinkwater was there to represent hospital management, his brief being 'to see that things went smoothly'.

'Will you be bringing them back?' he asked Steven.

'Do you want them back?'

'Not really. They're officially off-system. It's just a question of data protection.'

'We'll take care of that.'

SEVENTEEN

Steven phoned the surgery in Lamont Avenue and was asked if he was registered with Dr Cunningham. He explained who he was and asked if it might be possible to have a word with Dr Cunningham that evening. A long pause was ended by a suggestion that he come round after evening surgery. She should be finished by seven thirty.

Mary Cunningham proved to be a tall, studious-looking woman, somewhere in her forties, her hair starting to grey and the first lines of age appearing at the corners of her eyes and mouth. She looked over her glasses at Steven as he was shown into her consulting room by a receptionist who already had her coat on, ready to leave.

'Good of you to see me,' he said.

'I'm intrigued,' said Mary Cunningham. 'Unless you just want me to change the dressing on your hands,' she added, noticing his bandages.

'Accident with a steam pipe,' said Steven with a smile. 'Actually, no. I understand you knew Dr Neil Tolkien?'

'Neil? My God, that was a long time ago. Yes, we worked together on a drug rehabilitation programme not long after I'd qualified. I was young and idealistic.'

'And you're not any more?'

'Neither young nor idealistic,' said Mary. 'The passage of time I can do nothing about, but ideals tend to be modified through experience and the evidence of one's own eyes.'

'Sounds like there's a pretty serious change of heart in there somewhere?'

'Indeed. I now believe that the war against drugs – as they insist on calling it – is a complete waste of time and money, and has been for years.'

'A point of view I'd have no trouble at all in agreeing with,' said Steven. 'But when you worked with Neil . . .'

'We thought we could turn things round, rescue the fallen from the gutter, put addicts back on the straight and narrow, rebuild broken families . . .'

'With the help of the Northern Health Scheme, I understand?'

'It was very good,' said Mary. 'Gave us all the help we asked for in terms of medication, but we were fighting a losing battle.'

'One in which Neil lost his life,' said Steven.

'Poor Neil. Yes, he and his girlfriend, a nurse, both died. The police told us they'd got on the wrong side of some criminals who didn't like what the clinic was doing. They suggested we close it down.'

'And you did?'

'We did.'

'Why do you think they targeted Neil and his girlfriend and not you or your other partner . . .' Steven looked at his notes, 'Dr Mitchell?'

'Gavin Mitchell. He died a couple of years ago. It was pretty clear they targeted Neil because he'd teamed up with a journalist: the criminals feared exposure.'

'Do you believe that?'

The directness of the question seemed to take Mary by surprise. 'I'm not sure I understand . . .'

'It's a simple enough question,' said Steven with a smile designed to soften the impact of the observation.

'Yes, it is,' conceded Mary. 'Actually . . . I've always harboured doubts about Neil's death.'

Steven waited for more.

'Neil thought there was something wrong with the new health scheme. He thought some of our patients were dying when perhaps they shouldn't have.'

'Were any of those deaths ever investigated?'

'Yes, routinely, but there were never any suspicious circumstances. The deaths were always due to the various medical conditions the deceased were suffering from.'

'Despite the medication?'

'Despite that.'

'Thank you, Dr Cunningham, you've been most helpful.'

'Have I?'

Steven smiled. 'Enjoy your evening.'

'What time d'you think you'll get here?' asked a surprised Tally when Steven said he was planning on driving down to Leicester.

'Late.'

'Well, don't wake me.'

'Yes, dear.'

'My God, has it come to that?' said Tally, utterly failing to conceal the amusement in her voice.

True to her word, Tally was fast asleep when Steven got there. He found a note saying that there was food in the microwave: *give it two minutes*. He closed the kitchen door so that the ping wouldn't wake Tally, and helped himself to a beer from the fridge. He turned on the small TV and kept the volume low while he caught up on the news. The Tories and Liberal Democrats had agreed to form a formal coalition.

'After placing their respective principles on a small bonfire,' Steven muttered, as he removed his risotto from the microwave. 'There's nothing quite like the smell of power, is there, chaps?'

Half an hour later, he manoeuvred himself carefully and quietly into bed beside Tally. 'About time too,' she said.

Steven uttered a despairing, 'Oh, God, I was trying so hard not to wake you.'

'I know.'

'But now that I have . . .'

Over breakfast next morning Steven told Tally about meeting Mary Cunningham, and of her suspicions concerning Neil Tolkien's death.

'Pretty much what you suspected already,' said Tally.

'But there was one thing. She said that some of the deaths Tolkien was concerned about were investigated – presumably by routine PM – and nothing suspicious was ever found.'

'So either the bad guys devised the perfect crime or the good doctor's imagination was working overtime.'

'And James Kincaid's was too and their imaginations got them killed? I don't think so.'

'So where do you go from here?'

'Let's wait and see what emerges from the medical records. Are you going to be able to take a day off sometime soon – like tomorrow?'

Tally shook her head. 'I did try, but there's no chance until the weekend. My boss is away till Friday so I'll have to be there.'

Steven looked disappointed. 'Pity. But let's do something at the weekend?'

'That would be nice. Do you want to visit Jenny?'

'No, not this weekend. Let's have some *us* time.'

Tally left for the hospital and Steven drove back to London through pouring rain. The Porsche was not much fun to drive in wet conditions on the motorway, being low on the ground and ultra susceptible to the spray clouds thrown up by lorries. Steven decided to take an unscheduled break at a service station to get some coffee and a bit of a rest from the high level of concentration demanded by the drive. He had just come to a halt in the car park when his Sci-Med mobile rang.

'Steven? Where are you?' asked Jean Roberts.

'On my day off.'

'Not any longer. The Prime Minister has called a meeting of COBRA. He wants a Sci-Med presence.'

'Where? When?'

'Conference room A in the main Cabinet Office building in Whitehall. Three p.m.'

'I'll be there.'

'Good. I wasn't looking forward to telling the new government that neither you nor Sir John could make it.'

'What's all the fuss?'

'I don't know. There was no warning.'

'Exciting. I'll call in at the Home Office afterwards.'

'Maybe we'll have something for you on the medical records by then. The team supplied by the health department has been working through the night.'

Steven called in at his flat to shower and change. Jeans and sweatshirt were exchanged for dark blue suit, china-blue shirt and Parachute Regiment tie. He had been to a couple of COBRA meetings before but always with John Macmillan. Such meetings were called by government to discuss imminent problems of national significance, the composition of the committee varying with the nature of the emergency. Not only would he be on his own this time but the politicians present would be strangers to him – appointees of the new Prime Minister, including the new Home Secretary who was technically his boss.

Steven could feel the burden of expectation start to weigh him down. John Macmillan knew his way around Whitehall; he didn't. The fact that the new administration was a coalition was going to make it even more difficult to tell the organ grinders from the monkeys. But then that was going to be true for a lot of people, not just Sci-Med.

As he walked along Whitehall, trying to guess what the convening of COBRA might be about, he couldn't help but feel that this would be the perfect time for any faction wishing harm to the UK to strike. The ruling coalition comprised a party that had been out of power for over thirteen years and another who hadn't known it at all in living memory. Ministers would be not only strangers in their own departments but also alien to their new colleagues.

The civil service would, of course, keep everything running, and might even relish the chance of being even more in charge than usual with dependent strangers in their midst, but when it came to making big policy decisions under extreme or emergency pressure the test was yet to come.

'Hello, Steven. I heard you were back. Good to see you,' said a voice behind him as Steven climbed the stairs. He turned to see the head of MI5 with one of his colleagues.

'You too,' he replied automatically. Relations between 5 and Sci-Med weren't always cordial when 5 did the government's dirty work and Sci-Med shone a spotlight on it, with John Macmillan asserting that no one should be above the law – an attitude that had delayed his knighthood for many years.

Steven nodded to one or two familiar faces from the Metropolitan Police and the civil service. There was also a military presence, but the ministerial contingent from the Department of Health – the government department he usually had most dealings with – seemed to be entirely made up of unknown faces.

The deputy Prime Minister made apologies for the Prime Minister's absence without giving a reason, and got down to business straight away.

'Intelligence suggests that the UK will be subjected to a chemical or biological attack in the very near future.'

He had to pause to let the hubbub die down.

'How reliable is this intelligence?' asked the health secretary.

The head of MI5 said, 'We've had a tip-off from an anonymous source.'

'So it could be a hoax?'

'It could be. On the other hand, it might not be. We've been told that Islamic fundamentalists are behind it. We don't know much more than that.'

'Do we have any indication at all about the nature of the attack?' asked the Met commissioner. 'Gas? Chemicals? Anthrax?'

'I'm sorry. We don't know.'

'Which means we can't prepare,' said Steven.

'We can certainly tighten security at all airports and rail and ferry terminals,' suggested the commissioner.

'Our intelligence suggests they are already here,' said the head of MI5, a comment that provoked another hubbub. 'We think the terrorists are home-grown,' he clarified. 'Our colleagues in MI6 have heard nothing of an attack coming from outside the UK.'

'But you have no inkling at all of the nature of the attack?'

'I'm afraid not.'

'Which means we'll have to initiate standard emergency procedure in all our cities without telling the services what they're up against,' said the Home Secretary.

'Containment must be the immediate aim,' said the deputy PM.

'Let's hope it's a gas attack,' said Steven. 'At least that will be localised. If it's microbiological, the chances are we haven't got any hope at all of containing it.' He was immediately aware of the discomfort his comment had provoked.

'I don't think we need such negative thinking,' said the cabinet secretary.

Steven bit his tongue. He knew he was prone to saying more than was wise at such meetings, and had no trouble at all in imagining the kick on the ankle John Macmillan might have given him at that moment. Truth had to be approached in a more circumspect fashion in the corridors of power, which usually meant tiptoeing through a minefield of other people's egos and sensibilities.

'Our emergency services are the finest in the world and have been trained over many years for just such eventualities,' said the Home Secretary.

One of the Department of Health people, a confident-looking man named Norman Travis, Steven learned from his desk name plate, said, 'With all due respect, sir, I think the problem arises in not knowing exactly what "eventuality" we might be dealing with. As Dr Dunbar says, a gas attack will, by its very nature, be limited in area, and our services have been trained to deal with that sort of incident, but if it should turn out to be anthrax or even, God forbid, smallpox . . . we will have a much more challenging situation to deal with.'

That's how to go about it, Steven thought to himself. Travis even finished his comment with a disarming smile. Steven remembered that this was the man who had led the negotiations with the pharmaceutical companies over vaccine production to a successful conclusion.

'I think our experience with the swine flu pandemic will stand us in good stead,' said the deputy PM.

Steven shook his head slightly and looked down at the table as he kept hold of his tongue.

'But you don't agree, doctor?' challenged the cabinet secretary, who had noticed his reaction.

Steven lost the struggle. In for a penny, in for a pound. 'The handling of swine flu was a complete and utter disaster and one that we should learn from, not crow about.'

EIGHTEEN

'Perhaps you'd care to expand on that assertion?'

'Swine flu wasn't a real pandemic. It was a bad cold,' said Steven dismissively.

'People died from it.'

'People who would normally have died from ordinary flu because they had underlying medical conditions.'

'Not all.'

'All right, there were a few who died without having underlying conditions, but they were very few and far between, and their deaths were built up to justify the hype and create a totally wrong impression. It was a mess from the start. Advice was conflicting. Doctors squabbled over payment. Tamiflu was handed out to anyone who phoned a surgery – including the worried well – and anyone who was ill was told to stay away from hospitals and surgeries, the end result being that we have no real idea how many people actually caught swine flu. When I asked how many people went down with ordinary seasonal flu, they couldn't tell me because all cases of flu were being recorded as swine flu. We ended up with a mountain of Tamiflu, to the delight of shareholders in the company who make it. Frankly, a box of tissues and a hot toddy would have been a damn sight more use. What we learned from swine flu is how *not* to go about handling a pandemic. If swine flu had been smallpox we'd all be dead.'

The silence in the room seemed to go on for ever.

The cabinet secretary looked first to the health officials and then to the Home Secretary but failed to find anyone keen to put up a defence. 'Go on,' he said.

'The only defence against a virus attack is to vaccinate people beforehand. Once they're infected it'll be too late. We were actually better prepared to deal with outbreaks of infectious disease in the the first half of the twentieth century when we had hospitals specifically for that purpose and nurses trained to look after such cases. Now we have half a dozen fancy isolation beds in our big hospitals in case someone comes off a flight with a problem. Unless we're protected beforehand, we'll simply be overwhelmed. Sending in emergency service personnel wearing biohazard suits in vehicles with lights blazing and sirens blaring isn't going to help. It's a PR exercise. We'd be as well sending in morris dancers.'

Another awkward silence was broken by Travis. 'I think I must agree with much of what Dr Dunbar has said. The only real defence against biological attack is vaccination, but, as was pointed out earlier, if we don't know what is going to be used against us we will be forced into second-guessing the opposition. Not ideal. Apart from that, we are still painfully short of vaccines, although we hope this will change in the near future when Merryman Pharmaceuticals are fully up to speed.'

'So what do we do in the face of an imminent attack?' asked the deputy PM. 'Wait and see?'

'I think a gas attack is more likely than anything biological,' said a spokesman from the Ministry of Defence. 'Sarin, or some such agent. That sort of attack is a damned sight easier to mount than trying to infect a whole population and, of course, you get the all-important immediate terror factor.'

'Not sure I'm with you,' said someone.

'If you let off a sarin bomb in a shopping centre or on a tube train, you get an instant effect. People die; there is widespread panic. Press and TV gather round the incident. It's a big story. If you attempt to infect people by sending anthrax spores through the post, or spraying a virus into the air, there is no instant effect. Things take time to develop; people will spread out and fall ill in their own time. It will not even be clear to the man in the street that an attack has taken place, so the terrorists lose out in the propaganda stakes and we get more time to deal with it.'

'Makes sense,' said the deputy PM. 'Let's hope the terrorists see it that way too. I take it we are well prepared to deal with a gas attack wherever it happens?'

The question was directed at the Home Secretary, who assured him that contingency plans were in place in all UK cities.

The cabinet secretary turned to the head of MI5 and asked, 'Is there still a chance you might be able to stop this attack happening?'

'My people are working round the clock.'

'Are you absolutely sure that the attack is coming from within?' asked the Met commissioner.

'Eighty per cent.'

'So there is still reason for heightened security at entry points around the UK?'

'I think we must go for increased vigilance all round,' said the deputy PM.

Steven saw Travis whisper something in the new health secretary's ear. The minister nodded and said, 'With everyone's agreement, we'll approach Merryman Pharmaceuticals and – without giving details about why – ask them to step up all their vaccine production schedules to maximum?'

No one dissented.

'It won't take rocket science to work out what that's all about,' said one of the men in uniform – a colonel in the army.

'Indeed,' agreed the Home Secretary. 'But at least they won't know that we have no better idea than them about which ones will be needed.'

'Food for thought, ladies and gentlemen,' said the deputy PM, indicating that the meeting was at an end with a hand gesture that involved making a steeple with his fingers and then opening them.

Steven went over to the Home Office and found Jean Roberts looking expectant. She was too professional to ask directly what the meeting had been about but clearly hoped Steven would say something.

'A threatened gas or biological attack,' said Steven. 'Thought to be imminent.'

'Well, the warnings have been around for long enough,' said Jean. 'A case of when rather than if, as Sir John said more than once. Any idea what we have to look forward to?'

Steven shook his head. 'That's not known.'

'You know, I often wonder what aliens must think if they're observing our planet. The things we do to each other . . . Unbelievable.'

Steven nodded. 'How are the health department people getting on?'

'You can get the report from the horse's mouth. They're upstairs in room 211.'

Steven went upstairs and found a team of ten people hard at work going through the case notes of College Hospital patients. 'Hello, I don't think we've met. I'm Steven Dunbar.'

People smiled, and one woman got up and came towards him. 'Sophie Thornton.' She was in her mid forties, round-shouldered, with frizzy hair that seemed determined to escape from its bindings of several pins and a hair band. She swept a wayward strand from her eyes as she said, 'Pleased to meet you.'

'Any joy?' asked Steven.

'I think yes, but it's not straightforward.' She led the way over to two piles of files which had been weeded out from the rest and rested a hand on one of them. 'These people all fall into the categories Miss Roberts outlined – long-term sick, those over seventy years of age, people suffering from untreatable conditions – and all of them died within a year of being treated, either at College Hospital or in the surrounding area.'

'But?'

'Post-mortems were carried out on some of them, but there was no suggestion of suspicious circumstances in any of them.'

'Right,' said Steven thoughtfully. She'd confirmed what Mary Cunningham had told him. It has been the case with Tolkien's patients too. People who were costing the NHS a lot of money conveniently died once the Northern Health Scheme came into play, but there were no suspicious circumstances. 'Thank you, that's exactly what I'm looking for. How far are you into the examination?'

'About a third of the way.'

Steven looked to the two piles of records and made a mental calculation. 'So we could be looking at two hundred deaths, maybe two fifty?'

'Thereabouts.'

Steven nodded, then changed the subject. 'The election must have brought about big changes in your department. How are they affecting you?'

'Too soon to say, I suppose. There's not been enough time, but two ruling parties are going to make things . . . interesting.'

'I'll bet. I've just come from a meeting with some of the new people at Health. I thought Norman Travis was impressive.'

'He does seem to know what he's doing,' agreed Sophie. 'Unlike many, he actually has a particular interest in health matters and knows what he's talking about.'

'While others have health thrust upon them?'

Sophie smiled. 'I suppose it's to be expected when people have to move quickly from one ministry to the next.'

'Or from no ministry at all, as with the current situation. Rookies, the lot of them.'

'A bit like a Chinese curse,' said Sophie.

Steven saw what she meant. 'May you live in interesting times.'

He returned downstairs, deciding to use John Macmillan's office to have a quiet think about the day. Not one of his best. The progress he was making with his investigation was completely overshadowed by the prospect of a bio-terrorism attack. He had a particular loathing of the employment of microbes as weapons, seeing their use as the very epitome of evil. He thought about what Jean had said about alien observers and found himself agreeing. Human behaviour could be quite beyond comprehension.

It was impossible to think about such an attack without conjuring up images of the dead piling up in the streets as services were overwhelmed and society broke down, conceding defeat to a tiny, unseen enemy. As to which one . . . Would there be faces horribly disfigured by the eruption of smallpox pustules? The blue-black complexion of plague victims? The crippling paralysis of polio or the unstoppable bleeding of haemorrhagic virus infection? The answer was out there, and imminent if the intelligence was correct.

A knock came to the door, and Jean came in with coffee. 'Thought you might need this. What news from upstairs?'

Steven snapped out of his preoccupation. 'The Northern Health Scheme was killing people off, but we're no nearer knowing how they actually managed it.'

'An untraceable poison?'

'Maybe.'

'Maybe it was untraceable back then,' suggested Jean. 'Science has moved on . . .'

'A good thought,' said Steven. 'But we'd be talking exhumation.'

Jean shrugged her shoulders uncomfortably and said in a small voice, 'Maybe worth thinking about?'

'Not something to do without good reason; it always causes such distress to families. Maybe I'll mention it to John when I see him. I need to tell him about the COBRA meeting anyway. He should be part of what's going on.'

NINETEEN

'You look tired,' said John Macmillan when Steven sat down.

'Shouldn't I be saying that to you?' Steven's grin took a deal of effort.

'Things not going well?'

He explained about the COBRA meeting and the reported threat.

Macmillan's shoulders slumped forward as he let out a sigh. 'Strange,' he said. 'We knew this had to happen. But now that it's here on our doorstep the very thought of it is just as horrifying as if it had come out of the blue. Any idea what?'

'None.'

Macmillan echoed Steven's earlier thoughts regarding a chemical attack. 'We can cope with that, but microbes let loose on a largely unprotected population . . . doesn't bear thinking about. It could destroy the entire country.'

'Merryman are being asked to step up vaccine production, but it could well be too late.'

Macmillan nodded. 'We're always a bit too late in this country. It's a way of life . . . but when it comes to locking stable doors after the horse has bolted we have the most secure doors in the world.'

Steven was a little disturbed at hearing Macmillan sound so cynical. It was unlike him. 'MI5 are pretty sure the would-be attackers are "home-grown", to use their word.'

'So the disaffected of Leicester or Birmingham are seeking to wipe out the country they were born in . . . ye gods.' Macmillan looked Steven straight in the eye. 'Strikes me we're going to need all the good people we've got. I take it you will stay on at Sci-Med until . . . such times?'

Steven nodded.

'I suppose in the light of what you've just told me this pales into insignificance, but what's been happening with your investigation?'

'Everything's pointing to Carlisle and his pals being involved in mass murder back in the early nineties.'

Macmillan's eyelids shot up.

'They were killing off people who were costing society a lot of money.'

'A population cull?'

'That's what it looks like, but I don't know how they were doing it. Nothing was ever found in any of the bodies subjected to PM examination. Highly dependent people just conveniently died after being treated in the Northern Health Scheme area.'

'But they must have died of something.'

'Natural causes.'

'Which means what?'

Steven narrowed his eyes as he considered the question. He decided not to bring up Jean Roberts's suggestion of an unknown toxin. 'No,' he said slowly, 'they died of what they were expected to die of. They all had conditions that required treatment by either their GP or College Hospital . . . and they were all prescribed appropriate medication . . .'

'But they still died of their condition, so maybe . . .'

'They weren't treated at all,' Steven finished.

Macmillan nodded. 'They were culling the population by denying treatment to those who were perceived to be a drain on resources. So the question is, how did they manage to withhold treatment without anyone noticing?'

'That's where French's computer expertise must have come in,' said Steven. 'He must have come up with a program that would take into account the age and medical records of the patients. If you were on the wrong side of the line – too old, long-term sick, increasingly infirm, a drug addict or suffering from an incurable condition – the computer decided you got nothing.'

'And that's where Schreiber's pharmacy would come into its own. They must have come up with drug packaging that looked like the real thing but held pills or capsules that contained nothing but . . . sugar or chalk, useless placebos.'

'It was that simple,' said Steven with a final shake of the head. He exchanged a wry smile with Macmillan, a pleasing moment for both men, who recognised that they were still a good team and, more important, would continue to be. Nothing had changed as a legacy of Macmillan's illness.

'But we've no proof,' said Macmillan.

The men knew each other well enough for Macmillan to interpret Steven's look as comment about the age of the crime and the fact that the perpetrators were all dead, not to mention the new horror they were now facing. 'You should still carry on,' he said. 'I think we owe it to the people who died. Not least the journalist and the doctor who worked out what the bastards were up to.'

Steven nodded.

'Besides, it'll take our minds off what we have to look forward to. God help us all.'

Steven said, 'Schreiber's long dead, but French was alive and well right up until the meeting in Paris. If they were planning to reintroduce the scheme, the software must be around, probably in the Deltasoft offices.'

'A raid?'

'A raid,' agreed Steven.

'You'll have to clear it with the Home Secretary. French was a powerful man, a stalwart of the community and a big donor to the party.'

'You don't think . . .' began Steven hesitantly.

'Perish the thought,' said Macmillan. 'She's the Home Secretary.'

Steven resisted the temptation to point out that John Carlisle had been the health secretary, but Macmillan noticed he was biting his tongue. 'Charlie Malloy is coming to see me tomorrow. I'll ask him to have everything ready to go the minute you get approval from on high.'

Steven nodded his thanks. 'Good to have you back, John.'

'Thank you.'

Steven had anticipated a difficult interview with the Home Secretary. He wasn't disappointed. The fact that he had been more than forthright at the COBRA meeting didn't help.

'If your reputation for success didn't precede you, Dr Dunbar, I would be tempted to turn down your request and dismiss what you've just suggested as being too ridiculous for words. Are you seriously telling me that the government of the day was party to such an outrage?'

'No, Home Secretary, I'm not. I think the health department back then was infiltrated by others – I'm sorry I can't be more specific – but John Carlisle, the then secretary of state, was certainly part of the conspiracy, knowingly or otherwise.'

The Home Secretary diverted her gaze for a moment before saying quietly, 'I think it was "otherwise".'

'I'm sorry?'

'Carlisle called me before he died. His wife and I were friends when we were younger.'

Steven was aware of the pulse in his neck as a long silence ensued.

'I thought he was just trying to save his own miserable skin – and he was – but he came out with some ridiculous story about having his career ruined by other people when he was health secretary back in the early nineties. Claimed he was stabbed in the back by people he referred to as the Schiller mob, who were pursuing their own agenda.'

'But he didn't know what they were up to?'

'If he did, he didn't say – and that would have been the time to say it. If ever there was a time to show the strength of your hand . . . But I thought he was making the whole thing up, so I didn't probe. Mind you . . .'

Steven's eyes opened wide, encouraging the minister to say more.

'I have heard rumours from time to time about . . . some faction calling themselves the Schiller Group. But you know what Westminster's like. Rumours abound.'

'The Northern Health Scheme wasn't just the project of a few,' said Steven. 'It had powerful backing, not least from those who got John Carlisle elected in the first place and oversaw his rise through the ranks.'

'Well, it was all a very long time ago – not that that excuses any of it in any way if what you say is true – but I just wonder if this is the right time to be destroying confidence in the government?'

'Is there ever a right time?'

'Point taken,' conceded the Home Secretary with the merest hint of a smile. 'I will sanction your raid, but I must ask that you be discreet. Our country is by all accounts about to face one of the biggest crises in its history. The population must have trust in their leaders if we're to get through this.'

'Understood, Home Secretary.'

Steven returned to the Sci-Med offices and sat thinking for a moment, his hand resting on the telephone. It had been his intention to call Charlie Malloy and give him the go-ahead for a police raid on Deltasoft, but the Home Secretary's request for discretion was playing on his mind. She was right: this was not the time to unearth a huge scandal involving a past government minister.

A raid on Deltasoft would not in itself do so, but it would certainly attract the attention of the national press who would then see it as their business to find out what it was all about. He took his hand off the telephone while he asked himself a few questions. Would French have kept such sensitive software in the company offices and labs where others might stumble across it? Deltasoft had grown into a major player, successful and well respected. It was unthinkable that the entire staff would be complicit in some right-wing conspiracy.

French had been a very clever man; he would have worked out that keeping details of his illicit activities in a building full of computer experts in their own right might not be such a good idea. Maybe he kept it under lock and key, or whatever the computerised version of that was these days, but it might be even safer to keep it somewhere else. At home, perhaps?

Steven knew nothing about French's widow other than that she, like the other relatives of the dead, had not known anything about the Paris meeting. This suggested that she had not been part of the conspiracy. She could, of course, have been lying, but according to the police report she had been utterly shocked when informed about her husband's death, not only by the death but by the location – she had kept asking what he had been doing there, seemingly fearing that he might have been having an affair. She still could have been acting, thought Steven, but if not, it gave him an idea.

'All set to go?' asked Jean when he emerged.

'Change of plan. I need all you have on Charles French's wife, and I need the address of the family home.'

'Right,' said Jean, taken a little by surprise. Steven had told her of the Home Secretary's approval for a raid before he'd changed his mind. 'I have her on the database.'

She brought up the relevant information on her monitor. 'Here we are. Maxine French, aged forty-seven, parents both GPs in Surrey, a Cambridge graduate like her husband, only in

French and Italian, worked as a translator in the early years of their marriage but gave that up to become a lady of leisure when Deltasoft took off.'

'Did she have anything to do with Deltasoft at any point?'

'Not that I can see,' said Jean, checking her screen. 'She appears to have filled her time with charity work, served on several committees, chair of two of them, a pillar of the community just like her husband. She had a particular interest in underprivileged children. They both had.'

Steven held back a comment about the great and good and their charities. 'Address?'

'Clifford Mansions in Kensington. They have the penthouse.'

'Set up a meeting, will you?' Almost as an afterthought, Steven asked, 'Does the name Schiller Group mean anything to you?'

Jean narrowed her eyes. 'You know, I think it does. I'm sure I came across something recently to do with that but for the life of me I can't remember what.'

'Let me know if it comes back to you.'

TWENTY

James Black was last to arrive for the meeting he'd called of the Redwood Park competitions committee – he'd been caught in a traffic jam for twenty minutes.

'We were beginning to think you'd decided to up sticks and disappear,' said Toby Langton.

'Now why would I want to do that?' replied Black with a forced smile that contrasted with the worried expressions of the others.

'For God's sake, Sci-Med have the files from College Hospital. They're going through them as we speak,' said Elliot Soames.

'So much for taking Dunbar out of the game,' said Rupert Coutts.

'It wasn't a serious attempt,' said Constance Carradine. 'More of a spur of the moment thing when we heard he was going to search the cellars. An opportunity too good to miss. Anyway, a junkie got the blame. No harm done.'

'Aren't we missing the point here? Sci-Med are going to find out exactly what was going on in the north in the early nineties.'

'They may suspect something was going on but they won't know what,' said Black. 'People died, but that's what people do, especially sick ones.'

'I still don't like it,' said Soames. 'They're not stupid. They just might figure it out.'

'Even if they do, they're not going to be able to prove anything after all this time, and even if they could, they're hardly going to let the press in on it, are they? A coalition government hanging on by its fingertips would be swept away in the resulting storm of indignation, leaving us with the prospect of anarchy. It's little more than an academic exercise for Sci-Med. They'll pat each other on the back for working it out and then move on to more relevant matters like the threat that's hanging over our nation.'

'Aren't you overlooking the Paris meeting?' said Langton.

All eyes turned to him.

'If Sci-Med are bright enough to work out what the Northern Health Scheme was all about, they might figure out what the purpose of the Paris meeting was too – all the people from the Northern Health Scheme getting together again? They're bound to suspect that the whole business was about to be repeated.'

'Let them,' said Black. 'If French and co. had had their way, they'd be quite right, but they all died and so did the Northern Health Scheme. Although . . .'

The others found the pregnant pause unbearable. 'Although what?' prompted Langton.

'I've taken steps to provide some "proof" for Sci-Med if they're clever enough to find it.'

'Proof of what?' asked Rupert Coutts.

'Proof that Charles French and his colleagues were indeed planning a repeat of the Northern Health Scheme. They'll be well pleased with that.'

'You're enjoying this, aren't you, Mark?' said Constance with an air of disapproval. 'It's not a game. The future of our country depends on our success.'

'And it's in good hands,' said Black. 'But you're right. I do enjoy an intellectual challenge.'

'Frankly, I'd feel happier with Dunbar and his cronies out of the way,' said Constance.

'Me too,' said Soames.

'Dunbar and Sci-Med are no threat to us,' insisted Black. 'Sci-Med are on the verge of clearing up a twenty-year-old puzzle, with all those involved now dead. End of story. If we sanction any kind of action against them, it might signal that either we're not all dead, or we have something to hide and we think Sci-Med are getting too close. We can do without that kind of attention. Our project is on track and everything is going to plan. All we need do is keep our nerve. All right?'

One by one the others nodded their agreement.

'Good,' said Black. 'I'm told that Sci-Med were present at the COBRA meeting yesterday. I should think events of long ago are the last thing on their minds right now.'

Maxine French smiled as Steven was ushered into a stunning room with glass walls on three sides, all of them affording access to a magnificent roof terrace and breathtaking views beyond. Steven felt as if he had seen that smile before. It was the one that ladies of a certain class and political inclination used to put lesser mortals at their ease.

'Good of you to see me, Mrs French, and at such short notice. Your tireless charity work is well documented.'

'One does what one can,' said Maxine with a self-deprecating smile. 'But I am intrigued, doctor. What exactly does the Sci-Med Inspectorate do?'

Steven told her briefly.

'Science and medicine progresses at such a rate these days; I'm sure you must be kept very busy,' she said. 'But how exactly can I help?'

Steven was aware of his pulse rate increasing as he prepared to take his gamble. 'Your husband wasn't just a brilliant scientist, Mrs French . . . he also served his country in another capacity . . .'

'I knew it!' exclaimed Maxine with an expression that would have served a lottery winner. 'Charles was such a patriot. No one ever loved his country more than my husband. That's why he was in Paris, wasn't it? He was on secret business on behalf of the nation?'

Steven couldn't believe his luck. His gambit had worked so well he feared that Maxine was about to break into the national anthem. 'Yes indeed, Mrs French, Charles was working for the government.'

'I knew it . . . I knew it. It all makes sense now.'

'The thing is . . . Charles was holding some material that must not be allowed to fall into the wrong hands. His untimely death means that we aren't quite sure . . . where it is. I suppose I was hoping that you might be able to help.'

Maxine walked over to where a painting of an English land-scape hung over a rectangular marble fireplace set into the wall and housing living flames over a bed of cobbles. She swung the painting back like a door to reveal a safe, causing Steven to reflect on people's lack of originality, and to reckon that it would have taken a burglar all of thirty seconds to find and maybe another thirty seconds of threats before Maxine revealed the combination. Not very secure at all.

Maxine, however, was to prove him wrong. For a moment he thought the safe was empty when she opened it, but she removed something small and signalled that Steven should follow her outside to the terrace. He saw that she had a plastic card in her hand as she led the way to a small alcove among the plant pots. There she swung open a small trellis that was apparently on hinges and inserted the card in a hidden slot in the wall. It was swallowed like a bank card and a small screen appeared as a dummy brick facing slid back.

'Don't touch it!' warned Maxine as Steven leaned forward to take a look. Steven recoiled at the panic in her voice. 'It's a biometric panel,' she said, putting her own fingertips on it and holding them there for a few seconds. The panel slid back to reveal the contents of a small safe set into one of the apart-ment's concrete support pillars. Maxine retrieved a number of disks in plastic cases and handed them over to Steven. 'I think these are what you're looking for.'

'Thank you, Mrs French,' said Steven, trying to appear calm. He couldn't resist asking, 'What would have happened if I'd touched the screen?'

'It would have blown your face off, doctor.'

Steven silently reconsidered his earlier critical thoughts about the security arrangements. Even if someone had tortured Maxine to reveal the whereabouts of the disks she could simply have handed over the card, shown her attacker where the safe was and stood well clear.

He left the penthouse, thinking that he must have used up a year's luck all in one morning. He'd got exactly what he wanted without the need for police raids on Deltasoft or French's home. No damage would be done to public confidence through speculative press stories and Maxine could even return to her tireless charity work, secure in the knowledge that her husband's secret work on behalf of the nation would go on. Not.

'You look like the cat who got the cream,' Jean Roberts told him when he appeared in her office.

'A better than average morning, Jean. Could you get these over to the lab as quickly as possible?'

'Will do. I think the DOH people upstairs are just about finished.'

'I'll go and see them.'

Steven found the people from the Department of Health packing up and ready to move out. Sophie Thornton came over to speak to him.

'All done. We've arranged the suspect files alphabetically,' she said, indicating a bench by the window. 'Nothing new to report, just more of the same: people dying when perhaps they shouldn't have but with no sinister causes according to the PM reports.'

Steven thanked her and the rest of her team, and stood with them as they waited for the lift on the landing outside to say last farewells – a trait he recognised he had inherited from his mother, who had always made sure that no one left the Dunbar household without at least three versions of goodbye and usually a final wave from the window. Then he returned to the room and rested his hands on top of one of the folder piles.

Sophie's saying that they were in alphabetical order encouraged him to look for James Kincaid's father's notes. He found them without difficulty – a coal-miner who had retired with breathing difficulties due to his long years underground. A man who had finally contracted lung cancer and had died within three weeks of having an operation at College Hospital. Kincaid had been right to be suspicious. If death had been that imminent, surgeons at the hospital wouldn't have considered operating. The fact that they had, suggested a belief that, with the right therapy, life expectancy should have been a great deal longer than three weeks. Instead, French and his pals . . . or should he be calling them the Schiller Group after what the Home Secretary had said? . . . had decided that he was nothing more than a drain on resources. Expendable. Those to the right live, those to the left die.

TWENTY-ONE

Steven got his answer to the Schiller question in the morning when Jean Roberts announced, 'I've remembered why the name Schiller seemed familiar: it's what Charles French called his breakaway group at university when he left the Conservative club. The Schiller Group.'

'You're a star,' said Steven.

'I'm beginning to like working for you. Sir John never called me things like that.'

'He'll be back soon enough.'

With nothing back from the lab, Steven went for a walk while he thought about French and his student pals. Why had French chosen the name Schiller Group? Had it been coincidence or had it been devilment? Had he known about the real Schiller Group and been trying for some kind of recognition or inclusion, or had it just been chance? Either way it had been something that had attracted the attention of Lady Antonia Freeman's father, the judge who had uncharacteristically treated French with such leniency when he came before him on serious assault charges. That certainly suggested that French had gained membership of the big boys' club over it.

Later that evening, when Steven phoned Tally, he discovered that she had managed to get the following day off. 'We should do something,' he repeated.

'Any suggestions?'

'How well do you know North Wales?'

'Not at all.'

'Good, then I'll show you.'

'Isn't that an awfully long way?'

'I've got a . . .'

'Porsche,' supplied Tally. 'Oh, God . . . what am I letting myself in for?'

'I'll make an early start and pick you up at ten.'

The sun shone next day, making the drive along the North Wales coast a joy. Even Tally – no lover of cars or speed – seemed seduced by the wind in her hair and the throaty sound of the Boxster's engine. 'How come you know North Wales?' she asked above the noise as they slowed at the turn-off to Conwy.

'I trained here,' said Steven. 'Up and down these . . . mountains.' He deleted the expletive. 'I fell in love with it. It's a beautiful place . . . when it's not January, when you're not carrying a full pack and a weapon and the wind isn't driving horizontal rain into your face.'

'Like today,' said Tally.

'Like today,' agreed Steven, glancing up at blue skies. 'We'll have coffee and take a walk round the castle ramparts. You get great views.'

With Tally suitably impressed as they completed their circle of the castle walls, something she indicated with a smile and a squeeze of the hand, they returned to the car. 'Where to now?'

'Bodnant Garden, one of the most beautiful places in the world.'

'Not much to live up to then . . .'

There came a point in their slow amble through the trails of the beautiful gardens when Tally turned to Steven while they were crossing a little bridge over a tumbling stream. 'You're right,' she said. 'This is one of the most beautiful places in the world. Thank you for bringing me.'

'Where else would I bring such a beautiful woman?'

'You old smoothie,' Tally chuckled.

Steven grew serious. 'We're all right, aren't we, Tally? I mean, you and me?'

Tally paused as if a thousand thoughts were running through her head, before saying quietly, 'Yes, Steven, we're fine.'

'I love you.'

'I know.'

They drove on, ending up in Caernarfon, where they sat watching the yachts bobbing beneath the walls of another castle.

'You've gone very quiet,' said Steven.

'I was wondering when you were going to tell me why you could suddenly take another day off . . . not that I'm complaining. You've not hit the wall again?'

'Far from it,' he said with a smile. 'The investigation's all over bar the shouting.' He told her about the conclusion he and John Macmillan had reached regarding the withholding of treatment from people who were seen as a burden on the state. 'They pretended to treat them by giving them pills that looked like the real thing but contained nothing of any medical value at all. I'm just waiting for the confirmation to come back from the lab and then I think that will be that . . . just in time for all hell to break loose.'

'Can you tell me?'

Steven only paused for a moment. 'Intelligence believes the UK is in imminent danger of a biological attack from Islamic terrorists.'

'Oh my God,' murmured Tally. 'You've always said it was on the cards. How sure are they?'

'Very, but the key thing is they don't know what they're going to use.'

'So we can't prepare?'

'You got it.'

'Doesn't that make it even more odd that you're taking the day off? Or are we here to kiss each other's arse goodbye?'

Steven smiled. 'There's nothing I can do until it happens. MI5 and Special Branch are working their socks off trying to come up with more information from their sources, but until they do . . .'

'Life goes on as normal,' said Tally, thinking it was the stupidest thing she could come out with in the circumstances.

'Assuming we're given the time, there's one more thing I'd like to do to round off the investigation – assuming the lab comes up with the proof.'

'What's that?'

'I'd like to go up to Newcastle to visit the graves of the people who worked out what the Northern Health Scheme was all about all those years ago but didn't live long enough to get the credit. They deserve some kind of recognition. If it hadn't been for them, thousands more might have met an early death.'

'We should do that,' agreed Tally.

Steven drove back to London on Monday morning. He found the computer analyst from the Sci-Med contract lab waiting for him at the Home Office.

'Wanted to see you personally,' whispered Jean Roberts.

'Thought you'd better hear this from the horse's mouth,' said the man as Steven showed him through to John Macmillan's office and invited him to sit. 'It's quite straightforward really; it's software for controlling and directing the day to day workings of a large hospital pharmacy. Patients' details go in at one end along with a doctor's prescription. This is checked and assessed by the software, and the pharmacy is instructed to supply the relevant drugs at the other – either the prescribed medicine or an alternative if it's cheaper and just as good.'

'That's what we thought,' said Steven.

'There's a little more to it, however. I didn't see it at first but the software uses two pharmacies acting in tandem – let's call them A and B. A number of factors determine whether you will get your drugs from A or B.'

'Do you know what the factors are?'

The man nodded. 'There's a long list of medical conditions and other factors which will put you on the B list. I've printed them out for you. Not sure what it all means, but age is a factor. Maybe they need higher doses?'

Or none at all, thought Steven. 'Maybe.'

'There's also a disk containing a list of the hospitals and practices where the software is going to be introduced in the autumn.'

Steven couldn't believe his ears. 'Did you say *going to be* introduced?'

'Yes, September 2010 onwards, fifteen areas across England and Wales.'

So they *were* going to reintroduce the scheme, thought Steven. Macmillan's gut instinct had been right from the beginning. The thought gave him a hollow feeling. So what had the explosion in Paris been all about? He had to rethink his theory that the killings had been some kind of Schiller Group coup. It didn't look so feasible now. If the assassin had been one of the Schiller Group and lost his nerve over the reintroduction of the scheme, he would hardly have been likely to summon up the courage to murder six of his colleagues to stop it happening. There had to be more to it.

'Thank you very much,' he said to the computer man, who was getting up to leave. His mind was still elsewhere.

Steven left the office and went over to see John Macmillan. Macmillan's wife showed him in and told him John was on the telephone. 'He just won't do as he's told,' she complained. 'The doctors say he must rest, but . . . well, you know him.'

Steven nodded sympathetically as the sound of Macmillan's raised voice reached them. 'Ye gods, you must have some idea by now,' he was saying.

Steven deduced that Macmillan was complaining about the lack of progress being made by the security services. His last words before putting down the phone were, 'But every life in the country depends on it, man. Someone must know something. Get it out of them. We'll worry about their human rights later.'

'Well, you sound back on form,' said Steven, entering the room. 'I take it there's been no progress?'

Macmillan accompanied a shake of the head with an exasperated sigh. 'An attack like this needs infrastructure and planning; that means people – lots of them. It's not like a hit with explosives where a small cell can keep everything in-house. So why have our people drawn a complete blank? Not a whisper.'

'I agree; it is odd, particularly as they know they're home-grown.'

'Exactly. They must have people planted in all the relevant communities and yet they come up with nothing. Why?'

Steven took a deep breath. 'Best-case scenario, it's a false alarm. Worst-case scenario, they're wrong about them being home-grown. The hit's going to come from abroad.'

Macmillan took a moment to digest this before saying, 'I sometimes wonder where mankind would be if we'd never felt the need for religion. It's my guess we would have colonised the planets by now.'

'Pie in the sky has a lot to answer for.'

'I think it's the different fillings in the pie that are the problem,' said Macmillan. 'How are things?'

'Done and dusted,' said Steven. 'The disks confirm it *was* an attempt to cull the population back in the early nineties. A rough estimate says they ended the lives of about four hundred people between those being treated at College Hospital and in the surrounding practices.'

'I think I prefer "murdered",' said Macmillan.

'James Kincaid and his friends almost succeeded in exposing them but died in the attempt. The Schiller mob had to lie low for a while, and then, of course, the Tories lost the election and Labour came to power and stayed there for thirteen years. Now with another change of government they obviously felt it safe to have another go. They were planning to set the whole thing up again in a number of hospitals across the country, beginning in September.'

'But fate took a hand and blew them all to kingdom come,' mused Macmillan. 'Any more thoughts on that?'

'I just wish it had been fate,' said Steven. 'It's a loose end . . .'

'And I know how much you hate those,' said Macmillan. 'But maybe, in our current circumstances, we shouldn't look a gift horse too closely in the mouth.'

'You're right,' agreed Steven. 'In fact, I think they should make your gut instinct a national treasure. You were right in just about everything.'

TWENTY-TWO

The man came into the room at the back of the Edinburgh bungalow, carrying a box designed to transport bottles which he'd just removed from a large American-style fridge in the kitchen. He laid it down gently on the table in the middle of the room and removed a series of metal flasks. The two younger Asian men in the room couldn't take their eyes off them as they were lined up.

'The time has come,' said the older man. 'You both know exactly what to do. We have been over it many times in the past few weeks. You know where your targets are, and you know what to say to the caretakers or anyone else who asks what you're doing. You know what to do with these.' He indicated the flasks. 'You put on masks and gloves before opening them, and nothing must be spilled. Take great care not to contaminate yourselves with even the slightest drop. When you've finished your task, you drive south to the house in Northumberland to meet up with the others, and you'll be given details of your flights. You will not be returning to your families but they will know you are with the army of the righteous and you will live on in their hearts. Are you ready, my brothers?'

'I am,' answered Anwar Khan.

Muhammad Patel nodded, his throat too dry to say anything.

'You are both blessed. Your names will live for ever and your families will stand tall. The American imperialists and their

British lapdogs will learn that their greed for oil will not stop us reclaiming what is rightfully ours. The tide of filth that covers this country will be swept away by the pure waters of Islam. Do your duty. Allah is great. Praise be to Allah.'

The two men echoed the sentiment and opened their tool bags to pack the flasks inside, taking care to wedge them upright and cushion them with plastic bubble wrap.

The older man embraced each youth in turn and saw them to the door. He watched as they got into the white van with the Scottish Water logo on the side and drove off. Then, as he turned to go back inside, a woman's voice said, 'Oh, dear. Not having problems with your water supply, are you, Mr Malik?'

He turned to see his next-door neighbour, Gillian McKay, looking anxiously over the small hedge. 'No, no, Mrs McKay. My nephew works with the water company. He was in the area, just dropped in to say hello.'

'Oh, good. Maybe you could ask him next time you see him about the amount of chlorine they put in the water. Sometimes I'd swear my tea tastes like the swimming baths.'

'I'll certainly do that, Mrs McKay. But you can't be too careful with water, you know.'

Khan and Patel didn't speak during the journey to the north of the city where they stopped outside a fifteen-storey block of flats, one of four towers standing in close proximity to each other like giant skittles in a concrete alley. Khan parked close to the entrance and reached behind him to grasp a clipboard. 'Ready?'

'Let's go.'

The two men entered the graffiti-adorned ground floor of Inchmarin Court and paused for a moment as the lift doors opened to let a young woman with two small children get out and cross their path. Khan pretended to check his clipboard.

Patel swallowed and smiled at the woman, who ignored him as she turned to berate the smallest of her children, lagging behind.

Khan pushed the call bell for the caretaker and waited with his ear close to the grille.

'Who is it?'

'Scottish Water, here to check your pressure.'

'Naebody telt me anything aboot that.'

'We've had complaints of low water pressure from tenants on the top three floors.'

'They said bugger all tae me.'

'Do you want it checked or not?'

'Shit. Gimme a minute. I'll be doon.'

An elderly man appeared a few minutes later, grossly over-weight, wearing green corduroy trousers and carpet slippers, and carrying a large bunch of keys. He scratched at the grey stubble on his chin. 'This way.'

Khan and Patel followed him into the pump room, where the main water tank for the building was situated. From here water was pumped electrically up to three further storage tanks located on the upper floors.

'Great. No need for you to hang around, mate,' said Khan. 'It's a Yale. We'll see it's closed before we go.'

'Fair enough. Want me tae sign anythin'?'

'No, it's just a routine test. If there's a problem they'll send another team out.'

The caretaker shuffled off and Patel closed the door gently behind him. He stood for a moment with his back against it. 'He's seen us,' he said.

'Don't worry,' said Khan. 'We all look the same. Besides, we'll be on a plane to Pakistan before anyone comes calling.'

He and Patel donned the plastic coveralls they extracted from their tool bags and put on gloves and masks before gingerly removing two of the flasks and putting them down on the floor beside the big water tank. They worked on undoing the lid clasps before sliding the cover back to expose the surface of the water. Patel jumped as one of the pumps started up in order to replenish water being used on an upper floor. It stopped again after about ten seconds.

'Ready?'

Patel nodded.

The men picked up the flasks and undid the caps. Then, holding the rims very close to the surface of the water to avoid splashing, they tipped the cloudy straw-coloured liquid contents slowly into the tank.

'Done,' said Khan, replacing the cap on his flask and putting it down on the floor. 'I'll get the bag.' He brought over a heavy-gauge plastic sack – of the type used for garden refuse – and both flasks were put into it, followed by their gloves, masks and coveralls. Khan sealed the end with a series of knots, and the men slid the lid of the tank back into place.

They put the sack in the back of the van and drove the two hundred metres or so to the next tower block to begin the same ritual. It took them just under an hour and a half to do all four buildings in their schedule. At a little after eight in the evening they started heading east along the shore of the Firth of Forth on the first leg of their journey south.

Rather than join the A1 they stuck to the minor coast road and, after a few miles, stopped in one of the sprawling beach car parks which at that time was empty, the day trippers having gone home and the lovers not yet arrived. Khan dumped the sacks in the refuse bins outside the closed public toilets while Patel scrubbed off the Scottish Water transfers from the van. Using satnav directions, they continued heading for Northumberland.

At four in the morning a police patrol car stopped on the road outside the four tower blocks in Edinburgh. 'Notice anything strange?' the driver asked his colleague.

The officer, looking for signs of activity, said not.

'Lights in the windows,' said the driver.

'Jesus, you're right. It's like Hogmanay.'

'What d'you suppose they're up to?'

'Could be planning a revolution.'

The driver opened his window and listened. 'If they are, it's a quiet, orderly one.'

'Which suits us fine. Think I should call it in?'

'Nothing illegal about switching on lights during the hours of darkness . . . Mind you, if the Greens have their way . . .'

The patrol car drove on.

'God, I feel ill,' complained Neil MacBride as he returned to the bedroom in the flat he shared with his wife Morag and their two children on the fourteenth floor of Inchmarin Court. He'd just made his third trip to the lavatory in the past half-hour.

'Serves you right. How much did you have down the Doocot?'

'Just my usual. God's honest truth. Mind you, I had a pie . . .'

'God, how often have I heard that? Ten pints then you have a bad pie . . .'

'I tell you, I had three pints tops.'

'Come to think of it, I'm not feeling that brilliant myself.'

'Jesus!' exclaimed Neil, doubling up with stomach cramps. 'Christ, I'll have to go again.'

'Maybe it was that chicken we had at tea time,' Morag called after him.

'Mummy, I'm not feeling well. I've got a sore tummy,' said a small figure appearing at the door in pyjamas, clutching a teddy bear.

'Me too,' said another small voice from the bedroom next door.

It was a scene that was being played out in flats all over the four tower blocks. It was also being played out in five blocks of flats in Manchester, six in London and two in Liverpool.

At six a.m. Morag called the emergency out-of-hours service NHS 24. She couldn't get through. Neither could callers in

Manchester, London and Liverpool. The system was over-whelmed.

'In point two miles, turn left,' said the satnav voice. Khan slowed the vehicle, not that they were going very fast on the winding country road.

'Turn left,' said the voice.

'Where?' exclaimed Khan, straining to see through the darkness. The headlight beams were being diffused by drifting mist.

'Recalculating.'

'We must have missed it,' said Patel. 'I think there was a track . . .'

Khan reversed the vehicle slowly

'Turn left . . . Turn left.'

'There,' said Patel. 'It's a bit overgrown.'

Khan saw the opening and turned into it, shrubbery and branches scraping against the sides of the van. After a bone-jarring journey of a quarter of a mile over potholes that threatened to destroy the van's suspension, they saw the shape of a farmhouse appear against the sky. It was in darkness.

'Destination is on your left,' the voice confirmed.

'I thought someone would to be here to meet us,' said Patel.

'Looks like we're first.'

They found a key under one of the curling stones that flanked the front door. The house was cold and dark but the sound of a fridge compressor turning on in the kitchen assured them there was power: they turned on the lights. When they opened the fridge door, they found there was food too.

They were joined an hour later by the two who'd carried out the Manchester operation and two hours after that by the two from Liverpool. The young men who'd driven up from London joined them at first light, and they all congratulated each other on a successful mission.

Khan and Patel, who'd managed to grab a few hours' sleep, said they'd keep watch while the others got some rest.

'We're a good bit off the road here,' said one of the London pair. 'Mind you, I thought someone would be here to tell us what happens next.'

'Me too,' said Patel.

'They'll be here today,' said Khan.

TWENTY-THREE

'You woke me to tell me there's been an outbreak of gastro-enteritis in Pilton?' exclaimed Dr Alice Spiers, Director of Public Health for Edinburgh and the Lothians. She was less than pleased at being woken at three a.m. Her husband turned over and pulled the duvet up round his ears.

'How many?' was her next exclamation. The repeated answer made her sit upright in bed, now fully awake, her free hand rubbing her forehead nervously. 'The occupants of four tower blocks . . .' she repeated. 'How on earth . . .'

'The Western General and the Infirmary have both been over-whelmed. We just don't have the capacity for something like this,' said the caller, Dr Lynn James, communications director with NHS 24.

'No we don't,' agreed Spiers, trying to think ahead. 'Patients will have to be seen at home while we sort out some emergency beds and figure out just what has happened.' She was already out of bed and gathering her clothes to take to the bathroom. Her husband turned over again.

'There are so many I think there has to be an element of hysteria,' said James. 'But, on the other hand, some of them really do seem quite ill.'

'Too early for anything from the lab, I suppose?'

''Fraid so.'

Spiers held the phone between her shoulder and chin as she finished dressing. 'At the risk of being melodramatic, I think I'm going to call a major incident on this.'

'The numbers warrant it,' agreed James. 'But it does seem to be confined to the flats, which is a blessing.'

'We need a cordon round the buildings. No one goes in or out save for medical and nursing staff until we establish what's going on. I'll see to that if you alert GPs in the area. We'll have to get medical teams organised to treat people at home. I take it the Western and the Infirmary are on full alert.'

'Everyone has been called back on duty.'

'The water,' said Spiers. 'It had to be the water. They couldn't all have eaten the same thing.'

'But the sick are coming from four separate blocks of flats,' said James.

'And it wasn't in the mains or the whole area would be affected,' agreed Spiers. 'So four separate storage tanks were . . .'

'Poisoned?'

The major incident team assembled at the Western General Hospital at ten a.m. By that time, reports of similar outbreaks had come in from three other cities in the UK, putting beyond doubt the source of the outbreaks. 'We have been subjected to a terrorist attack,' announced the chief constable to the meeting. 'Blocks of flats in four cities have had their water supply contaminated.'

'Dare we ask with what?' asked the council chief executive.

'We don't know yet.'

'Do we know if it's going to be fatal?'

'We're not aware of any fatalities at the moment but I understand from the ID unit that several patients are very ill indeed. We hope to have lab results later.'

Neil MacBride, one of the very ill patients, and one of the first to be admitted to the Infectious Disease Unit at the Western General, drifted in and out of an uneasy consciousness, making it difficult for the staff nurse trying to get a saline line into his arm to find a vein. 'Hold still for me, Neil,' she murmured, once again avoiding a flailing arm.

Every bed in the unit was full, not that there were many. The days of epidemics were long past . . . according to political wisdom over the past thirty years. No politicians were involved in the hasty decision to open an empty upstairs ward for business.

A junior doctor, Dr Assad Hussain, seconded from another part of the hospital to help out in the crisis, came over to the nurse who was wrestling with Neil MacBride and held him steady while she got the drip line in. 'He really needs that,' said Hussain. 'He's dangerously dehydrated.'

'They all are,' said the nurse.

'This place stinks,' muttered Hussain.

'They've all got rampant diarrhoea,' whispered the nurse 'That's why they're bl— dehydrated, doctor.'

The young doctor smiled at the put-down but the smile faded from his face as he saw the bedpan on the floor beside the bed, waiting for removal to the sluice room. The cover over it had been dislodged.

'What are you doing?' hissed the nurse as she saw him kneel down to examine the contents.

'Rice water.'

'What?'

'I know I'm just another first-year idiot,' said Hussain, 'but I recognise the signs. I've seen it in my own country. This patient doesn't have gastro-enteritis . . . none of them do. They've got cholera.'

The diagnosis was confirmed by the lab a few hours later.

UK Under Cholera Attack was the message from every radio and TV station and newspaper during the next twenty-four hours, during which the first patients to die – forty-six so far – pushed the panic button even harder across the nation. The Prime

Minister appeared on television to appeal for calm, assuring the public that things were not out of control as messages on the internet were suggesting. Cholera was treatable and preventable. Supplies of vaccine would be available soon. Details would be given on radio and TV the moment they were ready. In the meantime, simple precautions should be taken. All domestic water should be boiled before use. Any suspicious activity, particularly near water supplies of any kind, should be reported to the police immediately.

'Do we know any more about how it happened?' Alice Spiers asked the chief constable at the second day meeting of the major incident team in Edinburgh.

'Yes, thanks to you pointing the finger so quickly at contaminated water as the likely source. Two days ago two Asian men turned up in a Scottish Water van at Inchmarin Court, saying that they were there to deal with a reported drop in water pressure. Needless to say, no such report had been made. They were shown to the pump room and must have infected the main storage tank. They went on to do the same at the neighbouring three blocks. Much the same thing in the other affected cities. All the attacks were targeted at flats using the same water supply system, where mains water flows into a large storage tank on the ground floor before being pumped up to auxiliary tanks on the upper floors. Contaminate the supply in the main tank and you affect the whole building.'

'I suppose we must expect more attacks,' said Lynn James.

The chief constable shrugged. 'It has to be a possibility.'

'I think it might be helpful if one of the medics among us told us exactly what we're dealing with here,' said the council chief executive, a comment that elicited sounds of agreement from several of the others.

'It's a very long time since we saw cholera in this country,' replied Alice Spiers. 'Personally, I haven't come across it in my career, even when I worked abroad. We were lucky an Asian doctor working here in the hospital recognised it so quickly. It's endemic in parts of India, and the sort of disease that you find breaking out after some natural disaster; a flood or an earthquake or anything that leads to a breakdown in hygiene standards – disrupted water supplies, leaking sewage pipes and so on. Contaminated water is the main cause of initial infection, but of course, once the disease is present, it can be spread in a variety of ways linked to poor hygiene.

'The disease is caused by a bacterium called *Vibrio cholerae*. It's a very serious form of gastro-enteritis, leading to severe dehydration, then shock and finally death if no action is taken. Replacement of lost fluid is vital. Patients can lose up to fifteen litres in twenty-four hours.'

'The Prime Minister said it was treatable. Are we talking about antibiotics?' asked the chief executive.

'Yes . . .' replied Alice Spiers hesitantly. 'It's a bit too soon to know about that . . .'

'I'm sorry?'

'Cholera is treatable with a number of antibiotics in the normal course of events . . . but, as yet, we don't know what we're dealing with here. The bug might have been . . . altered in some way.'

'Genetic engineering,' murmured the hospital's medical superintendent.

'With a terrorist attack, I'm afraid that is a possibility. We'll have to wait for a full lab report. Our labs are not used to dealing with cholera. We've sent samples off to Colindale for analysis. It might take a day or two before we know exactly what we're dealing with. In the meantime we have to concentrate on isolating the cases we have and rehydrating them. Nursing care is the thing that's going to save people. We'll also be giving broad-spectrum drugs and hoping for the best.'

'As instructed, we're keeping the cordon we threw round the infected flats in place,' said the chief constable. 'It's very upsetting for friends and relatives but, as I understand it, containment of the disease is all-important.'

'It is.'

'The thing is, not everyone living in the flats has been infected . . . My men tell me there are some perfectly healthy people there who are asking to leave, and you can see their point. It's not very pleasant being stuck in the middle of an epidemic.'

'I don't think we can allow it,' said Alice Spiers. 'Not yet, not until we get the lab reports and know exactly what's going on. The fact that they've been living in the same building makes them suspect. They may be healthy but they could be harbouring the disease – they could even be carriers without knowing it.'

'But maybe they'll contract the disease just by being there,' suggested the chief exec.

Alice Spiers conceded the point with a grimace. 'That's the downside,' she admitted. 'Ideally all the sick people should be in hospital, in isolation units being attended to by skilled nurses, but we don't have the capacity to deal with a full-scale epidemic. We have to do the best we can, and that means isolating and containing cases wherever they occur.'

'Doctors' surgeries and the NHS 24 phone lines are being overwhelmed by people thinking they've been infected. They have to go to the loo and start thinking the worst,' said Lynn James.

'I suppose we can't blame them. It's a frightening situation,' said the chief exec. 'What about the safety of the medical and nursing staff dealing with the patients?'

'Our travel clinics had limited stocks of cholera vaccine: we've used that for front-line people. It's all gone now and I don't know when we're going to get more. I think it's fair to say that demand exceeds supply right now, but I'm sure the government will be dealing with that.'

'Our immediate problem is a second wave of cases,' said Alice Spiers. 'There are bound to be people who were at the flats during the day of the attack on the water supply but didn't stay there. If any of them were infected before they left they'll be falling ill and passing on the infection to friends and family. Our teams are waiting to act to isolate and contain.'

'The trouble will be telling the genuine cases from the calls we're getting from people who just think they're ill,' said Lynn James.

'Operator common sense is going to be paramount,' said Alice Spiers. 'There's a world of difference between having cholera and thinking you might be sick. The degree of concern in the relative's voice should be the benchmark.'

'Something tells me things are going to get worse before they get better,' said the chief constable. 'What a mess.'

'Well, it's our mess, ladies and gentlemen,' said the chief exec. 'I suggest we get on with it.'

TWENTY-FOUR

'Well, now we know; the intelligence regarding a biological attack on our country has proved correct and we've been hit with cholera.' The Prime Minister was addressing the second meeting of COBRA in as many days. 'Four of our cities have been affected but we cannot dismiss the possibility that there may be more attacks. All the initial strikes were carried out on blocks of flats so the residents in those flats were the first to become infected, but we're now getting reports of cholera among the wider community in the four cities.'

'But with the same source being implicated,' interjected the health secretary. 'So far, they've all been people with some association with the flats – visitors, tradesmen, delivery men, a social worker in Manchester, a community nurse in Liverpool.'

'Has anyone claimed responsibility?' asked Steven.

'An Islamic fundamentalist group calling themselves Sons of the Afghan Martyrs.'

'Known?'

'No one's ever heard of them.'

'Do we have any more information about the strain of cholera?'

'Nothing back from the lab yet.'

'So we don't know if it's a genetically engineered variant.'

'Please God, not,' said the Home Secretary.

The Metropolitan Police commander asked the question that all the non-medical people present wanted to ask.

'Supposing it has been tampered with, what sort of things could we expect?'

'Resistance to antibiotics so we couldn't treat it,' said the consultant microbiologist with the Department of Health contingent. 'Increased potency of the enterotoxin the bug produces, making it even more lethal.

'What's an entero . . . ?'

'Enterotoxin. It's a poison produced by the bug which attacks the lining of the small bowel, leading to huge fluid loss. That in turn leads to severe shock and then death.'

'Supposing it has been tampered with in the way you suggest,' continued the Met commander. 'Does that mean that everyone who contracts the disease will die?'

'The fact that we couldn't treat it with antibiotics would be a setback, but it's not the be all and end all. It's the dehydration – the fluid loss – that kills. Replacing lost fluid in time can save lives.'

'So victims should be encouraged to drink,' said a self-satisfied-looking junior Home Office minister, as if completing the final entry in a crossword puzzle.

The microbiologist smiled. 'If only it were that simple. People with cholera are usually too ill to drink. Fluid loss has to be replaced through intravenous drip.'

'And that needs health professionals,' said the Home Secretary slowly, as if the implications of that were dawning on her as she said it. 'Which is just not possible. Why am I getting an image of people dying all over our cities, lying in pools of their own excreta?'

'That's a worst-case scenario, Home Secretary.'

'Which we will do everything in our power to avoid,' said the Prime Minister. 'If we go down, we'll go down fighting, so let's not have any more negativity. We must agree a plan of action. First, medical.'

The new health secretary, a little out of his depth after only a few weeks in the job, deferred to his colleague, Norman Travis, who said, 'We continue to isolate and contain outbreaks where they occur. We'll use wide-spectrum antibiotics until any contra-indications appear, and prime consideration will be given to replacing fluid loss in all cases. The wider population is to be given cholera vaccine.'

'Is there enough?' asked Steven.

'Merryman hasn't had much of a chance to come on stream,' said Travis, 'and frankly, cholera wasn't really considered as a favourite for biological attack, but things aren't looking too bad. Travel clinics across the country have limited stocks for immediate use but perhaps the best news is that one of our pharmaceutical companies, Lark Pharmaceuticals, which supplies cholera vaccine to the Third World, has substantial stocks which can be diverted for home use and used to vaccinate our most vulnerable citizens. In the meantime, Merryman will be working flat out and hopefully they'll come up with new stocks in time to vaccinate the rest of the population. A baptism of fire for them, but I'm sure they'll rise to the challenge.'

'What about distribution?' asked the Prime Minister.

'We're not going to go down the doctors' surgeries route as we did with swine flu. That was a bit of a shambles. We're going to set up central vaccination clinics in large halls and invite people to come to receive their jab.'

'Who'll staff these clinics?'

'We plan to ask final-year medical students to help out – properly supervised, of course.'

'I'm not sure of the legal implications of that, minister,' said a Home Office official.

'Nor am I,' said the Prime Minister. 'And right now, I don't care. Our country is under attack.'

Steven allowed a small smile of approval to reach his lips.

The deputy Prime Minister turned to the heads of the intelligence services, who had been quiet throughout. 'Do we have any more information about the perpetrators of this outrage?'

The head of MI5 looked slightly embarrassed at being forced to reply, 'In each case we're looking for two Asian men: they were driving fake water board vans.'

'So, eight Asian men in all. Descriptions?'

''Fraid not.'

The deputy Prime Minister looked at the head of MI6, who said, 'There's still nothing to suggest they came from outside the country. We continue to believe they're home-grown.'

'Maybe that'll work in our favour,' suggested Steven. 'They're probably young men: that means they'll have families living here. When they start to suspect what their offspring have been up to . . .'

'Good point,' said the Prime Minister, turning to look at the intelligence heads.

'Our ears are firmly to the ground, Prime Minister,' said the head of MI5.

'My people too,' said the head of Special Branch. 'Every rumour on the streets of the Asian communities will be followed up.'

'Good,' said the Prime Minister. 'The speedy apprehension of those responsible would do much to restore public morale, particularly if the relevant communities were to distance themselves from the criminals.'

'We're seeking talks with community leaders about it,' said the Home Secretary.

'Which just leaves law and order,' said the Prime Minister. 'To cut to the chase, the police will be seeking emergency powers and we will be granting them. Naturally we will expect that they be used sparingly and with discretion, but we cannot have anarchy on our streets.'

'I can't see people suffering from cholera posing too much of a problem,' exclaimed the junior Home Office minister, who seemed determined to make a name for himself while not having the intellect to make it for the right reasons.

'It's not the sick we have to worry about,' said Steven through gritted teeth. 'It's the well. If we operate a policy of isolate and contain, some people won't welcome being isolated and contained when all their instincts tell them to get the hell out of wherever they find themselves. But if we let them do that, they'll only spread the disease. They'll have to be restrained. Not an easy task.'

'And one which might escalate out of hand very quickly if the disease spreads,' said Travis. 'The police will be stretched.'

Someone suggested, 'Surely we can call on the military.'

'Not something we do lightly in this country,' said the Prime Minister. 'The idea of our soldiers in confrontation with our citizens fills me with horror. The circumstances would have to exceptional.'

'I think a full-blown cholera epidemic might just about fulfil that criterion, Prime Minister,' said the government's chief medical adviser.

'Then please God it doesn't come to that.'

Steven felt a hollow take shape in his stomach when he heard a number of people around the table say, 'Amen.'

'Exciting times,' a voice at Steven's shoulder said as he descended the stairs to leave the Cabinet Office. He turned to find Norman Travis there. 'I don't think we've met officially.' The two men shook hands.

'The kind of excitement I think we could all do without,' said Steven. 'On the bright side, you folks in the health department seem pretty much on the ball.'

'Nice of you to say so, but we've been lucky so far. Having a pharmaceutical company come up with large stocks of cholera vaccine was a big plus. I just hope the Third World understands when we commandeer them.'

'I just hope we're all around to hear their complaints if they don't,' said Steven.

'You sound like a glass-half-empty man.'

'I'm a realist,' said Steven. 'Cholera epidemics are practically impossible to contain when they occur naturally, but when we've got people deliberately contaminating our water supplies and the possibility that the bug's been genetically altered to make it even more lethal . . .'

'I take your point,' said Travis with a sigh as they reached the doors. 'We should get some lab results tomorrow, then maybe we'll see what we're up against.'

Steven took a taxi over to John Macmillan's place to bring him up to speed with what was going on. Macmillan was looking tired, his head resting on the back of his chair as he listened to what Steven had to say, his eyes closing for ten seconds or more at a time.

'Are you feeling up to this, John?' Steven asked. 'You seem very tired.'

Macmillan snorted then smiled as he again closed his eyes. 'Maybe confronting the slings and arrows of outrageous fortune for so many years is finally catching up with me, Steven,' he said.

'I need you to suffer them a bit longer, John. Whether it's nobler in the mind or not, I'm going to need your input on everything as this unfolds.'

Macmillan turned his head to look directly at Steven as if seeing some steely quality in him he hadn't seen before. 'Understood,' he said quietly. 'After all, I seem to remember lecturing you rather a lot in recent times about where your duty lay . . .'

'Damn right you did.'

'Fire away.'

When he'd finished, Macmillan still sat with his eyes closed but this time it was different; an intermittent twitch in his cheek muscle told Steven Macmillan was thinking, not snoozing.

'How many dead?' he asked at last.

'Fifty-four as of this morning.'

'And they would be mainly elderly or very young, along with a number who were immuno-compromised in some way – on steroids or anti-rejection drugs, for instance. Am I right?'

'I haven't seen the breakdown figures yet. Jean should have them when I get back to the Home Office.'

Macmillan continued to think out loud. 'Fifty-four . . . fifty four . . . out of . . . You know, it's my bet the genes controlling the enterotoxin haven't been tampered with,' said Macmillan. 'Otherwise there would be more.'

'Fifty-four's bad enough.'

'We must think dispassionately. We're not the newspapers. We're not here to throw fuel on an emotional fire.'

Steven accepted the slap on the wrist.

'Incubation period was a bit short: I would have expected longer,' Sir John continued.

'You sound as if you've come across cholera before.'

Macmillan nodded. 'I was a young man working for HMG in the Middle East in the early seventies. I saw the tail end of a cholera epidemic that had started in Indonesia in 1961 and crossed several continents. Bloody horrible disease, turns your whole world into a pit of filth and squalor. If it gets a grip here . . . God help us all.'

TWENTY-FIVE

'How was Sir John?' Jean Roberts asked when Steven got back.

'A bit tired but sharp as a tack,' Steven reported. 'He got caught up in a cholera epidemic in the days of his youth so his input is going to be valuable. He was asking about the fatalities. Do we have any details yet?'

'They're on your desk. Oh, and Lukas Neubauer phoned. Asked you to call him back.'

Lukas Neubauer was the director of biological sciences at the laboratories of Lundborg International, the private analytical service that Sci-Med used for scientific analyses when the occasion arose. It had been a long and happy association. Steven liked and respected the man, as he did anyone who was extremely good at their job. Lukas had proved himself to be the best on many occasions in the past.

'What's up, Lukas?'

'Thought you might like an unofficial update on the cholera strain.'

'Absolutely. How did you manage that?'

'I have a friend at Colindale.'

'Colindale?' exclaimed Steven. 'I thought Porton would be carrying out the analysis.' Porton Down was the government microbiological research establishment.

'I guess the enteric expertise at Colindale won the day,' said Lukas. He was referring to the Health Protection Agency Centre for Infections, a series of seventeen reference and support labs situated in North London. 'Or maybe they're both doing it.

Anyway, the news is that the bug is sensitive to the usual antibiotics. It hasn't been made resistant. They're proceeding on the premise that it hasn't been genetically altered.'

Steven breathed a sigh of relief. 'That's the first good news I've had in days.'

He started reading down the list of the people who'd died from cholera so far. Macmillan had been right. The most vulnerable had been the over sixties and a number of babies under a year old who'd failed to survive the effects of dehydration. There were also twelve people who had been taking steroids for a number of reasons and a kidney transplant recipient who had been on immuno-suppressive drugs to prevent rejection of the donor organ.

Steven got back to his flat a little after eight thirty after having had something to eat at his favourite Chinese restaurant, the Jade Garden, where, as always, he'd been warmly welcomed by the owner, Chen Feng, and given an update on how her family were all doing. She knew Steven was a doctor – she'd picked up on it the first time he'd used his credit card – but nothing about who he worked for or what he actually did. She would, however, on occasion probe for medical information or advice relative to family circumstances. Tonight, understandably, she had wanted to know how they could avoid getting cholera.

Steven, who'd phoned his own daughter earlier to apologise for not having managed to get up to see her for the past few weeks, had faced much the same kind of questioning from his sister-in-law Sue. He'd done his best to reassure her that living in a small village a long way away from the only city under attack in Scotland was the best defence she could have. He couldn't do the same for Chen Feng, however: her family all lived in London. Searching for something positive to say, he'd pointed out that she and her family, being in the restaurant trade, knew all about good hygiene practice and that was vitally important in guarding against the disease.

When he got in, Steven called Tally to talk about their respective days. He began with the news he'd got from Lukas.

'Thank God for that,' said Tally. 'You know, I'm also genuinely surprised. For some reason I felt sure they were going to discover the bug had been tampered with.'

'We deserve a break,' said Steven. 'And God knows it's a hellish enough disease without that.'

'The hospital's been asked to provide volunteer medical staff to help out with the mass-vaccination clinics.'

'And you volunteered?'

'Yes, I did. Rumour has it they're going to ask medical students to help out too if we don't have enough doctors and nurses to do the job, and we almost certainly don't.'

'It's no rumour,' said Steven. 'It's official.'

'Seems fair enough. Vaccinating people isn't rocket science.'

'Let's hope Health and Safety agree.'

'You don't think they'd try to stop . . .'

'Sorry, of course not. A bad joke.'

'When am I going to see you?'

'There's nothing I'd like more but we're having daily morning meetings of COBRA at the moment,' said Steven. 'I have to be there.'

'Of course,' said Tally. 'How's Jenny taking not seeing her daddy?'

'I spoke to her earlier. Sue's done a good job as usual in explaining to her why I have to be here.'

'Maybe we should both tie yellow ribbons to the old oak tree,' said Tally, immediately retracting it with, 'Sorry, I shouldn't have said that. Sometimes my tongue runs away with me. I know you have to be there . . .'

'Why so jumpy?' asked Steven.

'I've been reading up on cholera . . . in preparation. We all have. It's horrible. I'm just so nervous about the whole damned thing. How could anyone do something like this? It's beyond belief. It flies in the face of everything humanity is supposed to be about.'

'True, but not much surprises me any more about what people will do to each other.'

'How awful,' said Tally quietly. 'But I suppose you must have seen things . . .'

'That made me want to run off and live in a cave on my own? Yes. I've even tried it on a couple of occasions, but it didn't help. The right thing is to do what you can to make things better, even if it's very little.'

'I take it now would be the wrong time to point out that you didn't bother to vote.'

'Absolutely the wrong time. Were you put on this earth to annoy me?'

'No, just to stop you talking high-sounding crap.'

'Fair enough. I apologise.'

'No, I do. It's a self-defence thing. I'm trying to convince myself I'm hard enough to face up to wards full of children dying of cholera without collapsing on the floor in tears.'

'You need a distraction. I need your help. Leicester was one of the cities on the list of places the Schiller mob were planning to introduce their new health scheme in the autumn. I'd like to know how far they got with their plans, what infrastructure they managed to set up.'

'I'll ask around, see if anyone heard anything. But why?'

'I suppose I'm just making sure that the plan died in the bomb blast along with its designers. I'm checking there's no one else out there thinking about going ahead with it.'

'Of course, your theory about the person who placed the bomb,' said Tally. 'But surely no one could even consider such a thing while we're facing a cholera epidemic?'

'You'd think not,' agreed Steven. 'But maybe a few questions here and there?'

*   *   *

Anwar Khan and Muhammad Patel basked in the praise that was being heaped upon them, as did the other six young Asians. It was the first they had heard of the outcome of their attack as there was no radio or television in the farmhouse and no access to newspapers. The men had spent two nervous days and nights waiting as patiently as they could for word to arrive about the arrangements for leaving the UK.

'My brothers, you have been so successful that there has been a change of plan.'

Khan felt his blood run cold. He wanted to do his bit, but in his heart of hearts he dreaded being asked to don the belt of the martyr and blow himself up. He knew all about the promised pleasures that awaited him in Paradise, but . . .

'The Sons of the Martyrs ask that you carry out another attack before you leave for Pakistan and the hero's welcome you so richly deserve.'

Khan looked at Patel and saw the look of relief there before he averted his eyes. He had been thinking the same thing.

'We ask that you attack four more targets, this time in different cities, to capitalise on the fear and panic that is already out there and bring it to levels where the authorities will fail to cope. By the time the disease has rampaged through the land you will have established a reputation that will live for ever.'

'And then will we be allowed to join our brothers?' asked Patel.

'You will be flown out to the border camps as planned to help in the struggle to drive the infidel from our lands. After your success here, the British will be running scared: their withdrawal will be assured. The Americans will be left isolated as the Russians were before them, and soon Afghanistan will be free of them all.'

'Which cities, and when do we carry out the attacks?' asked Khan.

'You will be told when the time is right. In the meantime, I have brought more provisions for your stay. Patience, my brothers.'

The new government had learned lessons from the handling of the swine flu outbreak, where experts had made predictions that proved to be well wide of the mark. Those experts had found themselves in the firing line, and had clearly felt obliged to protect their professional backsides by citing the worst possible scenario with regard to case numbers and likely deaths. Once such figures had been uttered publicly, politicians had had no option but to proceed on them and act accordingly.

This time, the government set up a committee of four people to keep the public informed about the course of the epidemic and the measures being taken to counteract it. No one man would take the flak. The chief medical adviser, Dr Oliver Clunes, was joined by Norman Travis from the health department, Lydia Thomas, a junior minister from the Home Office, and Deputy Chief Constable Stella Mornington from Manchester city police. Each evening at seven p.m. the committee would appear on all terrestrial TV channels to give out information and answer questions sent in by viewers.

It had been agreed from the outset that, although health was a devolved matter in Scotland and therefore within the remit of the Scottish government, the current situation was considered more of a defence issue and therefore not devolved. The handling of the crisis would be overseen by the Westminster government.

The committee's first broadcast gave details of the planned vaccination programme, due to be operational by the Monday of the following week. The chief medical adviser gave a short summary of what cholera was and how it affected people – delivered in a dispassionate, academic way – before handing over to Norman Travis, who seemed more at ease in front of camera. He gave details of the counter-measures in a much more user-friendly way. The most vulnerable in society would be given protection first. All children under two years of age should be taken by their mothers to their GPs where they would be vaccinated with stocks diverted from travel clinics and military supplies all over the UK. All people over sixty years of age and everyone whose immune system had been compromised through the taking of suppressive drugs should attend one of the new mass-vaccination centres – a series of temporary clinics being set up in city halls all over the UK. They would be given vaccine diverted from the Third World aid programme until new stocks came on line, at which time the rest of the population would be invited to attend the mass clinics. Details of the location of these clinics would be given on local radio and TV stations and in local newspapers.

It was stressed that only people believing themselves to be healthy should attend the clinics. Anyone suspecting that they could be suffering from or had been exposed to cholera should seek help through one of the emergency lines which were now fully operational.

Stella Mornington, a pleasant-looking woman who exuded common sense rather than the air of authoritarian formality exhibited by many senior police officers when talking to the media – the reason she'd been chosen for the role – appealed for calm in the current emergency and urged people to go about their daily business as usual wherever possible. She stressed however that those not complying with emergency regulations in areas affected by cholera would be dealt with severely, as they would be putting their fellow citizens at risk.

Finally, Lydia Thomas, another pleasant-looking woman whose natural charm overcame any barrier her upper class credentials might otherwise have put up, gave details of the various helplines available and how they should be used.

TWENTY-SIX

Edinburgh, Tuesday 1 June 2010

'I hate to tempt fate,' said the chief executive of Edinburgh City Council, 'but I think we should give ourselves a little pat on the back.'

The other members of the major incident team did not disagree.

'I think we've been very lucky so far,' said Alice Spiers. 'We've managed to contain the outbreak, with only sixteen cases occurring outside the immediate vicinity of the flats. No more deaths in the past three days, and vaccination already started for the very young.'

'The mass clinics will open on schedule next Monday,' said the chief exec. 'Eight halls are to be used across the city, all staffed by volunteer medical and nursing staff with the assistance of medical students. The vaccine itself should be here some time on Sunday.'

'Civil unrest has been minimal,' said the chief constable, joining in the self-congratulations. 'Restriction on movements has been kept to a minimum, and I think the decision not to close all public places was the right one.'

'Mind you, the NHS 24 phone lines have been going like a fair,' said Lynn James, 'but that was only to be expected. People are naturally very worried, but we've been able to reassure them that the authorities are on top of things.'

'It could be the lull before the storm,' cautioned Alice Spiers. 'I hate to go all Scottish on you and look on the black side, but if there should be another attack . . .'

'Then all bets are off,' conceded the chief constable. 'Everything could change in an instant. We could be faced with blind panic all over the country.'

'Our hospitals and medical services could be absolutely overwhelmed,' said Alice Spiers. 'We're only getting by at the moment because we've managed to largely contain the outbreak to the flats where it originated and treat affected people in their own homes. I take it the police haven't arrested anyone for the attacks?'

'I'm afraid not,' said the chief constable. 'But if the perpetrators were home-grown as the intelligence services believe, they may well have returned to their communities where there's a good chance they'll be regarded with suspicion and even informed upon.'

'On the other hand, they could still be out there, planning phase two,' suggested the chief exec, whose early optimism had faded away.

'There's also the possibility that they may have contracted cholera and be dying in some lonely barn in the middle of nowhere,' said Alice Spiers. 'It takes skill and training to handle dangerous bacteria. It's the easiest thing in the world to infect yourself if you don't know exactly what you're doing.'

'A happy thought,' said the chief constable.

The chief exec smiled wryly. 'So we hope for the best and prepare for the worst, as someone once said.'

Forty-five miles away, Anwar Khan and Muhammad Patel were preparing to ensure that the chief exec's preparations would be justified. They had driven up from Northumberland to Waheed Malik's newly rented premises in Glasgow three nights before to receive instructions for their second mission. The success of their first attack had done much to dispel the nerves they had both suffered from last time, although in Khan's case these had been replaced by a different feeling of unease when he heard details of the target. It prompted him to ask questions.

'In Edinburgh it was just a case of gaining access to water

tanks in some old buildings,' he said. 'Pumping stations will be different. They'll have security.'

Malik shook his head. 'No,' he said. 'We have been monitoring the station for some time. There's no security. The water board doesn't do security.'

'But surely after what we did last time . . .'

'They've secured blocks of flats all over the country. That's the way security works in the UK. They prevent the same thing from happening again. There has been no new security put on water board pumping stations. We've been watching.'

'If you say so,' said Khan, still sounding a bit doubtful.

'Courage, brother. This time tomorrow you will have struck the blow which will damage morale so much that our victory will be guaranteed.'

Malik spread a plan of the pumping station on the table and went over the details again. 'Once more I remind you, the critical thing is that you introduce the solution to the pipe after it exits the blue valve of the filtration and chlorination unit located here.' Malik stabbed his finger on the map. 'Remember its location in relation to the door you'll enter by . . . here.'

'Which will be padlocked,' said Khan.

'The bolt cutters will make short work of that.'

'But are you sure about the perimeter fence?' said Patel, beginning to share Khan's anxiety. 'No barbed wire?'

'None,' replied Malik. 'Simple five-foot railings. You'll be over in a flash.'

'But there are houses nearby. What if someone sees us and raises the alarm?'

'They'll all be asleep at three o'clock in the morning and the station is located on a hill. You put the van in neutral and coast down the last two hundred metres. Then you sit and wait to make sure all is quiet.'

Khan and Patel had run out of questions; they sat in silence until Malik suggested they check they had everything they'd need in the back of the van.

'What time did you say we should leave here?' asked Patel.

'Ten o'clock. We don't want to risk disturbing the neighbours by leaving any later. Drive to the car park we decided on and wait there until it's time. It's only used by hill walkers so it will be empty at that time of night.'

The three men watched the TV broadcast of the government's advice and information panel at seven p.m., remaining impassive as Oliver Clunes, the government's chief medical adviser, reported to the nation that only thirty-eight new cases of cholera had occurred across the country in the past twenty-four hours.

'We have also heard from the laboratories at Colindale that the bacterium is sensitive to antibiotics,' announced Norman Travis. 'We're not out of the woods yet but it does look as if we could be getting the upper hand.'

Stella Mornington reported that the public had been behaving with the good common sense that the British were noted for in times of emergency, and very few arrests had been made for non-compliance with the emergency regulations.

Lynn Davies reminded the public about the helplines that were available, and urged everyone to find out the location of their nearest mass-vaccination clinic well before the commencement of the programme on the following Monday.

All four managed a smile as the programme ended, even the chief medical adviser, who made it look like an unnatural act.

'They won't be smiling tomorrow, my brothers,' muttered Malik, 'when they start drowning in rivers of their own filth. They'll be demanding that their troops be withdrawn from the Middle East and an end put to their imperialist adventure with the American pigs.'

*   *   *

Steven Dunbar had been watching the same broadcast at his flat in Marlborough Court. Tally phoned shortly afterwards. 'Well, what d'you think?'

'Things are looking better than I'd feared,' said Steven.

'Absolutely,' agreed Tally. 'I can't believe we're getting off so lightly – no disrespect to those who've died, but it could have been so much worse.'

'We should remember that the police haven't caught anyone yet; there could be a second wave.'

'Please God, no,' Tally sighed. 'That would just be too awful . . . God, it just doesn't bear thinking about.'

'Then let's not,' said Steven. 'We'll cross those bridges when we come to them.'

'By the way, I asked around to see if anyone had heard rumours about a new health scheme or changed pharmacy arrangements being introduced in the autumn but I drew a complete blank, I'm afraid. No one knew anything at all about it.'

'Thanks anyway. I've asked Jean to check out the other health authorities on the list, but if your lot haven't heard anything I guess the others won't have either. Maybe the Schiller mob didn't get that far before the bomber stepped in.'

'Maybe the bomber was a good guy after all.'

'I hope so.'

'I was just thinking this morning: if things continue to get better, maybe we'll get a chance to take that trip you suggested to Newcastle to pay our respects to the other good guys?' said Tally.

'That's a real possibility. There wasn't much to say at the COBRA meeting this morning. I think they'll be stopping them soon.'

'Good. Then maybe we can go on up to Scotland after Newcastle and spend some time with Jenny?'

'That would be nice.'

Although he meant it, Steven said it on autopilot. His attention had strayed back to Tally's reporting that no one in the Leicester health authority had heard anything about a proposed change to services coming in the autumn. The whole thing suddenly struck him as strange. If the Schiller Group were still discussing things back in February, when the outcome of the election would not be known until May, there wouldn't have been time to introduce a new health initiative by the autumn as the recovered disk had outlined . . . but did it matter now that the world had changed? Steven smiled as he remembered Lisa pointing out that he had the kind of mind that would find something suspicious on a bus ticket. A large gin and tonic and an early night were called for.

'Where are you going?' asked Patel. 'The car park is straight on here.'

'I want to drive past the pumping station.'

'What for? Someone could see us.' Patel sounded agitated.

'Relax. It's quarter past ten. There's plenty of traffic about and we're in an unmarked white van. I just want to make sure about the railings.'

'But Waheed already told you.'

'I know he did,' said Khan, checking his mirrors and slowing slightly as they passed the pumping station.

'See, exactly as he said,' said Patel. 'Five-foot railings. Now let's go to the car park like we agreed.'

'All right, all right . . . I just needed to be sure.'

Patel shot him a sideways glance. 'Don't you trust Waheed?'

'Of course,' said Khan.

Patel, unconvinced, shot him another nervous glance but didn't say any more. The unscheduled drive-by of the pumping station had already unsettled him more than enough.

The hill car park was as deserted as Malik had predicted, but Khan still took the precaution of driving head first into a parking place so that he and Patel were facing a clump of bushes. If he'd reversed in, any vehicle entering the car park would have caught them in the sweep of its headlights. Khan switched off the engine and they sat in silence for a few minutes, the only sound being contracting metal clicks from the van.

'Do you think we'll ever see our families again?' asked Patel.

'It's enough that they will be proud of us,' replied Khan.

'Yes, but—'

'Enough. We are soldiers on a mission. We must look forward, not back.'

'You're right. I wonder what the camps will be like? I've never been abroad . . . you?'

'No.'

'Our country . . . but we've never been there. Seems strange, don't you think?'

'Look—' Khan's angry response was cut short by a vehicle entering the car park, its headlights lighting up the shrubbery briefly, causing both men to sink down in their seats.

'It's slowing,' hissed Patel.

'It's a car park.'

Patel sat motionless, staring straight ahead while Khan monitored the car's progress in the van's mirrors. It circled round to the opposite side of the car park, its tyres crunching on the gravel surface, and extinguished its lights as it drew to a halt.

'As far away as possible,' muttered Khan. 'Guess what they're doing.'

Patel didn't respond. Humour was the last thing on his mind.

Conversation between the two men was uncomfortable and sporadic for the remainder of their wait, which was punctuated by the arrival of two more cars and the departure of the original one. 'Like rabbits,' muttered Patel when the third car drove in.

The last car left at one thirty a.m., allowing both men to get out and relieve themselves in the bushes. 'I thought they'd never go,' said Khan.

'Me too,' said Patel. It was the friendliest exchange they'd had.

At twenty to three, Khan, after checking his watch for the umpteenth time, finally said, 'It's time.' The words acted as a safety valve. Their enforced immobility, which had been acting as a magnifier of all things bad for both of them, had come to an end and they were finally on the move. The tension didn't return until they were drifting down the hill towards the pumping station in neutral.

Khan brought the vehicle to a halt and turned off the engine. They sat for a few minutes, watching the nearby houses for any signs of life, but windows remained dark and curtains were undisturbed.

'Ready?'

'Ready.' Patel reached behind him and brought the box containing the bacterial cultures into the front of the van rather than go round and open the back doors. Khan took it out his side, then Patel got out carrying the bolt cutters and both men pushed their doors gently to. They didn't want to risk slamming them and waking the neighbours.

Khan climbed over the railings first, dropping lightly to the grass on the other side, and turning to receive the box which Patel handed to him. Patel dropped the bolt cutters on the other side and climbed over to kneel beside Khan while they looked back at the houses opposite. Still no signs of life. In a spontaneous gesture, Khan held up his hand, inviting a high-five, which Patel performed with a smile.

Then both men were suddenly blinded as half a dozen searchlights were turned on and harsh male voices yelled at them from all directions. 'Armed police! Get down on the ground! Get down! Hands on your heads! Armed police!'

TWENTY-SEVEN

The headline news next morning was that terrorist attempts to contaminate drinking water at pumping stations supplying large parts of four major British cities had been foiled by police. It was not yet known whether other attempts had been successful or if the captured terrorists had been responsible for the first attack. The population was urged to remain vigilant. All water should be boiled until the all-clear was given.

There was an air of so-far-so-good about the COBRA meeting at ten that morning.

'I wouldn't like to go public on it right now,' said the Home Secretary, 'but I think we may have got them all. All pumping stations have been examined thoroughly and none report any signs of interference during the night. I think we have to congratulate the police and our security forces on a job very well done.'

'Was it a breakthrough or a tip-off?' asked Steven. He thought it was a reasonable question to ask but the slightly embarrassed looks that passed between the heads of MI5 and Special Branch and the Metropolitan Police commander seemed to suggest not.

The MI5 man cleared his throat and said, 'We did receive a tip-off, but it's not clear at the moment whether or not it came from one of our undercover people.'

'I see,' said Steven.

'I'm sure you appreciate the dangers involved in placing operatives in dangerous situations. We have to keep information about them as secret as possible.'

Even from each other, thought Steven, seeing what he thought might be a case of the right hand not knowing what the left was doing.

'No matter,' said the deputy Prime Minister, intervening. 'The main thing is we have eight terrorists in custody.'

There were murmurs of agreement round the table.

'Do we know anything about them?' asked Steven.

'First reports suggest they're home-grown and very young,' said the Met commander.

'And presumably Asian?'

'Yes, but born in the UK.'

'But they must have been subject to outside influence, and given assistance,' said Norman Travis. 'You don't exactly find cholera cultures in the cupboard under the sink.'

The MI5 head nodded. 'It's almost certain we're looking at disaffected youths being exploited by Islamic terrorists for their own ends.'

'After being recruited locally,' added the Met commander bitterly. 'This damned Afghan war is making it all too easy for these Fagin-like figures.'

'Be that as it may . . .' began the deputy PM, coughing to cover his embarrassment, 'it's a truly sad reflection on our society that British-born youths should feel so . . . un-British.'

The expression on the Met commander's face suggested that such social considerations were the last thing on his mind. 'Well, they'll have the rest of their natural lives to reflect on their Britishness or lack of it from behind bars,' he growled. 'Perhaps we should be more concerned with those who've died and those who might yet join them.'

'Indeed,' said Norman Travis. 'Our first priority must be to remain focused on stamping out the epidemic we still have on our hands. We can't afford to let down our guard even if we have – hopefully – deactivated its source.'

'Hear hear,' said several round the table.

'So we continue with the preventative measures we've put in place?' said the deputy PM.

Everyone agreed.

Steven walked back to the Home Office wondering why he didn't feel a whole lot better than he did. The capture of what looked to be the whole terrorist strike force was a major triumph, and yet he found himself feeling uneasy without knowing why.

'Wonderful news,' said Jean Roberts when Steven walked in. 'Aren't our police wonderful?'

'We are indeed blessed,' replied Steven, tongue in cheek.

'Oh, come on, Steven, I know you and Sir John have had your differences with the police and intelligence services over the years, but you have to admit they've come up trumps this time.'

'You're right; they have.'

'All the health boards you asked about have now reported back. None of them knew anything about any new scheme coming into operation in the autumn.'

'Thanks, Jean.'

Steven had barely sat down in his office when the phone rang.

'They've caught them! I can hardly believe it,' said Tally.

'It's real enough.'

'This is just what we need to get on top of things,' said Tally. 'It'll give us time to get everyone vaccinated so even if there's another attempt we'll be prepared. Is something wrong? You seem a bit distant.'

Steven struggled with a response. 'Something is wrong,' he confessed, 'but I don't know what.'

'I know that feeling,' said Tally. 'Sometimes I get it with the kids at the hospital. All the lab results are telling you one thing but you know in your heart that it's not the whole story: there's something else going on.'

'That's it exactly,' said Steven. 'The jigsaw looks complete but you're left with one piece in your hand.'

'Go and see Sir John,' said Tally. 'You and he have this thing . . . You can probably work it out between you.'

Steven called John Macmillan's home but was told by his wife that he was at the hospital having a check-up. 'Nothing wrong, I hope,' said Steven.

'Far from it. He wants to go back to work.'

Steven sympathised with her and made arrangements to call round later. He spent the next few minutes standing at the window looking out at the traffic, trying to decide what to do next. He took out his mobile phone and flicked through the contact list till he got to John Ricksen, then hesitated for a few moments before pressing the dial button.

'Ricksen.'

'John, it's Steven Dunbar. How are things?'

'Sci-Med calling MI5 to ask how things are? I don't think.'

'There's just so much cynicism in the world today . . .' Steven lamented.

That drew a laugh from Ricksen. 'Out with it, Dunbar. What are you after?'

'All right. I'd like to talk.'

'When?'

'Now.'

'You can buy me lunch.'

The two men arranged to meet at the Blue Boar, a pub by the river, at one o'clock.

Although not close friends, Steven and Ricksen, an intelligence officer with MI5, had crossed paths several times over the years, and had come to respect each other despite the lurking departmental rivalry which had MI5 believing Sci-Med had a little too much freedom to operate as they saw fit, and Sci-Med asserting that MI5 lacked imagination.

The two men shook hands, and Steven ordered a couple of

beers. 'You guys must be feeling pretty pleased with yourselves,' he said as they sat down. 'I take it it was 5 who made the breakthrough?'

Ricksen took a sip of his beer. 'Not exactly,' he said slowly.

Steven let his expression ask the question.

'It's all a bit embarrassing. The informant gave details of all four proposed attacks on pumping stations but our people on the inside knew nothing at all about any of them. The same goes for Special Branch.'

Steven frowned. 'If the operation was being kept that secret, how come one informant knew details about all four attacks?'

'Exactly. The information had to have come from the very top, but we've no idea who. That's a worry. It suggests that there may be home-grown terrorist operations out there that we know nothing at all about.'

'And MI6 are still certain they didn't come in from abroad?'

'Absolutely. In fact, we know that the eight in custody have never been outside the UK in their lives. All are under twenty – they're been-nowhere, done-nothing dumbfucks full of Islamic shit that someone rammed down their throats till they believed it. And here's the killer . . . They were all actually on our books.'

Steven's eyes opened wide. 'Now I can understand where the embarrassment comes in.'

'We keep an eye on all the young firebrands in the Asian communities who sound as if they may be destined to cause trouble. Mostly it's just running off at the mouth, but they invariably attract the attention of local recruiters and the next step can involve them disappearing for a "holiday" to the old country to see their roots for the first time – visiting Great-uncle Asif or some such crap. They actually spend their time in the training camps on the border between Pakistan and Afghanistan and come back ready for business – able to strip down a Kalashnikov blindfold and handle Semtex like it was Play-Doh. But these eight were different: they were obviously recruited, but not through the usual channels or we would have known about it, and none of them went abroad.'

Steven let out a low whistle. 'So the organ grinders are here in the UK, not just the monkeys.'

'That's what it looks like.'

'But one of them blew the whistle.'

'How lucky was that?'

Steven digested this comment in silence for a few moments before asking, 'I take it none of them is saying very much?'

Ricksen smiled wryly. 'I think the truth is that none of them knows very much. They're all low-level operatives, told exactly where to go and what to do, and all of them are so full of holy shit that they didn't question anything.'

'You don't think the fact that someone informed on them might change their outlook?'

Ricksen shook his head. 'Because none of them knows anything about the size of the organisation they were working for, they just assume that someone somewhere up the chain of command betrayed them and will get his just desserts in the life to come. One of them did say something interesting, though. He claimed he was set up.'

Steven saw the difference. 'Set up, not betrayed; that is interesting. Name?'

'Anwar Khan, caught in Glasgow, possibly one of those who carried out the attack in Edinburgh.'

As they sat with coffee, Ricksen said, 'I can understand Sci-Med's interest in the fact that it was a cholera attack but why the interest in who carried it out?'

'I wish I could give you a straight answer,' said Steven. 'I just have this feeling that something's not quite right. Ostensibly I'm looking at a terrorist attack on the UK using a biological weapon. But when I consider the overall picture, the bug they used, the people who carried out the attack, the fact that they were betrayed – or set up – there's something not quite right.'

'You mean they're going to hit us with smallpox while we're all patting each other on the back?'

'Christ, I hope not . . .'

TWENTY-EIGHT

Steven went over to see John Macmillan at four o'clock and found him in excellent spirits. 'A better day, eh, Steven? Not only have I been given the all-clear to return to work on a part-time basis but the security services finally get their act together and nail the terrorists.'

'It turns out they had little to do with it, John.' Steven told him what he'd learned at his lunch-time meeting with Ricksen.

'Damnation,' said Macmillan. 'I'd assumed that Special Branch or one of 5's insiders had come up with the goods.'

Steven said not. 'One unknown person, apparently in full possession of all the details of four separate operations, gave the lot away to the police.'

'But why?'

'Why indeed. It must have been someone at the top of the chain to have access to that much information.'

'So it won't take them long to figure out who it was. But the informer must know that, and yet he hasn't asked for police protection, I take it?'

'No.'

'So what had he to gain? It doesn't make sense.'

'Nothing has made any sense for weeks,' said Steven glumly.

'What else is troubling you?'

'One of the disks we recovered from Charles French's house outlined plans for a reintroduction of the Northern Health Scheme in the autumn. There wouldn't have been time.'

'Is that really relevant?' asked Macmillan, still thinking about the terrorist informant.

'I don't know,' Steven confessed. 'But . . . I'm beginning to think it might be.'

Now he had Macmillan's full attention. 'Go on.'

'Suppose we were *meant* to discover the plans for a reintroduction of the old Northern Health Scheme and where it was destined to happen.'

'But the disks French's wife handed over were genuine. The details agreed in every way with what we worked out happened in the north all these years ago.'

'But the plans for a relaunch of the scheme were listed on a separate disk,' said Steven. 'Someone could have added that for our benefit.'

'The end result being that we would see it as a failed operation . . .'

'And take no further interest in it . . . or them . . . or whatever else they might be planning on doing.'

'But they all died,' said Macmillan.

'Except the bomber,' Steven reminded him. 'The one thing that didn't make sense. An insider who destroyed the old guard in order to do . . . what?'

'Hopefully nothing while we're in the middle of a terrorist attack.'

'Which doesn't make sense either,' said Steven, a comment that made Macmillan raise his eyebrows.

'In what way?'

'Just about every way,' said Steven. 'Cholera was an odd choice for a bio-attack.'

'It's a horrible disease.'

'But there are worse, much worse, if *you* rather than nature are in the position of deciding which microbe to use.'

Macmillan conceded the point with a shrug.

'Where did eight disaffected Asian youths living in the Midlands get cultures of cholera from?'

'Presumably it must have been grown in laboratories abroad and brought into the country.'

'MI6 are adamant that they would have heard something about such an operation, and yet they heard nothing.'

Macmillan made a gesture with his hands indicating ambivalence.

'The cholera strain they used is sensitive to antibiotics, when it's the easiest thing in the world for a lab to make bugs resistant and therefore treatment harder. They didn't bother doing that.'

'Even we get a bit lucky sometimes,' said Macmillan with a half-hearted smile. When Steven's expression didn't change, he added, 'Fair enough, it is a bit odd. So why didn't they?'

'I'm still thinking about that.'

'Anything else?'

'The spread of the epidemic has been surprisingly limited.'

'I've been impressed with the way the authorities have responded,' said Macmillan. 'They've been on the ball from the word go.'

'I know they'd like to believe that, and people will take credit wherever they can, but, as you said, cholera is a horrible disease . . . and spreads like wildfire. Do we really put it all down to good management?'

Macmillan sat with one hand under his chin, his index finger tapping his lower lip as he appeared to think back to his own experience of seeing the full horror in his youth. 'Point taken,' he said. 'But what are you getting at?'

'I don't know,' admitted Steven. 'I just need to . . . share my angst.'

Macmillan smiled.

'And now, just as the terrorists are about to launch a second strike, someone shops the lot of them. As John Ricksen said, how lucky was that?'

'So where does that leave us?'

'All at sea.'

'And in which direction do you intend rowing?'

'I need to turn suspicion into fact,' said Steven. 'That means asking questions. I need to know if we were set up to believe that we foiled the Schiller Group's plans. If we were, it would mean they're still active.'

'In which case you could be putting yourself in very grave danger,' said Macmillan. 'I suggest you call a full code red on this and pay a visit to the armourer.'

Steven nodded reluctantly. He disliked carrying weapons, and only did so when his life could be in real danger, but there was no denying the truth of what Macmillan had said. 'I'll go round first thing in the morning . . . and then have another word with Maxine French.'

The next day, having duly signed for a Glock 23 pistol and a supply of .40 calibre ammunition and been fitted with a shoulder holster, he went into the Home Office and asked Jean Roberts to call Maxine French. Would it be convenient for him to pop over and see her some time – preferably that morning? He could tell by the expression on Jean's face that she was getting a positive response, and got up from his chair in anticipation.

'She'd be delighted to see you,' said Jean, putting down the phone. 'She suggests you join her for coffee at eleven.'

Maxine welcomed Steven and left him admiring the view while she made coffee and returned with everything on a silver tray.

'How can I help you, Dr Dunbar?'

'Mrs French, the last time I saw you you very kindly handed over some disks that your husband had been keeping safe.'

'Yes, government property, you said. Is something wrong?'

Steven still wasn't sure in his own mind how to approach the problem, but now, faced with the smiling Maxine French, he had to make his decision. He took a sip of coffee. 'Did anyone else have access to the disks you gave me?'

'Yes,' said Maxine, matter of factly, making the word music to Steven's ears. 'An executive called round from Deltasoft. He seemed to know about the disks, and said that when he was clearing Charles's office he had come across the latest versions, which Charles obviously hadn't had time to bring home. We exchanged them. I'm sorry. I should have mentioned it.'

'No problem,' said Steven. 'No problem at all.' He felt both relieved and apprehensive. The good thing was that he had made progress: he now knew for sure that Sci-Med had been set up to believe that there had been a plan to reintroduce the old Northern Health Scheme and it had ended with the explosion in Paris. There had never been any such plan, but knowing that now raised many more questions.

'Did you know the man who came to see you?'

'No, but he showed me ID. It's quite a large company,' said Maxine. 'And I wasn't involved in it at all. I think it fair to say I took as much interest in Charles's computer business as he did in my charities. Not-a-lot, as that chap on the telly used to say.'

Steven smiled and wondered about Maxine's marriage. He felt sure she'd been a loyal, supportive wife – probably the reason French had married her. She'd ticked all the boxes for service as a top-flight political animal's wife. He hadn't been looking for any sort of companion and she, coming from the same sort of background, hadn't expected to be one.

'Does the term Schiller Group mean anything to you, Mrs French?' He watched Maxine carefully for a reaction, but none was visible. She shook her head.

'Not in any meaningful way,' she said, a reply that Steven found strange: his facial expression said so. Maxine explained. 'I remember once at a dinner party we gave, one of the guests mentioned something about the Schiller Group and Charles told him to shut up. I thought it very rude of him but he was clearly very angry. I asked him about it later but he said it was something that didn't concern me – something he said rather a lot, if truth be told. But then, I suppose that was because of his government involvement?'

Steven gave a knowing nod. 'The price we all have to pay, I'm afraid, not being able to share things with our loved ones. Thank you, Mrs French. You've been a great help.'

He returned to the Home Office, feeling well satisfied with his morning's work. He was particularly pleased that he'd managed to find out what he wanted to know without alerting anyone to the fact, particularly anyone connected with the Schiller Group.

Steven reflected that this was the first morning since the start of the emergency that there had not been a meeting of COBRA. There was one pencilled in for the following morning – more a case of not wanting to tempt fate by calling a complete halt to them, he suspected – but it was a sign that fear was being replaced by optimism. The epidemic could have been so much worse, as he'd noticed the newspapers were starting to point out when he flicked through the copies on his desk. Some of them were already taking to task the consultant microbiologists across the country who'd been predicting something much more serious.

Steven noticed that they were largely the same experts who'd been asked to pronounce on the swine flu 'epidemic', and was reminded of some questions of his own he wanted to ask. He needed to speak to someone about the course of the cholera epidemic and considered calling an old friend at the London School of Hygiene and Tropical Medicine, but then he changed his mind. He needed something more than a strictly academic view. He called Lukas Neubauer at the Lundborg labs instead.

'Steven, you have some work for me?'

'Not right now, Lukas. I need to talk.'

'Talk doesn't put food in my children's mouths. We could do

with a big, juicy government contract down here. We're bored stiff doing DNA analyses for paternity suit lawyers and bacteriology reports for councils closing down Chinese restaurants.'

'Well, it keeps the Merc on the road,' Steven joked, alluding to the Mercedes Lukas drove.

'When would you like to come over, my friend?'

'This afternoon?'

Dr Lukas Neubauer, a tall, Slavic-looking man, welcomed Steven with a smile and a firm handshake. 'Maybe we can talk in the lab? I've got a couple of things on the go.' Steven perched on a lab stool and rested an elbow on the bench while he waited for Neubauer to transfer a rack of tubes from one water bath to another and start a stop clock. 'Now, what would you like to talk about?'

'When you found that the cholera strain was sensitive to antibiotics, what was your first thought?'

Neubauer pushed his glasses up onto his forehead and put his head to one side. 'I was surprised,' he said. 'But relieved too because it suggested the *Vibrio* had not been genetically altered.'

Neubauer's reply had been simple and to the point, so he didn't understand why Steven suddenly appeared spellbound. 'Steven? Are you all right?'

'Christ, that's it.'

'What's what?'

'That's what we were meant to think. Did Colindale do any further analysis of the bug's genetic make-up?'

'I don't think they did – everyone was so pleased that it was still sensitive to antibiotics. And, of course, it was quickly apparent that the enterotoxin had not been enhanced because people were recovering as long as they were kept hydrated.'

'Can you get your hands on the bug? I can go through the usual channels but it might be quicker if we bypass them.'

'I can ask my friend at Colindale. We have a licence to handle dangerous pathogens here so I can't see any great problem.'

'I need you to carry out a full analysis of it. Tell me everything you can as quickly as you can. Make it your number one priority.'

'What are we looking for?'

'I don't know.'

TWENTY-NINE

The evening broadcast from the advisory committee urged caution. People must remain on their guard against a disease which could still kill if given the chance. Water supplies were being kept under constant surveillance, but should suspicion be aroused the public were urged to report it quickly to the authorities. Arrangements for vaccination against cholera were proceeding as planned, and it was envisaged that there should only be a gap of around ten days after the first wave of vaccinations before the entire population could be protected. Together they would *wash away the evil.*

Steven had noticed the new government slogan appearing on posters in the city. Swine flu had had one too: someone in Whitehall believed that all epidemics should have a slogan. His mind strayed to what it might be if weapons-grade smallpox or bubonic plague came to call.

'Anything in from Lukas?' Steven asked Jean when he arrived at the Home Office in the morning.

'Nothing apart from a memo yesterday evening saying that the lab had the strain and would be working on it all night.'

'Let me know if anything comes in. I'm going over to Belmarsh prison after the COBRA meeting. I need to speak to the Asian who claims he was set up.'

'Aren't you going to say good morning to Sir John?'

'I'm sorry?'

Jean inclined her head towards John Macmillan's office, a gesture that made Steven break into a disbelieving smile. He knocked on the door and waited for a response before entering. 'Good to see you back. Does your wife know you're here?'

'She made a bit of a fuss, but frankly I think she's glad to be rid of me.'

'Well, I'm delighted to see you sitting there,' said Steven. 'Are you officially back at the helm?'

'No. Call me an interested observer until the medics sign me off completely.'

'I was just telling Jean I'm going over to Belmarsh to talk to Anwar Khan. If you were to attend the COBRA meeting instead of me, it would save some time.'

Macmillan smiled. 'You never were much of a one for meetings, were you, Steven?'

Steven concurred. 'There's quite a lot to tell you about, but it'll wait till later. Will you attend COBRA?'

Macmillan nodded. Steven set off for Greenwich and HMP Belmarsh, home to some of the most violent prisoners in the country. He paused at the door to check with Jean that full code-red status had gone through. This was important because, although Sci-Med agents always had the right to request assistance and co-operation from the police and many other authorities, having full code-red status entitled them to demand it with total Home Office authority should it not be forthcoming – not something to be used lightly, but a useful power when opposition was anticipated.

'The Home Secretary signed it yesterday.'

'Thanks.'

'Don't forget to remove your weapon before you try to enter the prison or we'll be seeing you on the six o'clock news.'

Steven had a brief meeting with the two MI5 interrogators on duty before his interview with Anwar Khan. 'None of them is saying anything,' one told him. 'They're shit scared but they're not talking.'

'It's not us they're scared of,' said the other. 'It's the Muslim mob in here. They've obviously been told they're dead if they say anything. It was a mistake bringing them here.'

'I agree,' said Steven.

'What's Sci-Med's interest?'

'The cholera,' Steven lied, knowing it would be a reasonable angle for Sci-Med to follow up on, and hoping it would defuse any animosity about his muscling in on security service territory. 'We'd like to know if they have a lab in this country.'

'So would we if you learn anything. Good luck.'

Steven remained seated when two prison officers brought in the nineteen-year-old Khan, his eyes betraying conflicting emotions. Steven guessed that fear was winning but currently defiance was emerging as a front-runner.

'What are you looking at?' the boy snarled.

'A loser?'

Khan made to move forward across the table but stopped himself when Steven didn't react at all. 'We'll see who the losers are,' he said, sinking back down in his chair.

'Indeed we will.'

'Our war is a holy war.'

'But what you don't realise, Khan, is that you were never part of it. You were set up just like you said you were. Weren't you? You were conned. They set you up, then blew the whistle.'

'Shut the fuck up.'

'Come on, son, you're the one who worked it out. Who set you up? At least make sure the bastard gets what's coming to him.'

'Fuck you.'

'Fair enough . . . but think about it. How many virgins do you get in Paradise when you're a loser who was set up from the very start? You're young, you made a mistake; someone used you and your friends. You're not going to get off after killing all those people but if you help us to get the brains behind it

. . . maybe, just maybe, your whole life won't be wasted in a place like this . . .'

'Fuck off.'

Steven returned to the Home Office.

'How did you get on?' asked Macmillan.

'He wouldn't say anything but I hope I planted a seed of doubt in his mind. I'm sure he knows he was set up, however much he might regret admitting it now.'

'You said earlier you had some other news?'

Steven brought Macmillan up to date with what he'd learned about the disks and told him of his request that Lukas Neubauer subject the cholera bug to a full analysis. 'I think that's why they didn't make it resistant to antibiotics, to stop us thinking it might have been altered at all.'

'Why would they want to do that?'

'I don't know,' said Steven, feeling his position weaken: he seemed to be saying that a lot.

'Well, your instincts usually serve you well. Meanwhile, I haven't been idle myself.'

'Really?' Steven immediately hoped he hadn't sounded too surprised.

'I've been checking through the things the computer's been picking up on.'

The Sci-Med computer was programmed to highlight any article appearing in the UK press with a scientific or medical content that might conceivably concern Sci-Med.

'An elderly woman living in Edinburgh, Mrs Gillian McKay, reported to the police that her next-door neighbour, a Mr Malik, had gone missing; she hadn't seen him for some days. When police checked the premises they found nothing amiss – he'd apparently just gone away – but they volunteered to check with Malik's relatives if Mrs McKay knew of any. She said Malik had told her all his relatives were back in Pakistan. Later, however, when a young reporter from the local paper came to see her, she remembered he had a nephew who worked for the water board . . . she'd seen the van at the house.'

'Oh, you beauty,' murmured Steven.

'She'd spoken to Malik about it: he was going to ask his nephew to investigate her complaint that there was too much chlorine in the local water. She claimed it made her tea taste funny.'

'Well, well,' said Steven, 'if you'll pardon the pun. Do we know what day the van was there?'

'We do,' said Macmillan, breaking into a grin. 'I checked the dates. The day of the attack on the Edinburgh flats. What's more, with the story being taken from a local newspaper, a report about a missing person . . .'

'The police didn't pick up on the nephew?'

'Apparently not.'

'Maybe we could hand it over after I've spoken to Mrs McKay?' suggested Steven. 'Actually no,' he said, having second thoughts. 'I could pass the info on to John Ricksen at 5. One good turn deserves another and all that . . .'

'Frightening,' said Macmillan with a shake of the head belied by a look of admiration. 'You put one over on MI5 and then get a round of applause from them. I suggest you get started.'

Steven decided to go up to Edinburgh that evening on the British Airways shuttle out of Heathrow. He wouldn't try to see Mrs McKay until the following morning, but he thought he might like to have a wander round the streets of Edinburgh. Although he'd never lived there, he knew it well enough. He and Lisa had set up home in Glasgow after their marriage and had often gone through to Edinburgh to see shows or just spend time there.

He'd also had occasion to visit the city several times in the course of his work with Sci-Med, so his memories were not all rosy and, in truth, he'd had some experiences there that he would rather forget. He'd found himself at cross purposes with Lothian and Borders Police on more than one occasion too, so rather than check into a hotel in the city he would keep a low profile and stay at a B&B recommended to him by Jean Roberts – Fraoch House in Pilrig Street, on the north side of the New Town. As one of the cities affected by the cholera attack, he wanted to get a feel for how Edinburgh was dealing with it.

If, as he suspected, he didn't get much out of Mrs McKay, and Lukas Neubauer had not been in touch, he thought he would go down to Dumfriesshire to see his daughter before returning to London. With this in mind, he bought some children's books for Jenny and his sister-in-law's children at the airport before boarding the flight. He was flicking through the pages of *Mother Goose* when the man sitting beside him said, 'I see you're a Booker Prize man.'

Steven laughed. 'Beats celebrity memoirs.'

'Tell me about it,' said the man. 'I've just been interviewing a couple.' He answered Steven's enquiring glance with, 'Liam Rudden, entertainments editor with the *Edinburgh Evening News*.'

The two men shook hands. 'Steven Dunbar. The book's for my daughter, honest.'

'Don't be embarrassed,' joked Rudden. '*Mother Goose* is a favourite of mine too. In fact I'm directing it at the Brunton Theatre this Christmas.'

'You're kidding?'

'No, I do a panto every year – the perfect antidote to interviewing too many celebrities. Panto's more realistic than some of them are. What line are you in yourself?'

'Civil servant,' said Steven.

Rudden gave Steven his card. 'Give me a call nearer the time. I'll sort out some good tickets for you and your daughter.'

'I may take you up on that.'

*   *   *

Steven's planned evening walk around the streets of Edinburgh came to an abrupt halt when the heavens opened and torrential rain had everyone running for shelter. He found his in the bar of the Roxburghe Hotel where he stayed until the deluge abated more than an hour later. The talk in the bar was about the weather and how unpredictable it was. Global warming found its proponents and opponents until, with nothing decided, the conversation changed to the terrorist attacks.

As most of the people were out-of-towners – businessmen on trips to the capital – Steven learned precisely nothing about how the locals were viewing them. He gave up eavesdropping and went back to Pilrig Street for an early night, winding his way downhill through the New Town, with the gutters still running like rivers and the professional premises closed and dark.

He was in a deep sleep when his mobile went off. It was Lukas Neubauer. 'Don't bother telling me it's two in the morning. I know it is; I'm the one still working,' said Neubauer.

'Fair enough. I'm impressed,' countered Steven. 'Is that what you phoned to tell me?'

'The cholera strain *has* been genetically modified.'

Steven was suddenly very wide awake, his mind filling with the possible horrors that could stem from that statement. 'In what way?' he asked in trepidation.

'A bizarre way,' said Neubauer. 'A cassette has been inserted in its genome. Basically it's a self-destruct mechanism.'

Steven struggled for words. 'You can't be serious.'

'I'm sure that's what it is,' said Neubauer. 'In the early days of molecular biology, people were worried about altered organisms escaping from labs, so scientists came up with ways of disabling such bugs if they ever did. This is a very sophisticated version of that. The bug has a requirement for an amino acid which is being supplied by a gene on the cassette, but the cassette has a limited life span. When it stops supplying the amino acid, the bug will die.'

'You mean the cholera was meant to die from the outset?'

'That's what it looks like.'

'Well, that explains why the epidemic isn't spreading like a forest fire,' said Steven. 'It was never meant to. What kind of a terrorist attack uses a microbe that's weakened instead of strengthened?'

'Happily,' said Neubauer, 'that's your problem.'

THIRTY

Steven had breakfast early at Fraoch House and walked up to Princes Street in sunshine. He felt he'd been cheated by the weather the night before and wanted to see Edinburgh do itself justice. Last night's rain had freshened the air and he found a spring in his step as he caught his first sight of the castle, high on its rock beneath a clear blue sky. If ever a building could be said to have seen everything, it was that one, he thought . . . and now a bio-terrorist attack.

He tried to put that thought out of his mind for the moment. Princes Street Gardens stretched out beneath him, empty at present but sure to fill up with tourists once they'd had their . . . The thought came to a juddering halt. There were no tourists to speak of. Tourist flights to the UK had all but disappeared because of the emergency. He passed some more time by having coffee at the one street stall that he found open – obviously to catch office workers on their way to work – and then started looking for a bus going to Corstorphine.

Thirty minutes later, Steven showed his ID to the woman who opened the door. 'Mrs McKay, I'm Dr Steven Dunbar from the Sci-Med Inspectorate. We specialise in finding missing persons. I wonder if I might have a word?'

The woman looked at him over her glasses and then said, 'Oh, you mean Mr Malik. Yes, of course, please do come in.'

Steven found himself in a time warp. He was sitting in the front room of a bungalow with furniture and décor that belonged to another age. The three piece suite in uncut moquette complete with crocheted chair-backs, the tiled fireplace, the standard lamp in the corner, the green Wilton carpet, all belonged in the aunt's house he had visited thirty-five years ago. It wasn't that anything was old or dilapidated; far from it. Everything was clean and polished and lovingly cared for but probably never used. Like the one in his aunt's house, this room had only ever been sat in on 'special occasions'. It smelt of furniture polish. Mrs McKay smelt of lavender.

'I take it Mr Malik hasn't come back?'

'No he hasn't, and if you ask me I don't think the police are looking very hard.'

Steven shook a sympathetic head and asked, 'Do you happen to know his first name, Mrs McKay?'

'As a matter of fact I do. It's Waheed. I don't know how you spell it but I heard his nephew call him that. I always addressed him as Mr Malik, of course.'

'Of course,' echoed Steven, thinking he'd like to give the woman a hug. Waheed Malik. He'd got the first name of those higher up the chain than the eight in custody.

'Would you care for some tea, Dr Dunbar?'

'That would be most kind, Mrs McKay.'

The genteel ritual continued, Mrs McKay returning with tea and fruit scones she'd baked herself. Steven was moved to remember a line from somewhere now long forgotten: *and the rain fell gently on the hats of the ladies of Edinburgh.* He was sitting opposite one of them.

'Can you describe Mr Malik for me, Mrs McKay?'

'Yes, of course. He was about the same height as my Angus. Oh, silly me, you never knew my Angus. Actually, it might be better if I showed you a photograph.'

Mrs McKay excused herself and left the room again, leaving Steven wondering if he could believe his ears. She had a photograph of Malik? He moved on from wanting to hug the woman to going through with the full marriage ceremony.

'Here we are. They're not very good, I'm afraid, but my grandson's only twelve. He took some pictures on his phone when he and his sisters were playing in the garden a few weeks ago. His father printed up a few and gave them to me. Mr Malik's in one of them. I think he'd come to the window to see what the noise was all about.'

Steven found the photograph. An Asian man was framed in a window behind two girls giggling on the lawn, one making faces at her brother.

'Do you think I could hang on to this for a little while, Mrs McKay? I'd like to make some copies,' he said. 'I think it could help enormously in the search for Mr Malik.'

'Then of course you must.'

Steven waved down the first taxi he saw on Corstorphine Road and asked to be taken to the airport. He was back in London and heading for the Home Office by two o'clock. On the way, he phoned John Ricksen and suggested they meet as soon as possible.

'What are you after this time, Dunbar?'

'I have a present for you . . . if you adopt a more respectful tone.'

'What is it?'

'Anwar Khan's controller for the Edinburgh attack.'

'You're kidding.'

'Fair enough. Maybe I should pass him over to Special Branch?'

'Wait. If you're serious, dinner's on me.'

'Is the right answer.'

Steven arranged to meet Ricksen later and went on to the Home Office, where he was relieved to find John Macmillan at his desk. 'Looks like you're back full time.'

'My wife's been trying to persuade me to think about taking a cruise to recuperate, as she puts it. I'm out of reach when I'm here.'

'Maybe she's right,' suggested Steven. 'You've been through a rough time.'

'It's mental stimulation I need, Steven, not cerebral atrophy.'

'Right, you're about to get some. The antibiotic sensitivity of the cholera strain was a ploy to make us think it hadn't been genetically modified. It has. Lukas found something inserted in its genome, something he called a cassette.'

'And what's that?'

'In this case, he tells me it's a self-destruct mechanism. The cholera bug is programmed to die out on its own.'

'God save us,' murmured Macmillan. 'So we're dealing with a group of Islamic fundamentalist extremists whom no one has ever heard of, who appear out of nowhere and attack us with a bio-weapon that is destined to die rather than kill . . .'

Steven pushed the photograph Mrs McKay had given him across the desk. 'The man at the window is Waheed Malik, the missing neighbour with the nephew who worked for the water board.'

'What a bit of luck. What do you plan to do?'

'I'll scan some copies and try running him against our own files but I don't think that'll get us very far. I'm going to hand him over to John Ricksen, as we discussed. I'm seeing him this evening.'

'Good show. There must be a good chance Malik knows more than the cannon fodder in Belmarsh.'

'At the moment, he's our only hope of finding out what the hell's going on,' said Steven.

He went home and took a long shower before wrapping his bathrobe round him and lying flat on his back on his bed to look up at the featureless white ceiling in search of inspiration. Try as he might, he could not figure out a reason for such an operation. The fundamentalists had carried out a near perfect attack using a horrible disease. They had created terror across the entire nation and had then shopped their own when they'd been in a position to deliver a killer blow. Now it seemed they had even planned the failure of their first attack by disabling the organism. It was bizarre, and he phoned Tally to say so.

'That's crazy,' was Tally's verdict, and not one Steven was going to argue with.

'Now I think I know how Alice in Wonderland felt,' he said. He told Tally about the lead he had brought back from Edinburgh.

'You've been to Edinburgh?'

'A flying visit. Sorry, I didn't have time to tell you.'

'It's like having a relationship with Lord Lucan.'

'C'mon, I'm much easier to find.'

'Marginally. Where am I going to find you next? I have a day off tomorrow. I tell you what, give me a clue and we'll call it an orienteering exercise.'

'How about your bed in the early hours of the morning?'

'Are you serious?'

'Never more so. I've got a date tonight and then—'

'You've got what?'

'With MI5,' Steven explained. 'I'm passing over the Edinburgh lead to them. I'm meeting one of their officers and then I could be on my way north to the arms of the woman I love.'

'Only if I get breakfast in bed tomorrow morning.'

''Tis a hard woman ye are, Tally Simmons,' said Steven in a cod-Irish accent.

'Take it or leave it, big boy,' replied Tally, doing Mae West no justice at all.

'Okay, you get breakfast.'

'Then we have a deal.'

Steven met John Ricksen in a riverside pub which had recently undergone a facelift and was now styling itself a gastro-pub. He hoped no *double entendre* was intended. Ricksen appeared to know the owner, and they were given a table with views of the river and dry sherry on the house.

'My only drink this evening,' said Steven. 'I have to drive later.'

Ricksen looked for a moment as if he were about to enquire where, but he didn't. Instead he asked, 'So, what have you got for me?'

Steven gave him the photograph.

Ricksen seemed less than impressed. 'What am I looking at?'

'The face in the window is one Waheed Malik.' Steven told Ricksen about the Corstorphine bungalow and the 'nephew' in the water board van on the day of the Edinburgh attack.

'How in hell's name did you come up with this?' exclaimed Ricksen.

'I have my methods, Watson. You know that.'

'Tell me about them, Sherlock.'

Steven told him about the missing person report.

'Jammy bugger,' said Ricksen.

'Not me, my boss.'

'Macmillan's back?'

'Yup. So tell me, what have 5 come up with?'

Ricksen made a face. 'Like I said before, we're not going to get anything out of the eight in Belmarsh. They don't know anything. They look like terrorists, they have names we expect terrorists to have, but their accents say they're English, from Leicester and Birmingham. They were looking for a cause because it was probably easier than getting a job, and some character stepped in and showed them the path to righteousness and martyrdom. They were recruited and groomed for a specific attack and then let loose without knowing up from down.'

'Let's hope Malik has form.'

'I'll drink to that. Pity you can't.'

As they finished their meal, Steven said, 'We've known each other quite a while.'

Ricksen looked at him, suspicion showing. 'What's coming next?'

'Have you ever heard of an organisation calling themselves the Schiller Group?'

Ricksen stayed quiet for what Steven thought was an unreasonably long time before he said, 'The answer is yes, I've heard of them, but that's about it.'

'Nothing more?'

'Right-wing political movement, obsessively secret, patriotic in a way that longs for the past, warm beer, the sound of willow on leather, a sense of order and decency as they see it, and woe betide anyone who gets on the wrong side of them – or so I'm led to believe.'

'Who led you to believe?'

Ricksen looked as if he'd rather not say any more but Steven's unwavering gaze persuaded him.

'A few years ago, one of our blokes succeeded in penetrating a National Front cell that seemed to be getting very ambitious in its plans to persuade Asians to consider leaving. He reported that it wasn't self-contained. An outside faction was behind it.'

'The Schiller Group?'

Ricksen nodded. 'We fished his body out of the Thames a few weeks later. No charges were ever brought, even though it was one of our own. Why are you asking?'

'A cold case I was working on before the terrorist attack.'

'I'd leave it cold.'

THIRTY-ONE

It was after one thirty in the morning when Steven opened the door to Tally's flat as quietly as he could and let himself in. He smiled when he saw the gin bottle and one crystal glass sitting on the table with a note that said, *Tonic in the fridge, sandwiches wrapped in cling-film.* It was just what he needed to help him wind down after the meeting with Ricksen and the long drive north. Ricksen hadn't told him anything he didn't already know about the Schiller Group, but the fact that even MI5 might back-pedal when it came to taking them on was more than a bit unsettling.

Thirty minutes later, Steven tiptoed through to the bedroom and pushed open the door, which wasn't closed.

'Who's there?' Tally asked sleepily.

'The Milk Tray man,' whispered Steven.

'Just leave them on the dressing table, will you? I'm expecting my boyfriend at any minute.'

Steven manoeuvred himself under the covers and snuggled up to Tally's back.

'I told you, my boyfriend is on his way.'

'We Milk Tray men like living dangerously.'

'Oh well then,' murmured Tally, turning to face him. 'I suppose if you're quick . . . so be it.'

'Breakfast is served, madam,' Steven announced, coming into the bedroom with a tray supporting boiled eggs, toast, orange juice and coffee. He laid it on the bed beside Tally and smoothed her hair back from her forehead as she sat up, smiling.

'God, I love you,' she said. 'It's so nice to see you again.'

'Snap.'

They didn't do anything specific, just spent the day together, strolling by the river and holding hands and laughing a lot, eating lunch and enjoying the wine they had with it before returning to the flat and going back to bed.

'Do you have to go back tonight?' They were lying in dappled sunlight coming through the curtains with the sound of grass being cut somewhere.

'I'm afraid so. John covered the last COBRA meeting but I don't want to impose on him too much. His wife's not happy about him coming back to work so soon. She wants him to go on a cruise.'

'What does he think about that?'

'He'd rather have root-canal treatment.'

Tally laughed. 'Is he fit to take the reins again?'

'I think so, but I'm not absolutely sure. Sci-Med is his life. He won't give it up easily, and nor should he while he's as sharp as he ever was. It was he who saw the significance of the missing person report up in Edinburgh.'

'But he might give it up if he knew you were going to take over,' said Tally.

'That really just came up because he thought he was going to die. That's no longer true.'

'Have you though about what you're going to do?'

'I'm going to keep on the Milk Tray job,' said Steven. 'The perks are fantastic.'

He warded off the rain of blows that descended on him. 'I'm sorry,' he said when Tally ran out of energy. 'I was avoiding the issue.'

'It's okay,' said Tally. 'I haven't changed my mind. You can't go back to kissing corporate arse. That just isn't you.'

'We'll talk again when things get back to normal.'

* * *

Steven was preparing to leave for the drive back to London when his phone rang. It was John Ricksen.

'What the hell are you playing at, Dunbar? If you think that was some kind of joke, I'm not laughing,'

'What are you talking about?'

'Waheed Malik: Anwar Khan's controller, you said. Jesus, you've made me look a right prat.'

'I gave you all the information I had. What's the problem?'

'His name's not Waheed Malik; it's Assad Zaman. He's one of ours.'

Steven stammered his disbelief. 'How can he be? What the hell was he doing in Edinburgh with Khan and a water board van?'

'We don't know that he was,' said Ricksen through gritted teeth. 'Khan was picked up in Glasgow with another guy called Patel. We've just been assuming the same two carried out the Edinburgh attack. Neither of them has admitted it or given any information about it.'

'All right, what was your man doing in Edinburgh with two unknown Asians and a water board van on the day of the attack?'

'If that's where the picture was taken,' said Ricksen sullenly.

Steven was angry now. 'Look, that picture was taken in Edinburgh. I know because I've been there. I stood on the spot where it was taken.'

'All right,' said Ricksen. 'I apologise. But what the hell's going on?'

'Why don't you ask Malik or Zaman or whatever his bloody name is, if he's one of yours?'

'We can't find him at the moment.'

'He's one of yours and you can't find him?'

'He's not a staffer. Turns out we've used him in the past. I'm told he was one of our insiders in the fundamentalist scene in Leicester a year or so ago.'

'So maybe he's been turned.'

'The fundos don't turn agents they catch; they cut them into little pieces.'

'So where does that leave us?'

'In view of what you've said, I'll put out a major alert for him.'

'I'll call you in the morning.'

Steven attended what was announced to be the last COBRA meeting for the time being. He couldn't help but feel he was the only one there who wasn't basking in a glow of self-satisfaction over being 'on top of things' as the deputy PM put it. No new cases of cholera had been reported in the past twenty-four hours, security at all reservoirs and water installations was tight, and vaccination of the infant population had already begun at surgeries across the country. Norman Travis took over to say that vaccination of top-risk people would begin in three days, and Merryman were on course to provide new supplies in three weeks' time for the remaining population.

Steven left the meeting with that now familiar hollow feeling in his stomach. There was something terribly wrong about . . . everything, but he couldn't say so. Norman Travis, who had been accepting the congratulations of some of the others over the health department's handling of the affair, detached himself and came downstairs with Steven.

'Isn't it strange how much things can change in such a short time? A week ago I wouldn't have put money on anyone's smiling today.'

'We've been very lucky,' said Steven.

'I know there can be no guarantee that there won't be another attack, but with Merryman coming on stream with new vaccines we should be in a much better position to defend ourselves.'

'You're right, and I understand your contribution to that has been invaluable,' said Steven.

'Some things are more important than party politics – as I

think the coalition is demonstrating. If you see something needs doing, you should get your head down and damn well do it.'

'Indeed,' said Steven with a smile.

'It was good to see John Macmillan at the meeting the other day, but we didn't get a chance to speak afterwards. Is he back full time?'

'Not quite.'

'Give him my best.'

Steven felt the need for fresh air and a walk. He needed to experience a sense of normality, see people going about their business, be assured that all was right with the world despite feeling sure that it wasn't. He was leaning on a rail watching the river traffic chug past when John Ricksen rang.

'They've found Zaman.'

'What's he saying?'

'Not a lot. He was swinging from a tree in the Clyde Valley.'

Steven closed his eyes. 'What's the thinking?'

'The brains think he must have started to feel guilty about working for us – maybe seeing the fuck-up in Afghanistan – and was really converted to fundamentalist philosophy. He was one of those chosen to run the cholera attack, but when he realised how many were going to die after a second hit he got cold feet and blew the whistle. It wouldn't be hard for the hierarchy to work out he'd been the one who'd done that so they strung him up.'

'Is that what you think?' asked Steven.

'I'm not so sure.'

'We should talk. Can you come over to the Home Office?'

'Give me an hour. There are a couple of things I have to do.'

John Macmillan asked Steven how the COBRA meeting had gone.

'Everyone was happy except me.'

'Did you tell them what Lukas came up with?'

Steven shook his head. 'I didn't want to be a party pooper. If I'd had any idea why they'd disabled the bug I would have, but I haven't. You?'

'No,' said Macmillan. 'Islamic terrorists don't do kindness. Doesn't make sense.'

'I've asked John Ricksen to come over. We need to talk.'

Macmillan raised his eyes.

'Waseed Malik was an MI5 informer. His real name was Assad Zaman. He was found hanging from a tree in Scotland in the early hours of this morning.

Macmillan slumped back in his chair. 'I'm beginning to think a cruise might be a better option.'

'MI5 think he was converted to the opposition. He ran the first attack but chickened out of the second and made the call that stopped it.'

Ricksen arrived and Jean Roberts brought in coffee.

'No calls please, Jean,' said Macmillan.

'Very good, Sir John,' she replied, winking at Steven on the way out. Normal service had been resumed.

'I've told Sir John what 5 thinks about the man we know as Malik and you know as Zaman, but I got the impression that you might have some other ideas,' Steven began. Ricksen seemed uneasy, and Steven guessed it was because Macmillan was present. 'Everything said here stays here,' he added.

'Something's not quite right,' said Ricksen.

'That's exactly the impression we have.'

'People are desperate to come up with plausible explanations for implausible happenings. We get a warning of a bio-weapon attack but we don't know where from. None of our sources know anything at all about it. Same goes for Special Branch. We're told the terrorists are home-grown – and they are – but no one knows anything about their masters. Zaman's involvement is not only a surprise to us, it's a surprise to the fundamentalist groups. Then his body is found – unmutilated. He still had his tongue. Very strange.'

Steven told Ricksen about the disabling of the cholera strain. 'They didn't want to kill too many people.'

'And our conclusion must be, gentlemen?' asked Macmillan.

'It wasn't an Islamic terrorist attack at all,' said Steven slowly.

THIRTY-TWO

Macmillan nodded. 'It's the only explanation. Some unknown faction recruited disaffected Muslim youths in our cities and groomed them to carry out the attacks, telling them they were acting for the Islamic fundamentalist cause.'

'Then they shopped them to the police to bolster the impression that it was Islamic terrorists who were responsible,' added Steven.

'But what on earth for?' asked Ricksen. 'And why use a weapon that's deliberately been blunted, if what you say's true?'

'To create the right conditions for . . . something else to happen,' said Macmillan. 'The people who died were expendable . . . collateral damage.'

'Working-class people in old council blocks of flats?'

'Oh, shit,' said Steven. 'It has to be the Schiller Group.'

Ricksen's expression suggested that he did not see this as good news.

'It's another Northern Health Scheme. They're setting out to reshape the population.'

'Reshape the pop—' stammered Ricksen.

'It's a long story, going back twenty years,' said Steven, unwilling to break his stride. 'They've been manipulating events to set it up all over again. That's what the killings in Paris were all about. It *was* a take-over bid. A new hierarchy with new ideas is in charge.'

'So what are they planning to do?' asked Macmillan.

'The mass vaccinations,' said Steven. 'It has to be that. The entire population is about to be vaccinated.'

'You're right,' exclaimed Macmillan. 'It does have to be that. The very young have been receiving what cholera vaccine stocks we had but the over-sixties are about to get the stuff that was bound for the Third World.'

'Or not,' said Steven.

'Are you suggesting they're going to kill everyone over sixty?' asked Ricksen, as if he were in the throes of a bad dream.

'Nothing so unsubtle, if the Schiller Group are responsible.'

'So how do we stop them? The whole operation is up and running with full government approval and we don't even know who "they" are.'

'Indeed,' said Macmillan. 'And what is particularly worrying is that it would be much easier for them to stop us.'

'And they must know we're onto something because of the alert 5 put out for Zaman,' said Steven.

'It must have been them who killed him to stop him talking,' said Ricksen. 'That's why it didn't look right.'

'We know from the cover-ups of twenty years ago that the Schiller mob was well represented in the police, so maybe informing them is not an option.'

'They must have a presence in 5 too,' said Ricksen, thinking about the National Front infiltrator who'd ended up in the Thames.

'Let's define our objectives,' said Steven. 'We have to stop the "vaccine" from getting to the mass-vaccination clinics all over the country. Its starting point is . . .'

'Lark Pharmaceuticals,' said Ricksen. 'They're diverting their overseas supplies.'

Macmillan hit the intercom button on his desk. 'Jean, we need to have everything you can get on Lark Pharmaceuticals as quickly as you can.'

'Lark may not be involved, of course. There might be a plan to swap shipments somewhere along the line,' said Ricksen.

'Then it's important we stop them setting out if we can,' said Steven.

'Easier said than done,' said Ricksen. 'Any word of such an attempt getting back to the Schiller mob and they'll simply change their plans.'

A knock came to the door and Jean entered. 'Something to be going on with,' she said, placing a thin file on Macmillan's desk.

Macmillan read in silence for a few moments before speaking out loud for the benefit of Steven and Ricksen. 'Lark Pharmaceuticals was formed in 1990 as an offshoot of Lander Pharmaceuticals but has never been listed on the stock exchange. It's a private company. Although the expertise came from Lander, private money from a body called the Wellington Foundation was used to set it up. It's run as a non-profit-making concern. What profits it does make from the sale of its pills and potions and diagnostic kits and so on is ploughed back into its vaccine programme for Third World countries.'

'So it's a charity?' said Ricksen.

'Not with a parent company like Lander,' said Steven. 'Lander supplied pharmaceuticals to the Northern Health Scheme.'

Macmillan continued. 'The head of Lark is Dr Mark Mosely, a previous associate of Dr Paul Schreiber, head of Lander Pharmaceuticals at one time.'

'Schreiber was deeply involved in the scheme. He ran the pharmacy at Newcastle College Hospital personally,' said Steven.

'Mosely, a brilliant molecular biologist, was recruited by Schreiber after getting his doctorate from Cambridge. He rose rapidly in Lander and was given the job of heading up Lark when it was formed. He's been there ever since.'

'Being funded by the Schiller Group,' said Steven.

'So it's Lark we're after,' said Ricksen.

'An outwardly respectable company, doing its level best to help Third World countries and commanding the admiration of all . . .' said Macmillan.

'Currently about to provide the vaccine necessary to protect some of our most vulnerable citizens,' said Steven.

'We need proof,' said Ricksen. 'Cast-iron proof before we can touch them, and that could take time . . .'

'Which we haven't got,' said Steven. 'We'll have to get the proof another way.'

'What do you have in mind?'

'Hereford,' said Steven. 'We don't waste time with polite requests and bits of paper: we hit Lark head-on with an SAS assault.'

'Jesus,' said Ricksen. 'Can you do that?'

'Steven is ex-Regiment,' said Macmillan. 'His old chums have come to our aid in the past. The question this time is . . . do we need MOD approval?'

'It could be argued that this is a civilian matter . . .' said Steven.

'Which might conceivably make it a Home Office affair,' said Macmillan. 'But this is big. We'll have to seek the Home Secretary's approval.'

Steven nodded. 'She's heard rumours about the Schiller Group in the past. It came up in conversation.'

'Good. Who approaches her, you or me?'

'You,' said Steven. 'I'll call Hereford.'

Macmillan was with the Home Secretary for nearly an hour. He returned looking tired and drawn. 'She will personally see that I am hanged from Tower Bridge if this goes wrong,' he said.

'But it's a yes?' asked Steven.

'With you hanging beside me,' continued Macmillan. 'But it is a yes. Have you spoken to your friends?'

Steven said that he had. 'I had confidence in your powers of persuasion. They'll be here at eleven this evening.'

'Are you going with them?'

'Yes.'

Macmillan's eyes asked the same question of Ricksen.

'If that's okay?'

'You bet,' said Steven. He turned to Macmillan. 'We're going to need Lukas Neubauer and the lab to be on stand-by throughout the night. I'll get the vaccine to him as quickly as I can.'

'I'll talk to him. Strikes me it's going to be a long night for all of us. I'll ask Jean to arrange some sustenance.'

Jean had not only come up with food and drink for them by the end of the afternoon but also some publicity photographs of the Lark Pharmaceuticals building. Steven was able to show these to the SAS commander who arrived at a service entrance to the Home Office at eleven p.m., one of twelve soldiers dressed in black counter-terrorist gear, travelling in four green Land Rovers. The others stayed where they were inside their vehicles.

Steven had to admit that neither he nor Ricksen had ever been inside the Lark building.

'Great,' said the man, who introduced himself as Tim.

'Relax,' said Steven. 'I'm not looking for subtlety here. I need you to hit that building like a train and secure it as quickly as possible. I don't think there will be too many people in the labs and offices at this time of night but if there are any, contain them but don't hurt them. I don't want anyone going anywhere or destroying anything. There will be people in the transport bays loading vaccine onto lorries. I don't want them or the vehicles going anywhere for the time being.'

'Understood. And if we meet resistance?'

'Overcome it,' said Steven. 'Minimum force. These people will be innocents doing their jobs. I just need everything to come to a standstill until we find what we're looking for.'

'Which is?'

'Let's say I've reason to believe that the vaccine supplies this company are about to send out are not what they're supposed to be. I need samples for our lab to analyse and, ideally, information about what's really in the vials. Last but not least I need any information you can get about the organisation responsible for putting it there.'

'The vials we can get from the loading bay,' said Tim. 'And we gather all files, disks, laptops from the exec suites?'

Steven nodded. 'The managing director is a Dr Mark Mosely. Concentrate on his office before anything else.'

It took Tim and his men eleven minutes to occupy and secure the Lark building. The personnel on site – mainly transport and loading staff, as expected – were herded into the staff canteen, given an apology, and asked to wait there behind locked doors until further notice. No one chose to argue with the black-suited, armed men wearing balaclavas.

Steven and Ricksen joined Tim in Mark Mosely's office. Tim watched while Steven made a thorough search of the room, selecting items to take back with him to London along with the vaccine samples obtained by the soldiers from the loading bay.

'Christ, I hope you're right about all this,' murmured Ricksen.

'You and me both,' replied Steven.

'Make that three of us,' Tim chipped in. 'The boss isn't putting this operation through the books.'

'Could get a bit busy under Tower Bridge,' said Steven, a comment that passed over the heads of the other two.

'Ready?' asked Tim.

Steven took a last look round the office. 'I'll just make sure there aren't any wall safes . . .' He was thinking about Charles French's penthouse.

He hadn't really expected to find anything under the various pictures on the wall but when he moved *Ville d'Avray* slightly to the left with his fingertips he took a step back in surprise when an entire wall panel slid open.

'What the f—' exclaimed Ricksen. 'What is it?'

'A lift,' said Steven, slightly bemused.

'But there's a lift just outside the door,' said Tim.

'Could be an executive lift,' said Ricksen. 'You know what these guys are like . . . executive this, executive that.'

Steven pressed the single button at the side and the lift door slid open. He looked inside. 'One button. Only goes to one floor.'

THIRTY-THREE

Tim looked at the inside of the lift and decided they could get four into it. He called in one of his soldiers and told another where they were going.

It was a tight squeeze: Steven was very conscious of the smell of gun oil from the soldier's automatic weapon which was only inches from his nose as the soldier held it flat against his chest. 'Ready?' he asked, then pressed the button.

After what seemed a very long, slow descent, the lift bounced gently on its cables as it came to a halt and the door slid back to reveal brightness.

The two SAS men leapt out, moving to opposite sides and levelling their weapons at the four white-coated people working in what was clearly a basement lab. They froze. Tim signalled to his soldier that he was going to check what appeared to be a smaller room at the far end of the lab, and Steven watched as he kicked open the door.

A man was sitting at a desk. 'What the hell?' he exclaimed.

'Over to you,' said Tim over his shoulder to Steven.

Steven presented his ID. 'Dr Steven Dunbar, Sci-Med Inspectorate.'

'Dr Mark Mosely. This is my research lab. This is an outrage. Get out of here.'

'Keep an eye on him,' Steven told Tim as he left the small office to start examining the lab. 'Very nice,' he murmured, admiring the quality of the equipment. 'A state of the art molecular biology lab . . . and some well-qualified people, I'll bet,' he said, eyeing the four nervous people standing motionless under the watchful gaze of the soldier.

He opened the door of an incubator and removed one of the Petri dishes from it. He angled it to read the writing on the lid. '*Vibrio cholerae*. Well, that answers a few questions. Is this where you made that ingenious cassette?'

The way that the four scientists averted their eyes suggested that it was.

'It's hardly surprising that a company making cholera vaccine should have cultures of cholera, is it, Dunbar?' Mosely called out.

Steven returned to the office. 'Your vaccine is going to be analysed before it goes anywhere, Mosely. And if it should turn out to be something other than cholera vaccine – as you and I know it is – you and your Schiller Group are going down for ever and a day.'

Mosely's hand shot out and thumped down on a white button set in a red mounting on his desk. Nothing happened.

'Damn,' said Mosely with a small smile. 'The floor was supposed to open and drop you into a pool of hungry crocodiles.'

Steven didn't like the smile on Mosely's face. The man was in no position to be making jokes . . . but he seemed to think that he was.

Ricksen, who had been rooting around in the lab, had just come up behind Steven. He said, 'There was one of these buttons on his desk upstairs too . . . I need the card that opens your safe, Dr Mosely.'

Mosely opened a desk drawer and, holding the card between two fingers, handed it over without comment. Steven followed Ricksen outside and watched him place the card in the safe's reader slot. The door opened to reveal a glass panel. Ricksen was about to touch it when Steven yelled, 'Get back!' It was the same kind of panel he'd seen in Charles French's place. 'It's biometric.' He called to Tim. 'I think we need Dr Mosely's assistance here.'

Tim ushered Mosely out of his office and Steven took pleasure from the change of expression on the Lark executive's face. 'Open it.'

'Screw you.'

Tim primed his weapon.

'You wouldn't dare.'

'You know, Mosely, I think it just might be a night for daring . . .' said Steven. 'Open it.'

Mosely placed his hand on the glass surface and it opened to reveal a number of disks. Ricksen took charge of them and went through to Mosely's office to scan their contents. Mosely was put under guard with the scientists while Steven continued inspecting the lab, until Ricksen returned with a broad smile on his face. 'Bingo! Schiller membership, the lot.'

Steven said to Tim, 'I think we have what we came for.'

Steven and Mosely were the last to come up in the lift. Despite holding a gun on Mosely and having possession of the disks, Steven was disturbed to see what he could only construe as a look of self-satisfaction on Mosely's face. It was the expression he'd noticed in the office a little while earlier. It had slipped when the disks were discovered but it was back. Steven motioned with the Glock that Mosely get out first, and the man acknowledged with a nod. As he stepped out, he raised his hands above his head.

The scientists from the basement lab, the SAS men, Steven, Ricksen and Mosely were all now standing in the glass-fronted hall of the building, preparing to leave. Mosely moved forward and faced the glass doors, his hands now resting on his head. 'Well, well, well,' he said, loudly enough for everyone to hear. 'Here we all are, the managing director of Lark Pharmaceuticals and four of my staff, being held at gunpoint by armed terrorists intent on stopping life-saving vaccine getting to the British public . . .'

Steven frowned, but before he could reply the world outside erupted in a blaze of lights and loudhailers.

'Shit, the button on the desk,' said Ricksen.

'Correct,' murmured Mosely. 'A direct alarm to the police, indicating we were under terrorist attack. I think they've done rather well, don't you?'

Steven could see dozens of armed response officers and rows of police vehicles outside. In his mind's eye he could see what the police were seeing and it didn't look good. Twelve black-clad men brandishing automatic weapons, four white-coated men huddling together in fear, and Mosely with his hands on his head.

'We're not carrying ID,' said Tim.

'I'll go out,' said Steven.

'Yes, why don't you, Dunbar?' said Mosely smugly.

Ricksen interrupted. 'Think, Steven. Those guys out there are itching for an excuse. Look at them. They're running on pure adrenalin and now they have the chance to confront real terrorists face to face. They'll mow you down as soon as you reach for your ID.'

'Keep your guns trained on this lot,' Tim ordered his men. 'It's the only thing keeping us alive.'

Steven knew that was true. The fact that he still had his gun in his hand and his proximity to Mosely were probably the only things that had stopped the police marksmen from targeting him already. 'I'll have to go out,' he said. 'It's the only way to stop this ending in bloody mayhem.'

Mosely looked as if he might be about to ignore Steven's gun and make a move away from him. 'You wouldn't really shoot me, Dunbar, would you?'

'No, *I* would,' said Tim flatly. 'And that's a fucking promise.'

Mosely believed him.

A new sound joined the general cacophony outside, that of the whirring blades of a helicopter, its down-lights illuminating a chosen landing spot in front of the building. The police, not sure what was going on, moved out of the way, forming a semi-circular perimeter of waiting, armed officers. As the 'copter's engines died a loudspeaker crackled into life, filling the night air with the sound of a woman's voice.

'Attention, attention, this is the Home Secretary speaking. You have been misinformed. The men inside the building are not terrorists: they are SAS soldiers. I want everyone to lay down their weapons.'

No one moved.

'I am going to come out now. When I give the signal you will all lay down your weapons, both inside and outside the building.'

The helicopter door opened, and a woman, accompanied by a man Steven could see was John Macmillan, got out and moved away from the aircraft, followed by searchlights.

'Christ,' murmured one police officer, 'it *is* the Home Secretary.'

'I'd know those shoes anywhere,' said another.

The Home Secretary spread her arms as if in a scene from a passion play, then dropped them. All arms were laid on the ground.

Mosely thought he saw the chance to pick up Steven's gun, but Steven felled him with a single punch. It was over in the wink of an eye.

'Bet that felt good,' murmured Tim.

The Home Secretary took over the police address system and asked that all commanders come to her immediately. After a bizarre series of introductions involving Sci-Med, MI5, the SAS and the police, she said, 'When I was wakened by the police and told that Lark Pharmaceuticals was under attack by terrorists, I contacted Sir John and he organised a helicopter from City Airport to bring us down immediately. Thank God we were in time.' She turned to Steven. 'I take it your suspicions were correct?'

'It looks like it,' said Steven. 'We'll know more when the vaccine is analysed.

'In that case, Sir John,' she said, turning to Macmillan, 'the jury will remain out on Tower Bridge until it has been. Now I'm going home to bed.'

It took Lukas Neubauer and his people two days and nights to come up with the answer he brought to the Home Office.

'It's definitely not cholera vaccine,' he said at once, getting sighs of relief from Steven and Macmillan. 'It's a dodgy adjuvant.'

'A what?' asked Macmillan.

Steven was also looking puzzled, but for a different reason. He said, 'Adjuvants are substances you add to vaccines to provoke a better response from the immune system.'

'Correct,' said Neubauer. 'But this particular one has a bit of a bad reputation. It was banned because scientists thought it was damaging the immune system and might even be provoking auto-immune disease. At the concentration I found in the Lark vials it would certainly damage the immune system.'

'Making the people who got it much more likely to develop a range of illnesses.'

'And much less likely to survive them. You'd be lucky to see out the next three or four years.'

'So people would not be living longer and longer after all,' said Macmillan thoughtfully. 'The life expectancy of anyone over sixty would drop like a stone, and a burden would be removed from the state . . .'

'But what a state,' said Steven.

'Agreed,' said Macmillan. 'And a good reason for you to continue with Sci-Med.'

'We'll see.'

The information contained on the disks recovered from the Lark laboratory led to the Schiller Group's becoming a proscribed organisation in the UK and a wave of arrests and sudden resignations, many at quite senior level. Norman Travis was one of those arrested.

Steven and Tally made their trip to Newcastle to seek out the graves of the people who'd died in the nineties in the abortive attempt to expose the Northern Health Scheme for what it really was. Macmillan had promised that they would be given national recognition, but for the moment flowers would suffice.

After visiting the burial place of Dr Neil Tolkien they arrived at the cemetery where James Kincaid, the journalist who'd started the original investigation, and Eve Laing, the nurse who'd fallen in love with him, lay side by side. Steven felt a lump come to his throat as he watched Tally arrange the flowers. When she stood up, Steven expected to see sadness in her eyes but found something else that he couldn't quite fathom.

'Steven . . . my mother was two days away from receiving that vaccine.' She looked at the ground before saying, 'Your country needs you, Dr Dunbar . . . even more than I do, damn it.'

And then Tally reached up and gave Steven the kind of kiss not normally thought appropriate in cemeteries.